FOLLOW THAT STAR

A
SADDLE
HILL
CHRISTMAS
MYSTERY

ERIN LANTER

To Billy, who has always been my biggest fan.

FOLLOW THAT STAR

PROLOGUE

HEART POUNDING, THE intruder inserted the key into the lock of the jewelry case and slid the door to the side. Hundreds of diamonds twinkled under the display lights. With sweaty palms, the thief nimbly removed each piece from the display case. Using something that looked like miniature pliers, the settings were expertly loosened. The gems didn't stand a chance of staying where they'd been so lovingly placed.

Pausing briefly at a diamond tennis bracelet boasting dozens of small diamonds, the gloved hand plucked it off the display stand, and taking only a moment to admire the craftsmanship and the bracelet's flawless beauty, slipped it quickly into a coat pocket. One after another, each piece was removed and tampered with, ensuring no customer would ever be pleased with their purchase.

Satisfied that the creator of these masterpieces would face humiliation and financial ruin once word spread about his shoddy work, the criminal closed the jewelry case, locked it, and slipped out, confident no one would ever know someone had been there.

CHAPTER ONE

BEADS OF SWEAT popped up on Marian Bright's upper lip as she hauled the box of Christmas sweaters from the attic. It was Thanksgiving evening, and the Christmas season would officially begin at midnight.

This was Marian's favorite time of year. A spirit of goodwill seemed to miraculously take over even the grumpiest members of the human race, including the ones that scowled the other eleven months of the year.

Heaven knows we all need a break from those people, Marian mused as she descended the final rung on the pull-down ladder leading from the attic.

She dropped the box, leaned against the closet wall, and wiped the sweat from her face with her sleeve. At seventy-two years old and just five feet two inches tall, Marian was only slightly bigger than the box she'd just lugged down the rickety old ladder.

This was the first year she'd had to carry it herself, and her first Christmas as a widow.

Poor Roger, Marian thought, with the familiar pang of loneliness. He loved the holidays, though for him Thanksgiving was the highlight and the season went downhill from there. He'd always taken great pleasure in the celebration of a holiday that was dedicated to just being thankful for what you have, though he could never get over the irony that the very next day the entire country spiraled into a shopping frenzy trying to acquire more stuff nobody really needed. Each year Roger would sit in his favorite chair beside the fireplace and shake his head at the seemingly unquenchable thirst the citizens of this great country seem to have for more useless gadgets.

"Just one year," he'd say, "I don't want to hear about some poor soul getting trampled to death in the name of a good deal."

Unfortunately, a heart attack while Roger was working in the flower bed seven months ago erased that possibility.

The pain of missing Roger never seemed to go away. Sometimes it eased up, then surprised her at the strangest moments.

Today had been especially hard. She made his favorite Thanksgiving meal, but without him there to share it with, she was as miserable as she'd ever been. She was thankful for all the Thanksgivings they'd had together, but this one felt empty. As soon as she had the dishes cleared and the leftovers put away, she'd turned on the dishwasher and started a task she knew would lift her spirits: unpacking her Christmas sweaters.

It was one of her favorite Christmas traditions, and for the first time in fifty years Roger wouldn't be there telling her how ridiculous it was that she owned a Christmas sweater for every day of the season.

As she opened the box, Marian began humming, "It's the Most Wonderful Time of the Year." Satisfied her collection was in good shape, she pushed the box from her bedroom to the laundry room. The first sweater would make its appearance tomorrow. Each year she bought one new Christmas sweater, retiring the oldest in the collection, feeling slightly guilty that after so many years of faithful service, it would be cast aside in favor of something new.

Isn't that the way it always is? Marian thought, then wondered how Roger's opinion had traveled from the great hereafter and lodged itself in her brain. Over the years they'd seen many of their friends' marriages end for the same reason. Trading in the old version for a newer model.

With the washing machine going full tilt, she walked to the living room, lit a fire, and grabbed her laptop.

She settled into Roger's favorite chair—the one that still held faint traces of his aftershave—and propped her feet up on the ottoman as her computer booted up. She was about to participate in what she hoped would be a new Christmas tradition.

After Roger died, the lonely nights had been so difficult. She'd try to watch TV or read a book, anything to distract herself. Then, one evening in midsummer she'd stumbled across a chat room for people with Christmas names. She'd always loved her name; so much so that when she and Roger were married, she'd kept her maiden name. At the time, that had been unheard of. Roger, ever the traditionalist, had been furious. He'd insisted it wasn't proper to not take her husband's name.

"But Roger," Marian had protested, "think about it. Marian Smith. That's so dull! How do you expect me to live with such an uninspired name?"

Eventually he'd stopped pressing the issue, and she continued to live happily as Marian Bright.

After logging into the chat room, Marian saw that many of the regulars had already posted. To her chagrin, several of them were already dreading the season.

One member posted: *All year long, nobody notices my name,*

but as soon as Christmastime rolls around, suddenly having the name Sylvia Bell is a riot. If things weren't going so well at work right now, I'd turn into Scrooge himself!

Another member responded: *At least you only have to worry about it at Christmas. Who would have thought there were real people with the last name Claus? My coworkers keep coming to my office to give me their Christmas lists. If I wouldn't lose my job, I'd tell them exactly what they can do with their precious lists…*

Marian chuckled softly as her fingers flew across the keyboard. *Now, now. Let's not be cross about the names our lovely parents have given us. We have been entrusted with a beautiful gift, and it's up to us to spread Christmas cheer to all we meet. Sylvia, you bring joy to each person that laughs because of your name. We need more laughter in our broken world. Take pleasure in being able to provide it. And dear Mr. Claus, please don't lose the twinkle in your eye. You have a wonderful opportunity to teach the world to be merrier. Instead of telling your coworkers to do you-know-what with their Christmas lists, try surprising them with an unexpected treat.*

Just as Marian was about to press the button to post her encouraging remarks, she pulled her hand away from the keyboard. She chewed her thumbnail, hoping for a Christmas miracle.

And Holly, if you're out there, please consider taking me up on my offer. This Christmas will be terribly lonely for me, and I would love for you to come spend the season with me. Please think about it. We might be good for each other. I've sent my address to you in a private message.

Marian pressed "post" and stared at the flames flickering in the fireplace. The last couple posts from Holly Berry had been upsetting, and she couldn't help but worry that if things didn't change, the poor girl might end up finding herself in trouble.

CHAPTER TWO

DISHES CLATTERED AS Kristopher and Nicholas Jingle cleared the table. The cleanup after Thanksgiving dinner marked another holiday survived by the Jingle family.

"Tomorrow is the big day," James, the patriarch of the Jingle family, announced happily.

"Mmm-hmm," Kris agreed as he carried the platter holding leftover scraps of turkey to the kitchen.

Worry lines deepened around James's mouth. "Aren't you excited?"

Kris returned and collected the goblets that thirty minutes earlier held his mother's famous spiced cider. "Of course. How could I not be?" Again, he disappeared toward the kitchen, and again returned to collect more dishes.

"Of course he isn't excited, Dad," Nicholas chimed in. "Look at him. He's Ebenezer Scrooge in the flesh."

A flush of red crept toward Kris's receding hairline. "I am not," he defended.

"Oh, yes you are," Nicholas insisted. "You hate Christmas."

The red deepened. "I do not."

"Nicholas, stop picking on your brother," Patricia, their mother, ordered. "He loves Christmas just like we do."

Nicholas snorted. "Right."

"He does," James said halfheartedly. "He's just different than we are. He's...*peculiar*."

The sound of dishes crashing into the sink preceded Kris's reentry into the dining room by mere seconds. His red face had darkened to crimson, making his strawberry-blond hair fade to pink. "I'm peculiar?" he demanded. "You people keep this house decorated for Christmas all year long and *I'm* peculiar?"

"Settle down, Kris," Patricia soothed. "The holidays are stressful for a lot of people. That doesn't mean you're peculiar."

Nicholas snorted again, louder this time.

The family was silent while they finished clearing the table. Tension hung thick in the air as the brothers worked side by side. Always different, Kris had an interest in literature far beyond "'Twas the Night Before Christmas" and theater that had nothing to do with *A Christmas Carol*. Nicholas, on the other hand, was a carbon copy of their father. He hummed Christmas carols all year long and worked primarily as a Santa in commercials and at parties. While his wife, Suzanne, was the breadwinner, Nicholas moonlighted in pointing out to the rest of the family that Kris didn't belong. He even went so far as to ask Kris to have his DNA tested to make sure they were biologically related.

"Why don't we all sit down and watch a Christmas movie together?" Patricia suggested as she filled hand-painted poinsettia glasses with eggnog.

"No thanks," Kris said. "I've got to get home."

"But we always watch a Christmas movie together on Thanksgiving evening," James protested. "It's a family tradition."

"Like I said, he's a Scrooge. Charles Dickens had him

pegged a hundred and fifty years before he was ever even born. Kris doesn't care about Christmas or our family traditions."

"Will you stop it?" Kris demanded. "I like Christmas. I really do. But I don't like what this family has made it into. The tree stays up all year round and you even have fake snow sprayed on the yard in the summer. I'm surprised you even celebrate Thanksgiving. If all this isn't bad enough, you petitioned the town to officially change the name of this street to Santa Claus Lane."

"I know. Isn't it wonderful?" James said, a merry smile finally spreading across his face.

"No, Dad, it isn't wonderful. At least not for the Benowitzes next door."

James waved a hand at his son. "Oh, please. They love it."

"They're Jewish, Dad. They don't love it. And our last name? What possessed you to legally change our last name to Jingle? It's ridiculous!"

"Bite your tongue," the elder Jingle growled, rising from his red-and-green plaid recliner. "You would do well to watch what you say in this house."

Kris rolled his eyes. "I've got to go."

Crossing the room, he gave his mother a quick hug and a kiss. "Happy Thanksgiving, Mom." With that he turned and walked out the front door, slamming it shut behind him.

"Can you believe that?" Nicholas said, pointing toward the door. "You gave us the wonderful gift of Christmas memories all year long, and he is nothing but ungrateful. I still can't believe we're even related." Nicholas settled onto the sofa and shook his head.

James rose from his chair and sat next to his youngest son. Patting Nicholas's hand, he said, "That it is, son. That it is."

Patricia selected one of the favorite Christmas movies from the DVD collection and settled on the other side of Nicholas. It was a tradition they'd had since the boys were small. Back then, Kris had enjoyed it as much as the rest of them. Now he wanted nothing to do with it.

She tried to focus on the movie and feel the same joy about Christmas as she had in years past, but, having the heart of a mother, knew she wouldn't be genuinely happy until they brought their lost little sheep back into the fold.

Two hours later, the movie was over and Nicholas had gone home to his wife, Suzanne, who insisted on spending Thanksgiving with her brother who lived two hours away. The house was dark except for the twinkling lights on the Christmas tree in the corner of the living room. Even they did nothing to cheer Patricia. She looked at them for several long moments before turning the lights off and going to bed. Perhaps they had all done a bang-up job at alienating poor Kris. The year-round Christmas thing had been fun at the beginning, but she could now see that it was driving a wedge between the family. Even she had lost some of her enthusiasm for the holiday.

Climbing between the flannel sheets, Patricia was careful not to wake James. Whatever conversation he'd want to have was certain to end as a venting session about Kris.

"Where did we go wrong, Patty?" James's voice was muffled by the pillow.

I don't want to talk about it! Patricia shouted in her mind.

"We've got one good son, one that holds to our family values. Then we've got Kris. What happened to him?"

"I don't know, dear," she said through an exhale. She wasn't in the mood for this.

"We must have really messed up raising him. We got it

right with Nicholas, though. Maybe we would have been better off if Nicholas had been an only child. Although that would be impossible, considering that Kris came first."

Patricia winced. She loved her boys. Both of them, no matter how different they were.

"I don't know, dear," she repeated. "Maybe he's just tired of the charade." Then she whispered, "God knows I understand that."

James didn't hear her remark. He was snoring softly beside her, a smile on his bearded face. He'd clearly forgotten his disappointment in their oldest son, at least for the moment. Patricia frowned. She was certain that if she looked hard enough, she'd be able to see the sugar plums dancing around his head.

CHAPTER THREE

KRIS JINGLE SLID his key into the lock of his apartment door and swung it open. This Thanksgiving had been terrible, the worst one yet. The only thing he could think of to give thanks for was that he wasn't still stuck at his parents' house with Nicholas being viewed as the family outcast.

To think, I'm the odd one in the family, he thought incredulously. All the ridiculous Christmas stuff they do all year long, and *I'm* the odd one out.

He caught a glimpse of himself just inside the door. Tall, lean, balding. I don't even look the part they want me to play.

He thrust his jaw forward. Then so be it.

Dropping his keys on the table in the small entryway, he glanced around the tiny apartment. It wasn't much to look at, but at least it was quiet and filled with his own non-Christmas stuff. He wasn't even planning to decorate at all this year, not even a tree.

Kris smiled unconsciously. The family would go crazy if they knew.

He was different, yes. He admitted that. His interests

ran deeper than simply decking the halls and fa-la-la-ing all year round.

Gazing at the framed portrait of Shakespeare above his fireplace, Kris asked, "What would you think of all this nonsense?" He half expected an answer from the great bard.

When he told his family he had to go, it wasn't just because of Nicholas's teasing or his father's anger and obvious disappointment. It wasn't even because the fake Christmas spirit that oozed out of every pore in their bodies made him nauseous.

He had a test to study for.

Kris had been taking night classes for the past year. His dream was to teach Shakespeare. It was a dream he never even considered sharing with his family. For all they knew, he was just an unmotivated slob that didn't put any effort into getting better at something. What they couldn't seem to grasp, though, was that playing Santa was the *only* thing he didn't care about.

He sank his lean frame into his worn armchair and picked up a copy of *Hamlet*.

"They'd probably think it's a story about a baby pig," he muttered.

Though he knew the play backward and forward, he studied more. His class would be tested next week, and he was determined to know it better than old William himself.

Then, when he was out of school and had a teaching position, maybe, just maybe, his family would be proud of him.

Kris shook his head. That would never happen.

CHAPTER FOUR

RALPH STOCKTON EXCUSED himself from the table and walked toward the basement door.

"Where are you going?" Brenda, his wife of three years, demanded.

"To my workshop. I've got to put the final touches on the special Christmas piece I'm designing. I'm unveiling it tomorrow, and I have to make sure it's perfect."

Ralph owned the only jewelry store in Saddle Hill, Kentucky. As a child, his dream had been to be a diamond miner. Claustrophobia and his bulky frame put an end to that dream. Instead, for the past thirty years he'd settled happily into designing and creating beautiful pieces for his customers to wear. Now fifty-three, he owned his own store. The store was his baby.

Unfortunately, business had been down the last several years and some months he'd barely been able to pay rent or buy supplies for new pieces. He was hoping his spectacular new design would sell well enough to get out from under the cloud of debt he'd been under.

"When do I get to see it? You shouldn't be keeping it a secret from me," Brenda pouted.

"Not much longer, sweet cakes," Ralph soothed. "I promise you'll see it as soon as it's finished."

"I hope so. Didn't we promise never to keep secrets from one another?"

"Yes. In due time, my dear," he assured her, then lumbered down the basement stairs.

Brenda tapped her bright red fingernail on the table. Ralph had been spending a lot of extra time in his workshop lately. *Whatever he's working on must be stunning.*

She stood, back straight, and flipped her dyed blond hair over her shoulder. At forty years old, she knew she could still turn heads. Even when no one was around, she was careful not to let her posture slump. *A good habit is far too easy to break,* her mother always warned.

Collecting the dishes from their meager Thanksgiving dinner, she scraped the bits of food from their plates into the garbage disposal and flicked it on. As the blades liquefied the already unappetizing food, she wondered how long she would have to go on playing the part of the happy, devoted wife. Sure, Ralph had his good qualities. For one thing, he owned a jewelry store. When they met and she realized he was unattached, she'd nabbed him before anybody else got the chance. At thirteen years her senior, she thought it was fairly obvious why she married him. He hadn't caught on, though, and still made his clumsy attempts at romance. In a way, she kind of felt sorry for him. He actually believed he had a prayer of holding on to her.

When they met three and a half years ago while they were both vacationing in Miami, she'd barely given him a second glance. With his thinning hair and middle-age paunch, it was no wonder he was still single at fifty. He certainly wasn't much to look at, but when she heard him on the phone with his gem supplier, she decided maybe a second glance wouldn't kill her. It hadn't been hard to charm him. After only a few months of their long-distance relationship, he'd put a ring on her finger. Insisting on a short engagement because she couldn't stand the thought of being away from him any longer, they'd married three months later.

Now she was the queen of Stockton's Jewel Palace, a tiny store that barely brought in enough money to pay the rent. It wasn't the lifestyle she'd envisioned when she married a man that was up to his elbows in diamonds.

And this town! It was so dull. She'd lived most of her life in the big city, and at first she'd thought a quaint life in Kentucky would be just the thing to keep her young. Instead, it sucked the life out of her. Besides the complete lack of sophistication, there were no men to choose from. Married or not, she'd vowed to keep her options open, but all the men were either married or had the charm of a troll. The good ones hightail it out of town as soon as they can. Not that she blamed them. She would too if it weren't for that blasted "till death do you part" thing.

How long until I've paid my debt and can actually get out of this God-forsaken place? she'd asked herself dozens of times.

She turned off the garbage disposal just in time to hear Ralph whistling happily. Though muffled, she thought the tune was "God Rest Ye Merry Gentlemen."

If nothing else, he is merry, she admitted. It made her sick.

Brenda turned off the light in the kitchen and went upstairs to change into her pajamas. If Ralph was going to work as late as he had been the past couple weeks, there'd be no use waiting up for him. She climbed into bed and clicked the TV on. *It's a Wonderful Life* was on.

She groaned. If only I could have gotten to see what my life was going to look like before I ever walked down that stupid aisle, she thought grumpily, I could have saved myself three years on that silly man and his rotten little town.

CHAPTER FIVE

RALPH LISTENED CLOSELY for any movement upstairs. He'd heard Brenda's footsteps on the stairs leading to their bedroom, but none since. *Maybe she'll fall asleep before I'm finished working on the piece,* he thought hopefully.

Once upon a time he'd really loved Brenda—or at least thought he had. Sure, they'd only been married three years, but it seemed like forever—and not in the comfortable, familiar way most couples do. The first time she'd walked over to him in that bar on the beach, he thought he'd hit the jackpot. No woman had ever looked at him like that. She seemed interested in him and loved hearing about his work. He'd been flattered. She was beautiful and way out of his league.

But she'd persisted, and he soon found himself proposing to her with the biggest diamond in his store. They'd been happy.

So he thought.

Now it seemed like all she did was complain. She didn't like small-town life, had trouble making friends, and even though she tried, couldn't hide her disappointment in the gift he'd given her for her birthday. He thought she would love a day at the spa. What woman wouldn't?

These days it was easier to spend the evenings by himself in his workshop. His special Christmas design made it easy. He'd work on it at the store during the day when business was slow and at home in the evenings. It had to be perfect. All his hopes for saving his store were riding on this one piece.

Unfortunately he didn't have the funds to buy all the supplies at once. Instead, he'd decided to make it a special-order piece, and the clients could choose their own metal and stones. That way, he wouldn't sink deeper into debt and each piece would be truly unique. The customer could make it as inexpensive or extravagant as they wanted.

People loved unique, one-of-a-kind things, he reasoned. This plan will work.

He made a large version of the piece, a star made of white diamonds with yellow diamonds shooting off from it. A shining star. The original would stay at the store, and the copies the customers ordered would be made significantly smaller and could be attached to a necklace or charm bracelet.

Brenda had been pouting for weeks that she hadn't been able to see what he was working on. Ralph told her he wanted to make sure it was perfect before she saw it, that he wanted to impress her. She didn't have to know that he missed the good old days when he used only his instincts to create pieces, and that he didn't care what her opinion was. She always wanted to give her two cents, and if he'd taken her advice, he'd have been out of business ages ago. Brenda often confused gaudy with beautiful, and her taste wasn't nearly as sophisticated as she thought.

Choosing to relish the impending success his star would

bring him, he pushed aside the frustration with his bride and launched into another whistling fit. This time it was "We Three Kings."

Star of wonder, star of night, star with royal beauty bright…
Just the thing for Stockton's Jewel Palace.

CHAPTER SIX

THE FLAMES DANCED as Joe Adler and Nadine Dobbs watched the crackling fire.

Nadine held her hand in front of her face. "I still can't believe it," she breathed. "This is going to be our last Thanksgiving as singles. By this time next year, we'll be Mr. and Mrs. Adler."

Joe smiled and nodded. He'd proposed to Nadine after dinner, over a piece of her homemade pumpkin pie. To his surprise and delight, she'd readily accepted. In his mind it had been a long shot that a girl like her would agree to marry him. He couldn't imagine another day in his life without her, and wondered how he'd managed for thirty-five years.

To him, Nadine was the epitome of class and beauty. With a delicate bone structure and flawless skin, large brown eyes and hair the shade of a latte heavy on the milk, in Joe's mind no other woman could hold a candle to her. Though she was thirty-two, she looked like she could have just graduated from high school. Even the poise with which she walked and the care she took with her work spoke volumes about the kind, generous person she was.

He, on the other hand, knew he could only be described as average. Average height, average weight, average looks. No one would notice him in a crowd, and many times someone he'd just met forgot him as soon as he left their field of vision. Average Joe. To make matters worse, he'd had dreams of being a police officer, but hadn't passed the physical. His childhood scoliosis had come back to bite him. That failure caused any remaining self-confidence he had to disappear.

Until Nadine came along, that is. She remembered him and everything about their first conversation. She thought he was handsome, and now she was wearing his engagement ring. It was almost too good to be true.

"I don't think we should have a long engagement, do you?" Nadine was saying. "I've always wanted a winter wedding, and I definitely don't want to wait until *next* winter. I was thinking sometime in January. I know that only gives us a month or two to plan the wedding, but I think we could make it work. Do you think it's too soon?"

Joe was still smiling and nodding, basking in the good fortune of meeting Nadine before somebody else swept her off her feet.

She knitted her eyebrows. "You do think it's too soon? I suppose I could be a spring bride, or even a summer one. Whatever it takes, just so I see you standing at the altar waiting for me."

"What? Sorry. I was distracted," Joe said sheepishly.

"I said that I always wanted a winter wedding, but that we could postpone it if you thought January was too soon," Nadine repeated.

Joe's eyes widened. "Of course January would be fine. The sooner the better, actually," he said hurriedly. "I don't want to give you time to change your mind."

Nadine squealed and stood from her seat to throw her arms around Joe, then lowered herself into his lap. "It will be a small wedding, just family and a few close friends. Hopefully we'll have the good fortune of a light snow falling. I'll wear a white fur cape over my dress. Won't that be wonderful?"

"It really will," Joe agreed. "I can't wait." As he spoke, he was certain he'd never said more honest words in his life. "But first we have to survive Christmas. Tomorrow is going to be crazy, isn't it?"

Nadine sighed. "It always is. I suppose it's a good thing, though. A lot of the stores really depend on the day after Thanksgiving to keep them afloat. I'm really worried about Ralph this year. If he doesn't sell enough, I don't think his store will be there next Christmas." She held her hand up again. "Although, I think you've done your part to keep the doors open."

Joe ignored her comment. "Well, I dread it. I wish everyone would just stay home in bed."

Joe was a security guard at the Saddle Hill Mall. Nadine was the pastry chef at the Rose Petal Café, a small bakery in the same mall. Both knew they wouldn't have a chance to catch their breath tomorrow.

"Don't start getting grouchy already, Joe. The season is just beginning," Nadine gently warned.

"I'm sorry, my sweet. It's just that not a year goes by when I don't have to break up a fight over some stupid toy. Last year an elderly man was pushed down on the floor over a toy robot. A *robot*," he repeated. "People just forget the whole meaning of Christmas."

"I know." Nadine glanced at her watch. "I've got to get going," she said, lightly kissing him, then raising herself from his lap.

He wrapped his arms around her slender waist and pulled her closer. "Two months. We'll be married in two months."

Nadine nuzzled his neck. "I know. It's just all so incredible." She kissed his forehead and whispered, "Now, I really have to go."

Joe reluctantly let go of her. "Will I see you tomorrow?"

"Only if you stop by the café on your lunch break. Other than that, I'll be swamped. All that shopping makes people hungry, and they get grumpy if they don't get their sugar fix."

"I'll try to stop by. Maybe you can make me a sandwich or something."

"Sandwiches aren't exactly my specialty, but for you, I'll make an exception." Nadine slipped her coat on and said, "I have to be at work at four o'clock tomorrow morning, so I need to get home for some shut-eye." She stood and walked toward the door. With her hand resting on the doorknob, she turned and said, "Goodnight *Mr.* Adler," then opened the door and walked out into the night, leaving Joe sitting alone by the fireplace.

"Goodnight *Mrs.* Adler," he said to the closed door.

Not much longer, he thought. Soon she will be here to stay. He smiled as he stood and disappeared down the hall to the bedroom he'd share with Nadine in two short months.

He knew he'd have sweet dreams tonight. Dreams that had nothing to do with the Christmas sweets Nadine would be busy baking tomorrow. Shortly after Christmas, as long as nothing went wrong, she would be Mrs. Joe Adler.

CHAPTER SEVEN

NOW THAT THANKSGIVING was practically over, it was time to survive another Christmas season. Holly Berry pushed her chair back from the rickety desk in her living room and walked the short distance to her bedroom. Christmas had been terrible for her since her parents split on Christmas Eve when she was seven. Now the joy of the season was forever hitched to memories of heartbreak and loss. Barely on speaking terms with either of her parents, she usually spent the holidays alone, ducking her head and waiting for them to be over. New Year's was more her kind of holiday. After all, who couldn't use a fresh start?

If her parents' hostile divorce hadn't made the holiday hard enough, they'd saddled her with a name that made her the butt of every Christmas joke under the sun. Enduring the mocking at Christmas was one thing, but June was quite another. Having hair the color of a fire engine didn't help, either.

As a child, she'd learned that isolation was the best way to keep others from hurting her, so she'd spent the majority of twenty-five years as a loner. Unfortunately for her, that very isolation is what led her to make one bad decision after another. A good support system could have kept her from shoplifting and dropping out of college. At least that's what the court-mandated counselor had said.

For once in her life, Holly just wanted things to go her way, to have somebody that cared about her and would help her start a better life. She just wanted to not have to struggle.

Her parents certainly didn't fit the bill, but maybe someone else did.

Since the Christmas season would officially start tomorrow and the jokes poked at her would be kicked up a notch, Holly had gotten on the Christmas name support group website to see if others were already suffering because of their names. Even though she didn't know any of them personally, the camaraderie was encouraging.

Holly had been surprised that Marian Bright had addressed her directly, then left an even more personal note and her address and phone number in a private message.

She seemed to be genuinely concerned about me, Holly thought. Maybe I should take her up on her offer. I understand what it's like to be lonely at Christmas, and this will be her first one alone in fifty years.

Holly twirled her bright red hair around a slender index finger and chewed her bottom lip. It was worth a shot, she decided. Grabbing a suitcase from her closet, she quickly pulled jeans and sweaters from her dresser drawers. Then she turned toward the cramped bathroom and dropped her toiletries into a smaller bag. In less than thirty minutes, she was finished packing.

For the second time that evening, Holly logged into the website and typed a quick message: *Marian, I'm on my way. I should be at your house around midnight. Holly.* Sure, she had Marian's phone number, but this felt less committed. If she changed her mind halfway there, there would always be the chance Marian hadn't checked the website.

She's so trusting, Holly thought. She has no idea who I am but is willing to let me come into her home and stay with her for an entire month. For all she knows, I could be planning to rob her blind. If this was three months ago, I probably would have. Holly shook her head. A month in jail was all it took to make her want a new start.

Grateful for Marian's blind trust, Holly double-checked to make sure all the lights in her crummy little apartment were off and locked the door behind her.

Marian lived about four hours away in Saddle Hill, Kentucky. If she made good time, Holly should be there just before midnight. Still uncertain about whether or not she'd actually follow through with the trip, she shifted the car into reverse and backed out of the parking lot.

If nothing else, the next several weeks would be an adventure.

At 11:58 p.m., Holly pulled into the driveway of a small ranch-style home. The street was lined with bare trees and cheery streetlights. If there had been snow on the ground, it could have served as the backdrop for a Christmas card.

Taking a deep breath, Holly grabbed the suitcase from the backseat and made her way up the front walk and rang the doorbell. Not quite sure what to expect of her hostess, Holly was pleased when a birdlike woman in a red and white flannel robe answered the door. She looked like everyone's favorite grandmother.

"Come in, dear," Marian said with a warm smile and stepped aside so Holly could enter. "To be honest, I'm surprised you came."

"No one is more surprised than me, Ms. Bright. Thank you for inviting me." Holly shifted uncomfortably in the entryway of the cheerful home.

"Please make yourself at home." Marian swept a hand toward the open living room. Boxes of Christmas decorations were spread on the floor, ribbon and garland hanging out of many of them. "Excuse the mess. I wouldn't usually start decorating Thanksgiving night, but when I got your message I decided to get a jump on things. The house isn't completely decorated yet, but the guest room is all ready for you."

Holly followed Marian down a narrow hall and stopped outside the bedroom Holly would be using for the next several weeks. "I think you'll find everything you need in there. You'll have your own bathroom, so just make yourself comfy."

"Thank you. I really do appreciate this, Ms. Bright." Tears stung the backs of her eyes. "I haven't felt this welcome somewhere in a long time."

Marian reached out and squeezed Holly's hand. "Please call me Marian. We're living together for the next month, so we might as well drop the formality." Wrinkles creased around Marian's eyes as she smiled. "Now, I've got to get to bed. I have to be at work at five o'clock tomorrow morning. You'll find everything you need for breakfast in the refrigerator. Goodnight, Holly." With that, Marian turned and walked the few feet down the hall to the other bedroom and closed the door behind her.

After putting on her pajamas and settling on the four-poster bed that smelled like a freshly cut pine tree, she slid between the red and green patterned flannel sheets, wondering exactly what she'd gotten herself into.

33

CHAPTER EIGHT

THE FIRST DAY of the Christmas season dawned cold and clear. Marian swung her feet over the side of the bed and promptly slid them into her slippers. Her alarm wasn't set to go off for another seven minutes, but she couldn't bear to lay in bed any longer. It was time to get to work spreading Christmas cheer to the masses.

This would be her sixteenth year playing an elf for all the children that came to sit on Santa's lap. It was a role that suited her perfectly. With her small size and merry disposition, she was a natural. To think she enjoyed being a mall elf this much at the age of seventy-two would amaze anyone who didn't know her. Those who did know her weren't surprised in the least.

Marian took a few moments to stretch her back and legs. The spirit was willing, but the rest of her was becoming arthritic. A few minutes later, her joints were as loose as they were going to get, and she started getting ready.

Each year, Santa started showing up earlier and earlier. This year, his first day had been November first. Being a mall

Santa was a decent-paying gig, and men of all ages lined up for the honor, willing to start as early as possible. Marian was sure that Santa would soon be sitting in his chair right next to the ghosts and goblins on Halloween. After all, the stores already had Christmas decorations for sale by then.

Not Marian, though. She was a purist. Christmas season began at midnight after all the Thanksgiving festivities were over, and not a second sooner. To her, Christmas was more magical when celebrated for a limited time. She'd only made an exception and decorated a bit early this year because Holly was there.

Donning her robe, Marian shuffled quietly down the hall toward the kitchen, careful not to wake her sleeping houseguest. Though she'd never laid eyes on the girl, Marian felt an instant kinship with her. Perhaps it was the Christmas name, or the fact that this Christmas would be a lonely time for both of them. Whatever it was, Marian was certain they'd have a jolly time together for the next twenty-nine days.

After a quick cup of coffee complete with eggnog creamer and a piece of toast cut into the shape of a Christmas tree, Marian jotted a quick note for Holly, encouraging her to come to the mall for the kickoff of the town's Christmas festivities, sure to include that it was a celebration she wouldn't want to miss. She signed it "Merry Marian."

Satisfied she was helping Holly get off to a good start, she went back to her bedroom to get dressed. Her costume awaited.

From the back of her closet, she pulled out a green full-body leotard, complete with a green felt tunic that had bells around the bottom hem. Most of the other elves complained about the ensemble, but Marian was thin enough to feel comfortable in it, no matter how tight the leotard. Besides, she reasoned, the tunic covers the important parts, anyway. Over the tunic she slipped on the first Christmas sweater to make an appearance this season. It was a bright red number with leaping white reindeer across the chest. This was her oldest and would be retired next year.

She slipped on her pointy-toed elf shoes, careful to slide her feet when she walked to keep the bells around the ankles from jingling.

Stepping out into the cold morning air, she inhaled deeply, the chill burning her nose as she looked up at the sky. Still dark, there wasn't a cloud in the sky to cover the millions of stars that twinkled above her.

What a great day to be alive, she thought, then slid behind the wheel of her Buick.

Twenty minutes later, after weaving her way through the crowd already lined up outside the mall, Marian quickly walked around to the employee entrance and unlocked the door.

An early bird shopper saw her unlock the door and shouted, "They're opening that door!"

A small group broke off from the crowd and charged in her direction. Heart pounding, she slipped inside and pulled the door shut quickly behind her, reengaging the lock just as an enthusiastic shopper tugged on the handle.

"Even in Saddle Hill," Marian muttered to herself as she marched toward the center of the mall, where every employee was expected to be at five a.m. sharp.

Marian made it to the meeting with fifteen seconds to spare.

"Okay, everyone," Winston Marshall, the mall manager, bellowed from his perch in the middle of the group of dedicated mall employees. "I want to see everyone smiling today, even if the customers get rowdy. It's your job to spread the joy of the season, whether you feel like it or not. From what I gather, this Christmas has the potential to be one of the most lucrative ones in the past several years. I want to make sure that happens, so I don't want to hear about any bad attitudes from you."

He paused briefly, just long enough for the audience to nod in agreement. "Very well. Okay, troops. Man your battle stations."

It was common knowledge that Winston had enlisted in the army several years ago, only to find out he had a heart murmur during processing. He received a medical discharge and was sent home. He never got to serve his country, but when he became manager of the Saddle Hill Mall, he finally got his chance to be a commanding officer. Always referring to his employees as "troops," he insisted that each and every one pass daily inspection.

Behind his back they called him "The General."

Unfortunately for the employees, he believed he and Winston Churchill were kindred spirits, even though the shared name was where the similarity ended.

He descended the makeshift platform that would now serve as Santa's Workshop and strode with his back straight toward his office, signaling that everyone should begin performing their assigned duties.

With that, the group disbanded.

"Nadine, your smile is even brighter than usual," Marian remarked, catching Nadine Dobbs's arm. "You must be excited to be here baking your glorious pastries for the hordes."

Nadine laughed softly and shrugged. "It pays the bills. Besides, some people are very generous during the holidays.

But that's not why I'm smiling." She leaned closer to Marian and whispered. "Joe and I got engaged last night."

"Oh, how wonderful!" Marian crowed, then glanced at Nadine's hand. "What a lovely ring. Is it one of Ralph's?"

Nadine nodded. "It's just beautiful. He did a marvelous job with it."

Winston glanced over his shoulder at the lingering employees, then snapped his fingers and pointed in the direction of the bakery.

Nadine rolled her eyes. "I better get back to work. The General has spoken."

"I'll come by the café at lunch. Maybe I can catch Joe. I'd love to congratulate Joe on his choice of ladies." Marian winked then watched as Nadine glided back to the bakery.

Even with flour all over her chef's coat and powdered sugar on her nose, Nadine practically glowed.

If only everyone had such a sunny outlook on life, Marian thought, we wouldn't have to wait until Christmas to see the good in people.

CHAPTER NINE

RALPH STOCKTON GAZED lovingly at the white and yellow diamond star in the protective glass case. His labor of love during the past several weeks had paid off. In his mind, it was the most beautiful thing he'd ever created. Heck, it was the most beautiful thing *anyone* had ever created. So far, no one else had seen it, and he wanted to treasure the last few minutes alone with his masterpiece.

Even the ring Joe Adler had purchased for Nadine Dobbs wouldn't match the beauty of the star. As he was leaving the employee meeting, Ralph had noticed Marian Bright admiring Nadine's ring. He unconsciously smiled. Nothing gave him greater pleasure that seeing others enjoy and appreciate his work. That was what drove him to create the most beautiful and best-quality jewelry he could. Ralph hoped his reputation as a fair and conscientious jeweler would help him sell even more this year than in Christmases past.

He glanced again at the star.

The doors would open in three minutes, and throngs of shoppers would dart to and fro in search of the best deal.

Fortunately for him, the location of his store ensured they must pass him first. He hoped that meant he'd get some orders for the star before the consumers started spending their money on pieces of junk they didn't really need.

Just moments before the door opened, his cell phone rang. At this hour, it could only be one person.

"Good morning, Brenda," he said. "You're up early."

"You didn't show me the piece you've been working on before you left this morning. I wanted to be the first to see it," she whined.

"I'm sorry, my love," Ralph soothed. "You were sleeping so peacefully and looked just like an angel. I didn't want to disturb your sweet dreams."

"When do I get to see it? Surely you aren't going to put it on display until I do."

Panic flitted through Ralph's midsection. He could hear the footsteps of the shoppers thundering toward him. There was no way Brenda would be able to see that star before anyone else. She'd be livid, and impossible to live with if she didn't get her way.

On the other hand, he reasoned, if I take it off display, I'll miss the prime opportunity to get orders for the star. The store depends on it.

"Of course not, dear," he lied. "I wouldn't dream of showing it to anyone else before you see it."

Several people filed into the store, most of whom stopped to ooh and ahh over the star.

"It's beautiful," remarked a large woman with an equally large handbag and hair dyed an alarming shade of red.

"I've never seen anything like it," said a girl in her teens, who Ralph was sure wouldn't be able to afford to buy the star for at least another decade.

Bursting with pride, Ralph turned his attention back to his phone call. "Brenda, I've got to go. They've just opened the doors and I need to be out on the floor greeting anyone who might want to buy my jewelry. Try to get down here as soon as you can. I can't keep the new design a secret for much longer." With that he disconnected the call and turned toward the people admiring his handiwork.

"Where are these?" asked a middle-aged woman, pointing toward the star.

Ralph slid his phone back into his pocket, and with a smile on his face, approached the inquiring woman. "These are special-order pieces. They are truly one of a kind. You choose your metal and the type of gems you want in it. No other will look exactly like the one you select," Ralph beamed.

"That sounds wonderful," someone murmured.

"I'd like one," said the lady with the large handbag and red hair.

"Me, too," chorused four more voices.

"Of course," Ralph readily agreed and pulled out the paperwork for the customers to fill out.

This is going even better than I'd imagined, he thought happily.

One by one, the customers handed him their forms, and he tallied the cost of the metal and gems to give them a final total.

Pleased that they'd be getting something no one else had, the ladies exited his store in search of more good deals.

I guess my being in the red this year is actually helping business, he mused as he was once again alone with his star.

Otherwise, every one of the stars would look the same and the uniqueness would be lost.

He began whistling the first few bars of "We Three Kings."

As another group of shoppers entered the store, Ralph smiled at the thought that the Star of Bethlehem wasn't the only magical star this Christmas.

CHAPTER TEN

BRENDA MORRIS-STOCKTON HUFFED and tossed the phone onto the bed beside her. Ralph had promised she would be the first to see the new piece he'd been working on for the Christmas season. Now she was certain he was going to put it on display before she got to the store.

When she married a jeweler, she'd imagined being showered in jewels for every holiday and special occasion. Diamonds are a girl's best friend, after all.

Only Ralph, of all people, didn't seem to know that. Aside from the engagement ring he'd given her and a few small trinkets of no real value, she'd gotten squat in the jewelry department. He kept trying to be creative.

She hated it.

Instead of living in the lap of luxury, she was stuck in a tiny house in a tiny town. She glanced around the room in disgust. Everything was so dated. They even slept under a quilt instead of a plush down comforter with a designer duvet.

How primitive, she thought.

The entire house was in need of remodeling. It still had the look of a bachelor pad, just as it had been since Ralph moved out of his parent's house thirty-five years ago. Brenda swore he hadn't replaced so much as a towel since then. Now, every time Brenda tried to freshen the place up, Ralph groaned about how much money she spent.

"Don't you know it takes money to get good stuff?" Brenda would argue.

He always countered with the same remark. "And don't you know it isn't stuff that makes life grand?"

Around and around they went until Brenda would stomp out of the room, certain she'd married a cross between a simpleton and a caveman.

As she laid in bed thinking about how her marriage to Ralph had caused her to miss three years of the finer things in life, she pulled a loose thread on the quilt Ralph loved so much. Something about it being a family heirloom.

What a sap, she thought bitterly. He claims to care about people instead of things, yet he's going to put his top-secret piece on display for all the world to see before I get so much as a glimpse of it.

Or maybe he won't, the little voice in Brenda's mind said. If nothing else, Ralph is a man of his word.

Brenda shrugged and nestled deeper into the bed, pretending she was surrounded by soft goose down. Ralph wants me to come to the store and see his latest creation. He's made me wait this long. Now he can wait.

Pulling the quilt up to her chin, "Silver Bells" played in her mind. She smiled drowsily. That was what she'd always called a college friend of hers around Christmastime. If my life is pathetic, Brenda mused, I can only imagine how dreadful Sylvia Bell's is.

She sighed, taking comfort in that thought as she drifted back to sleep.

CHAPTER ELEVEN

SYLVIA BELL STRETCHED and wiggled her toes under the heavy down comforter. A soft snow was falling on Park Avenue and her favorite Christmas song was playing on the radio. It was going to be a magnificent day. Yesterday had been wonderful, her favorite Thanksgiving so far. It had been a tough year for her and her company. Her employees resented her for making them work on Thanksgiving but had made the most of it.

As their company-wide Thanksgiving lunch came to a close, she stood with a glass of champagne and announced they were free to take the rest of the day off, and that they could have today off as well. Cheers echoed off the walls of the conference room as her employees rose and practically knocked her down as they surrounded her in a group hug.

It had been a tough year for them, too.

But they'd been building a fashion empire. Everyone sacrificed and everyone was rewarded. Now, their new line was being released today, just in time for the Christmas rush. It was a reason to celebrate.

Make that a *season* to celebrate.

Finally, she urged herself out of bed and walked across the heated floor of her penthouse to the kitchen. She brewed a pot of coffee and plucked the single chocolate-covered donut from the box on the counter.

There would be no diet today.

She smiled broadly, revealing a row of perfectly white, perfectly straight teeth as the scent of coffee filled the kitchen. She loved mornings.

Turning to grab a mug from the cabinet, Sylvia caught a glimpse of herself in the microwave door. Again, she smiled. She liked what she saw. A mane of wavy black hair cascaded around her perfectly symmetrical face. She was tall and slender. Finally, she'd hit the jackpot in the looks department.

It wasn't always this way, she remembered. A mess all the way through college, the other girls made fun of her frizzy, uncontrollable hair and the ten extra pounds she could never seem to get rid of. It all came to a head when her roommate, Brenda Morris, found out Sylvia wanted to go into fashion. Brenda told Sylvia she'd never make it, that she wasn't pretty enough to ever be taken seriously in the fashion industry. On her particularly mean days, Brenda had called her "Cow Bell."

If only she could see me now, Sylvia thought bitterly.

In direct rebellion to that awful nickname, Sylvia had named her clothing line "Jersey Belle." Everyone thought it was a nod to Sylvia's New Jersey roots, and she never bothered to correct them. A Jersey was actually a kind of cow. It was her own passive-aggressive way of sticking it to Brenda that she'd found success in the fashion world after all.

The coffee maker gurgled, alerting Sylvia that it was finished brewing. She shook the thought of Brenda Morris from her head. Today was a day of celebration, and she was going to eat, drink, and be merry. There was no room for thoughts of a college bully today.

Deciding a trip was in order for the long weekend, Sylvia settled down at her computer to look up small-town Christmas festivals. After all the long hours and hard work she'd put in this year, she was finally going to let her hair down. It would be glorious to finally get some peace and quiet away from the city and deadlines.

She remembered that one of the members of the Christmas name support group raved about her town's Mountain Craft Festival. Sylvia tapped her finger on her desk. What was the name of that town? Ah, yes. Saddle Hill, in Kentucky.

She entered the town into her search engine and was rewarded with pictures of a quaint town and advertisements for the Craft Festival this weekend.

Who would imagine that a city girl like her would be heading to a small town in the Bluegrass State? There were no skyscrapers or subway stations or designer boutiques.

It looked perfect.

Several minutes later, Sylvia's plane ticket was booked and she was busily tossing her most comfortable clothes into her Louis Vuitton suitcase. She only had an hour to get to the airport and Black Friday traffic would make it take forever.

When her driver buzzed to say he was waiting for her in the lobby, she took one last glance around the apartment. She wouldn't see anything like it for two glorious days.

Rolling her suitcase behind her, she glanced at the picture from fifteen years ago on an end table in her living room. Her hair was frizzy, her face round. That was the girl that had been teased mercilessly all through college.

With the all-too-familiar ache of rejection, Sylvia wondered whatever became of Brenda Morris. She'd always been so certain she was going to make it big somewhere. With her ruthless attitude and willingness to do whatever it took to get ahead, Sylvia was certain Brenda had succeeded.

CHAPTER TWELVE

CHRISTMASTIME AT THE Jingle house was in full swing. A fire crackled in the fireplace while Bing Crosby crooned in the background. It was a typical Friday morning for them.

"Patty dear, you've really outdone yourself this time," James Jingle said as Patricia flipped the pancakes on the griddle. "Can I have a few more?"

Patricia looked at her husband of more than forty years. James wore red long johns, red flannel pants, and suspenders. His full snow-white beard and rosy cheeks completed the look. He was Santa Claus incarnate. He also seemed to be taking his job of getting plump for the holiday season seriously.

"They'll be ready in a few minutes," she responded, pleased that her first attempt at eggnog pancakes appeared to be a success. She wore a red fleece robe with white trim, her mostly gray hair swept up into a bun. A suitable Mrs. Claus.

It was hard to remember what they looked like before Christmas hijacked their lives.

"Wonderful! They're just what we need to kick the official Christmas season off right," James enthused. "Heaven knows we need a bit more cheer in this house after Kris did everything he could to ruin it for us."

Patricia's hand tightened on the spatula. Take a deep breath, she reminded herself. "You know, James," she said cautiously, "we might have come down a little too hard on him. After all, he is thirty-seven years old. There comes a time when we have to let our children make their own way in the world." She flipped the pancakes once more to make sure they were a perfect golden brown.

James pounded his coffee mug on the table. "It's a family tradition, Patricia. He knows that, and he knows what's expected of him in this family. He is to be a good Santa, a jolly Santa, and to keep Christmas in his heart all year long."

Patricia winced. He only used her full name when he was angry. "I suppose," she conceded. "I just hate to see the rift this causes between Kris and the rest of the family. There will come a time, I'm afraid, when we will have to decide which is more important; playing Christmas three hundred and sixty-five days a year or having Kris in our lives."

James shook his head tightly. "Kris is deciding that for us by alienating the family and everything we hold dear."

"Is he Santa at the mall today?" Patricia asked, hoping the question would remind James that Kris hadn't abandoned the tradition altogether.

James grunted. "Yeah. He started at eight o'clock this morning. Back when it was my full-time gig, we started at six a.m. on the dot."

"I remember dear," she said in a soothing tone, "but Winston pushed the time back because so few kids were showing up that early. I mean, what parent in their right mind would drag a sleepy kid out of bed at that hour just to sit on Santa's lap?"

James's mouth formed a hard line. "The kind of parent that's serious about Christmas. The kind of parents we are." He looked pointedly at Patricia. "Or at least used to be."

She pretended not to notice the implication. Sliding the spatula under each pancake, she put them on a plate and carried them over to her not-so-jolly husband.

He looked at the three perfectly golden circles. "Never mind. I've lost my appetite." The legs of the chair screeched on the floor as he pushed away from the table. As he stood, he said, "I will want some Christmas cookies later." Then he walked, shoulders slumped, into the living room. He was a disgruntled Santa carrying the weight of the world.

She sighed. Trying to get James to see the other side of the argument was useless.

Patricia picked up his dirty plate and carried it to the sink, then walked back to the table and settled into the chair James had just vacated. She picked up the fork and cut a wedge off one of the pancakes. It was delicious, or it would have been if her stomach wasn't twisted into knots. She didn't have an appetite either.

She scraped the uneaten pancakes into the garbage and loaded the breakfast dishes in the dishwasher. She needed to find a way to talk to Kris. One way or another, the family had to find some common ground. If they didn't, she feared the last Christmas was, indeed, the last Christmas they would spend together as a family.

Patricia went to the bedroom to change into an appropriate Mrs. Claus outfit. As she closed the bedroom door, Perry Como launched into "There's No Christmas Like a Home Christmas."

As the door clicked shut, she heard James say, "I know, Perry. But these kids just don't get it."

CHAPTER THIRTEEN

"BUT I WANNA sit on Santa's lap next!" a little boy cried as he waited for his turn to give Kris Jingle his Christmas list.

The line to see Santa wove around the Christmas displays in the center of the mall and halfway down to Stockton's Jewel Palace, which was at the farthest end of the mall.

It was only eight o'clock in the morning and the impatient boy was near the end of the line.

Kris stretched his neck from side to side. He could already feel the tension creeping up the back of his neck and wrapping around his head. Who on earth brings a child to see Santa this early in the morning? One more look at the line of children answered the question for him: at least half the town.

They should be home in their jammies watching cartoons, Kris complained to himself. Not that complaining had ever done him any good. It had only ever made him an outcast and had gotten him accused of being a grump.

A portly child with rosy cheeks and uncontrollable curls made her way up to Kris. She had bright eyes and a beaming smile. He groaned. This one was going to hurt.

"I want a doll with a stroller, a crib, a changing table, a bassinet, and a bunch of clothes," she said before she was fully settled on his lap.

"Is that all?" He was already in a bad mood.

She looked up at him and blinked innocently. "No. I also want a doctor's kit, and shoes and clothes for myself. Oh, and I'll also need diapers for the doll," she added cheerily, as if asking for twenty things in the span of six seconds was the most natural thing in the world for her. She rattled off a half dozen more items on her wish list before batting her baby blues at him. "I promise I've been good all year."

"I'm sure you have," Kris mumbled, then nudged her until she took the hint and vacated his lap.

The girl walked over to Marian Bright, who was holding a basket of candy canes and had a permanent smile on her face. She pulled one from the bunch and handed it to the child, who curtsied in front of her.

"Merry Christmas, dear," Marian said, then guided the girl back to her mother.

Taking a few steps to her right, she leaned close to Kris. "You have to smile. These kids are here to see a jolly Santa, not the Christmas grouch. Perk up." Marian's smile didn't fall during the gentle scolding. "The day is just beginning."

"Don't remind me. I wasn't born with your cheery disposition," he grumbled, then turned his attention to the ever-growing line of children.

"I find that hard to believe, Kris. I know your mother and father very well. They're about as cheery as people can get."

"I know. It's awful." Kris shook his head. "Now, if you don't mind, I'd like to start moving these kids through. Some of them have a list longer than my arm." He took a deep breath and muttered, "It's going to be a long day."

One by one, the children sat on Kris's lap, their endless requests drowning out the cheerful music playing in the background. After an hour, Kris had had enough.

"Santa needs a potty break," he announced to the children. "I will be back in fifteen minutes," he said over the protests of dozens of kids.

Maybe some of the parents will decide they don't want to wait and take their little angels home, he hoped. Or better yet, they'll do some shopping and come back when Nicholas is on duty.

The corner of Kris's mouth twitched. That would serve him right. Let all these parents bring their kids back after they've been shopping all day and the whole family is on the verge of a meltdown. Then we'd see how jolly Nicholas really is.

Fat chance of that happening, though. Nicholas would be cheery for no other reason than to spite Kris.

Locking himself in the bathroom stall, Kris leaned against the door. Thirty more days and Christmas would be over. Everyone will be sick of the decorations, the music, and even the presents. Kids will have lost interest in their new toys after about five minutes, and the parents would be saddled with sky-high credit card bills from buying this worthless garbage for the little darlings.

What's the point of it all? Year after year, why do people keep thinking this is the true meaning of Christmas?

The timer he'd set on his watch beeped, alerting him that his fifteen minutes of solace was up.

Just as he reached toward the latch to unlock the stall door, a small head poked under the divider in the stall. "Santa! Guess what I want for Christmas?"

"Get in line, kid," he grumbled as he washed his hands and headed back toward the crush of the season. The little peeping Tom in the bathroom had erased any joy he might have gotten from his few minutes alone.

"Thanks a bunch, you wretched little snot," Kris muttered as he approached Santa's Throne with the same enthusiasm he would if he was going to the electric chair.

CHAPTER FOURTEEN

MARIAN TRIED TO hide her concern for Kris Jingle. He was in even lower spirits this year than he'd been last Christmas, and that was saying something. For some reason, Kris always seemed to ooze melancholy this time of year.

What an odd duck, Marian thought, watching kid after kid climb onto Kris's lap. He's not at all like the rest of his family.

She'd been playing the part of an elf at the mall for the last sixteen years, most of them side by side with Kris Jingle. Each year he seemed less and less enthusiastic about his role as Santa. It was so bad this morning that Marian wondered how he kept the gig at all, or why he'd even want to with the kind of attitude he had.

Sure, he'd been sitting in that very chair with kids spouting their endless requests at him since November first, but there was still a month to go before he could hang up his boots and big shiny belt. At this rate, he'd never survive.

And neither would she if he didn't stop being such a downer.

"Santa Claus is Coming to Town" began playing over the loudspeaker. Kris visibly tensed.

Whatever his problem is, it has something to do with being a Santa Claus. It has to. He doesn't seem to dislike Christmas itself too much, it's Santa he seems to hate. I guess I shouldn't be surprised, though. His parents are nice, and I've always gotten along with them, but they do take Christmas to the extreme. As far as they're concerned, there are no other days of the year worth celebrating if it's not Christmas day. My Roger always thought they were a peculiar bunch.

She continued her internal monologue, all the while absently handing out candy canes and smiles to the youngsters that stopped by.

Marian glanced at her watch. It was only nine-thirty, and Kris was the Santa on duty until two o'clock when his younger brother, Nicholas, would take over.

Boy, those two are like night and day, she thought, shaking her head. Nicholas is just like their father. He can't get enough Christmas. It's obnoxious, actually, she mused. Working next to Nicholas was almost as bad as working with his father.

Suddenly thankful she was working with the least jolly of the Jingle clan, she realized she hadn't been paying attention when she handed a candy cane to Winston Marshall, the mall manager. His scowl told her she and Kris needed to get their act together soon, or Kris's grumpiness was going to pale in comparison to the wrath of The General.

CHAPTER FIFTEEN

WITH A PRACTICED military carriage, Winston turned on his heel and marched back toward his office.

These people are going to ruin me, he thought, as he tilted his head and forced himself to smile at the shoppers bustling around him. At least *they* aren't trying to put me out of business.

His bi-hourly inspection of the mall employees certainly didn't provide that kind of comfort.

At the Rose Petal Café, Nadine and Wanda darted around like they hadn't been expecting such a large breakfast crowd. Wanda shouted orders to Nadine, who appeared to be off in la-la land and seemed to take her sweet time restocking the bakery case.

Joe had been walking around almost aimlessly, paying little attention to what was going on around him. He'd only glanced half-heartedly through the window of Whipple's Wicks, Carla Whipple's candle store. For all Joe knew, a customer could have gone crazy and thrown a dozen of the candles onto the floor, shattering glass everywhere, and he'd never even know it.

Then there was Kris. How he could be the biological child of James and Patricia Jingle was a mystery. *What am I going to do with him?* Winston wondered for the fiftieth time that morning. Every day for the past three weeks, Kris sat on the throne in front of Santa's Workshop looking like he'd just eaten a truckload of sour grapes. If he didn't straighten up soon, parents were going to stop bringing their children to sit on Santa's lap. Winston wouldn't stand for it.

I could always fire him, he thought.

A wave of panic washed over him as he thought of the backlash he'd face if he fired a Jingle. Though he was no longer the sole Santa and hadn't wanted to work twelve-hour shifts in several years, James Jingle still carried a lot of weight in this town. He was the unofficial, and in his own mind, the official, spirit of Christmas in Saddle Hill. There was no way he'd stand for his eldest son being let go from the role James felt they were all born to play.

What should I do? Winston wondered, chewing his thumbnail. He quickly jerked his hand away from his mouth. It was a sign of weakness when someone displayed that kind of nervous habit.

He concluded there was no good option but to ride out this Christmas season, and consider making changes for next year. Surely there were younger, cheerier men who'd want the gig.

Marian was a pro and would make the transition easy, although he wasn't quite sure what had gotten into her this morning. Paying so little attention to the children, and not even noticing when she gave him a candy cane instead of a child wasn't like her. If Kris was dragging her down too, perhaps letting him go couldn't wait until next year, after all.

He'd just have to deal with the temper tantrum James Jingle would throw at him.

The one bright spot in Winston's morning had been Ralph Stockton. Bright, cheerful, jolly Ralph hadn't taken the smile off his face since he walked through the doors at a quarter to five this morning. That's the kind of attitude we all need, Winston thought. Ralph, even though he's facing bankruptcy and would lose his business if his new design doesn't sell, is still smiling. If Ralph can have a positive attitude even when he's facing losing everything he's worked so hard for, why can't everybody else?

Let's just hope he sells enough, Winston thought, mentally crossing his fingers. If he doesn't, we won't see that smiling face around here anymore, and we certainly can't afford to lose him.

CHAPTER SIXTEEN

AT TEN O'CLOCK, Brenda Morris-Stockton hopped out of bed and went to the closet. She wanted to look dazzling. Most of the people that had been out shopping all morning would look haggard, at best.

Not that the vast majority of them look much better than that even on their best days, she thought smugly. That's the thing about a small town. You've got one or two hairdressers that do a mediocre job, but customers flock to them and then rave about their new 'do like they just stepped out of a salon on Park Avenue.

Brenda wouldn't settle for mediocre. Since she'd married Ralph, she'd been driving two hours to a decent salon every six weeks. It was taxing, but worth it. She looked better than anyone in town. Too bad Ralph didn't see the value in it. He just complained about how much it cost to keep her looking that way.

After selecting a red sweater she knew hugged her curves in all the right places and a pair of jeans that did the same, she hurried to the bathroom where she went through her typical morning beauty routine. An hour later, she emerged looking effortlessly perfect. The other women would hate her, and she'd let them. They didn't need to know she had to work for it.

A quick spritz of her intoxicating perfume and she was ready to fulfill her role as queen of Stockton's Jewel Palace.

"On second thought, maybe I should wear some jewelry," she muttered to herself. "It might make people buy more things at Ralph's store. He certainly needs the business."

Taking an inventory of her jewelry box, she decided on a white gold and diamond encrusted snowflake pin and a pair of diamond studs. No need to look gaudy, she told herself. Not that she had enough jewelry for that.

At eleven o'clock, the sun shone brightly against the brilliant blue sky. She grabbed her designer coat and slipped her feet into her most expensive boots and walked to her Mercedes, the one splurge she'd been able to talk Ralph into. He was so practical he still drove a fifteen-year-old Chevy.

Suddenly and inexplicably, she was filled with the Christmas spirit. Again, she began softly humming "Silver Bells."

Why does that song keep popping into my head? she wondered as she guided her car into the mall parking lot.

Finally, at eleven-fifteen, Brenda breezed into Stockton's Jewel Palace. She was shocked and pleasantly surprised to see a large crowd gathered at the display cases.

All this and he hasn't even unveiled the new design.

The crowd shifted, making a gap between several of the shoppers. There, on top of one of the display cases, Brenda saw a three-inch by three-inch white diamond star with yellow diamonds shooting from the sides and points.

The *nerve*, she thought angrily. I was supposed to be the

first one to see his new design, and there it is, on display for the whole town to see.

"Ralph!" she bellowed above the pleasant chatter of the shoppers. A few turned to look at her, then went back to admiring Ralph's handiwork.

Ralph looked up from his station behind the cash register. "Just a minute," he said, then looked back at the paper in his hand. Ralph smiled and nodded as a customer spoke to him, then took a credit card from the woman and swiped it. "It's going to be just lovely," he remarked. "The stones you have chosen will complement each other beautifully." He gave the card back to the woman, then she signed the receipt and left the store, smiling.

Another satisfied customer, Brenda thought bitterly.

Pushing through the crowd of shoppers, Brenda demanded, "What is the meaning of this?"

"The meaning of what, dear?" Ralph asked with a look of childlike innocence on his face.

"Don't play stupid. The meaning of this." She waved her hand around the store, stopping when she was pointing at the star.

"You mean selling jewelry? That's what I do for a living. I thought you knew that." The corner of Ralph's mouth twitched.

"You know exactly what I mean," she huffed, then pointed at the star. "Is that your new design?"

"It sure is, and people love it. I'm taking orders so quickly I can barely keep up. My hand has a cramp from filling out order forms," he said, gently massaging it.

"Poor you," Brenda snapped. "I was supposed to see it before the rest of the town. You promised."

"What time is it?"

Brenda glanced at her watch. "Eleven-thirty. Why?"

"What time did the store open?"

"Five o'clock."

"The store opened more than six hours ago, yet you didn't even bother to drag yourself out of bed until now to come look at it. I'm trying to stay in business here, and I couldn't wait to unveil the one thing that might keep me from going under until you decided to grace me with your presence. Now, if you don't mind, I have a business to save." Ralph turned and plastered a smile on his face, then greeted an elderly gentleman who was admiring the star. "Is there anything I can do for you this morning, sir?" The irritation in his voice that had been present only a minute ago was gone.

"I'm just looking at this wonderful star," the man said. "The thing is, I don't think I can afford something like that. I sure would like to figure out a way to get it for my wife for our anniversary in January. It'll be our fiftieth. She's been really sick, and I want to do something special for her."

Ralph placed a hand on the old man's shoulder. "Why don't you come right over here. I'm sure we can work something out." He guided the man toward a small desk in the corner of the showroom.

Work something out, my foot, Brenda fumed. If Ralph hadn't been so generous with his customers, the store wouldn't be in trouble to begin with.

Inching closer to the star, Brenda looked at it in more detail. She had to admit it was good. Breathtaking, actually. It was probably the best thing Ralph had ever designed. The attention to detail was magnificent.

"That must be worth a fortune," she said under her breath.

There were a lot of diamonds in that star, and somebody could make a truckload of money by selling it.

And to think, he's essentially leaving it right out in the open, where anybody with sticky fingers could take off with it. Let's just hope that nightmare doesn't come true, she thought, then turned to walk toward the Rose Petal Café.

One of Nadine's cinnamon-chip scones was just what she needed to lift her spirits. That and a one-way ticket out of this town.

CHAPTER SEVENTEEN

HOLLY BERRY WAS greeted by swarms of shoppers as she walked into the Saddle Hill Mall.

So much for Smalltown, USA, she thought.

She clutched her purse close to her slender body and tried to get her bearings. Marian had told her to come to the center of the mall, but how was she supposed to pick out one tiny little woman in a sea of faces? Children were everywhere, their eyes wide with excitement. Disheveled parents looked exhausted. In front of the crowd, Holly saw a Santa coax a little boy of about three years old off his lap.

He's adorable, Holly thought. The boy, not the Santa. The Santa was scowling.

Her eyes followed the little boy over to a grinning elf who handed him a candy cane. Holly squinted. If she wasn't mistaken, that elf bore a striking resemblance to Marian Bright, her gracious hostess for the next month.

Tucking her elbows close to her sides so she didn't knock one of the bright-eyed tots unconscious, she wove through the tightly compacted crowd and scooted up beside Marian.

"You didn't tell me you're an elf," Holly said, the corners of her mouth turning into a small smile.

Startled, Marian turned, then returned the smile when she saw Holly. "I am. Sixteen years and running. Did you sleep well?"

Holly nodded. "I did, thank you. Christmas has always been a hard time for me, and I'm looking forward to finally being able to celebrate it appropriately." She looked at Kris. "Although I think I'll have a better shot at it if I keep my distance from him."

Marian chuckled warmly. "Don't worry your pretty little head about that, dear," Marian assured her. "Celebrating Christmas is what I do best. Not even a grump like Kris Jingle can ruin it for me. Are you planning to shop while you're here? The Mountain Craft Festival is on the other side of the mall."

Holly shook her head. "I don't have money for that, I'm afraid, but I am interested in some seasonal work if you know of anybody that could use some help."

"Of course. Lots of people need extra help in their stores around the holidays. You'd think people would be looking to make extra cash and would be willing to pick up the hours, but instead almost everybody is shorthanded."

"That's good news for me, though. Any idea where to start?"

Marian glanced at her watch. "My break is coming up in a few minutes. Why don't you wait for me, and during my break we'll get some lunch at the Rose Petal Café. After that, I'll take you around to some stores and we'll see if anybody could use you."

Holly nodded in agreement, then stepped out of the way so the shiny-eyed kids could get candy canes from Marian. If her memory was right, her mom and dad took her to see Santa once, and they'd had to practically drag her to sit on his lap. She'd cried the whole time.

One look at the long line of impatient children confirmed they didn't have that problem.

A little girl of about five with pigtails and a ruffled blue dress slid off Santa's lap, then walked over to Marian for a candy cane.

Marian signaled to the Santa that she was leaving, then slipped an awful-looking Christmas sweater with a reindeer leaping across the front over her elf costume and took Holly by the arm. "I've been handing out candy canes nonstop for the past four hours, without so much as a trip to the restroom. I need to make a pit stop there, then we'll head over to the Rose Petal Café. I'm starving!"

Before she could agree, Marian whisked her down a corridor toward the ladies' room, and a few minutes later, they were off again, this time to fill Marian's empty stomach.

The smells coming from the café were divine, and Holly was almost sorry she'd already eaten.

"Would you like anything, dear?" Marian asked, already sizing up the menu posted on the wall.

"No thanks. I ate before I came."

"Okay. Find a table for us while I order. In about two minutes, this place is going to be standing room only."

Holly took her cue and wove between the tables, searching for unoccupied seating. In the far back corner, a table for two had just been vacated. She quickly claimed the seats and wiped the crumbs off the table, then rested her chin on her hands while she waited for Marian.

This Christmas might not be so bad after all, she thought as a total stranger smiled at her. The people here seem so nice, too.

A few minutes later, Marian settled into the chair across from Holly. "My sandwich will be ready in a minute. I know you said you didn't want anything, but I ordered one of Nadine's orange-cranberry scones for you. Her pastries are not to be missed."

Just as the waitress slid a tray containing a sandwich, a steaming bowl of soup, and Holly's scone onto the table, Holly began, "I really appreciate you taking your lunch break to help me find a job. Funds have been a bit low lately, and I could really use the cash."

"Of course. Think nothing of it. I'm happy to help," Marian said, taking a giant bite of her sandwich.

Holly leaned across the table and lowered her voice. "The thing is, I've got a record."

"Record?" Marian asked, a tomato hanging from the corner of her mouth.

"Police record," Holly whispered. "For shoplifting. I'm fairly certain no one is going to want to hire a shoplifter to work in their store."

Marian nodded. "I see. I could tell from your posts in the support group that you'd been in some trouble. Do you still do it?"

"Shoplift? No, that's why I'm short on cash."

Marian thought a moment, then said, "I'll still take you to some stores. If I vouch for you, someone will give you a chance. As long as you promise not to steal from them. The last thing I need is my reputation getting ruined. I'm an elf, for crying out loud!" She winked at Holly and took another bite of her sandwich.

"I promise. I've put that behind me." Holly put her hand over her heart for emphasis.

"Good. Give me another minute to finish my lunch and we'll set out. I can take you to Carla Whipple's candle store. She pays well and she's a nice lady, but being in there all day with so many different scents can cause quite a headache. Frankly, I don't know how Carla can stand it."

"How about if we consider that a last resort?" Holly said.

"Wise choice. I'll take you to Stockton's Jewel Palace. I heard in the ladies' room that Ralph is up to his eyeballs in business today, and can barely take all the orders he's getting. He might just be desperate enough to hire someone on the spot," Marian suggested, then practically drank her soup, downed her coffee in a few gulps, then stood. "Let's go."

As the pair left the table, the woman who'd smiled at Holly when she first sat down smiled even wider.

Brenda Morris-Stockton was desperate to get out of this town, and now she knew just how to do it.

CHAPTER EIGHTEEN

SYLVIA BELL'S FLIGHT touched down at LEX at exactly 12:07 p.m. She stretched her legs and slid the book she'd been reading into the tote she had stored under the seat in front of her. For the last several minutes, she'd watched the expansive green fields and pristine white plank fences get closer as the plane descended. The dots became horses, many of them thoroughbreds that raced around the world.

She already liked Kentucky, and was more than ready to start the long, quiet weekend celebrating her hard work over the past several months.

When the passengers were free to move about, Sylvia stood and quickly grabbed her small suitcase from the overhead bin. She slid the straps of her tote over her shoulder and extended the handle of her carry-on and was herded slowly down the center aisle of the small jet.

I'm a long way from New York City, Sylvia thought as she made her way through the small Lexington airport. As she passed baggage claim, she noted that the noon news was on the TV above the luggage carousel. The feature story appeared to be the various Christmas festivals taking place around the state. Sylvia was delighted to see that the one she'd chosen to attend in Saddle Hill was featured.

Unconsciously smiling, she walked toward the exit. Once outside, she inhaled deeply. It wasn't as cold as New York, but the air was clean and crisp.

This is going to be a great weekend, Sylvia thought as she exhaled, her breath forming a small cloud in front of her face. Excited to get started on her adventure, she turned and walked quickly toward the rental car agencies. She had a two-hour drive ahead of her, with miles of picturesque countryside awaiting her.

Thirty minutes later, car key in hand, she loaded her suitcase into the trunk of the car. She typed the address of the inn into the GPS and carefully pulled out of the parking lot.

It would be so nice to be away from the bustle of the city, from the demands of everyday life. For the next three glorious days, she'd be in a sleepy little town where she didn't know a soul.

She flipped through the radio stations until she found one playing nothing but Christmas music and turned up the volume. Singing loudly to Dean Martin's rendition of "Let it Snow!" a fat snowflake landed on her windshield.

Again, Sylvia smiled. "Just don't turn into a blizzard until I get where I'm going. Then feel free to dump buckets of snow on me."

CHAPTER NINETEEN

WITH A GROWLING stomach, Joe Adler squeezed through the crowd in the Rose Petal Café. He glanced around wearily, wishing somebody would leave so he'd have a place to sit.

He'd spent the whole morning on his feet, walking from store to store ensuring nothing went awry. Every two hours, he'd had to dodge Winston's disapproving scowl that communicated to Joe that he should be doing more. Unless he was a superhero, Joe wasn't sure how he possibly could. The only security guard for the entire mall, there was no way he could be everywhere at once. He was spread too thin as it was, and doing a detailed check of each individual store was impossible. Winston was particularly peeved that Joe had missed a fight in the lingerie section of one of the department stores—a fact Winston had tracked him down to report immediately.

The veins in his neck had bulged as he relayed the account to Joe that there had only been one bra left in a size 38JJ, and apparently a disagreement between two women about who'd had their hand on it first came to blows.

Joe's mouth twitched. He was actually sorry he'd missed that one.

Winston made it perfectly clear that he was sorry, too, and yelled at Joe for not being there to break it up. The General became even more upset when Joe explained that the reason he missed it was because he'd been helping an elderly man carry his numerous purchases to his car at the time.

Winston didn't want to hear it. He went on for several minutes about how Joe's job was to keep shoppers safe and prevent theft, not provide transport service for customers who bought too much.

Joe didn't mention he felt it was necessary to escort the man to his car for his own safety. With his frail form, Joe had been worried he'd be crushed or trampled, or at least knocked down by the throngs of shoppers. He also didn't mention it was Winston's fault in the first place for being too cheap to hire another security guard.

Winston had made his point loud and clear: Being a good citizen wasn't in Joe's job description.

It wasn't until a child was separated from his mother that Joe was able to escape the berating. Duty called, after all.

A hand on his arm pulled Joe from his thoughts. He looked down into the smiling face of Nadine. It was a welcome sight after Winston's dirty looks.

He bent quickly and kissed her forehead. "Hi, sweetheart. How's it going in here today?"

"Not too bad, I suppose, but Wanda is in a special kind of mood," Nadine replied, then with her eyes sweeping the dining area, said, "I think we're even busier than last year."

"I have no doubt about that," Joe said. He thought the whole mall looked busier. "I was going to grab a sandwich and steal a few minutes of your time, but it looks like you don't have a few minutes to spare. There's nowhere to sit, anyway. I'll just grab something from the food court."

"You will not," Nadine challenged. "That stuff isn't even real food. Follow me." She curled a finger at Joe, leading the way and weaving around occupied tables toward a door marked "Employees Only."

As they entered the kitchen, the smell of warm sugar filled his nose.

"Sit," she commanded playfully as she pointed at the small table in the corner of the kitchen. "You can sit at the chef's table." She winked and walked toward the counter covered with bread and various lunch meats and toppings. "What are you in the mood for today?"

Joe's eyes twinkled. "Besides you? How about a BLT?"

Nadine smiled and got to work. "How are things going out there? She asked, waving a knife in the general direction of the mall. "As busy as it is in here, I can only imagine what it's like in the stores." Nadine piled bacon on one piece of bread, a piece of cheese on the other, and put it on the belt to run it through the toaster. Joe always wanted cheese on his BLT.

"It's okay. Not as violent as last year, and as far as I know, no one has been knocked down. I did get yelled at for helping an old man to his car, though."

"Let me guess, The General?"

Joe nodded. "He said he wasn't paying me to help people carry their bags."

"No, we wouldn't want to actually help someone," Nadine snorted and pulled the sandwich halves from the toaster, piling them with lettuce and tomato, then stacked the halves together. She speared the sandwich with an extra-long toothpick with a red and green cellophane ribbon at the end, then slid the sandwich in front of Joe.

"Aren't you going to join me?"

Nadine glanced around then plopped into the other chair. "I can only sit for a minute. Wanda will have my head if I leave her alone out there for too long."

Joe took a bite of his sandwich, some melted cheese finding its way onto his chin. "I've been thinking about you all day."

Nadine sighed and handed him a napkin. "I've been too busy to think about anything other than giving these people what they want. I swear, I think people get ruder and more entitled every year."

Joe put his sandwich down, wiped his fingers on the napkin, and reached across the table for Nadine's hand. "Soon the Christmas mania will be over, and it will just be us, planning our wedding."

Nadine smiled. "I still can't believe it. Two months, then you will be all mine."

"If we even decide to wait that long. Early January sounds good to me." Now that it was official, he couldn't imagine waiting a day more than he had to. "Let me see how that ring looks on you again," Joe said quietly, remembering that Nadine wanted to hold off formally announcing their engagement until the Black Friday rush was over.

She pulled her left hand out of the pocket of her chef's coat and glanced at her hand before extending it to Joe.

She gasped.

"What?" Joe asked, alarm creeping into his voice.

"The ring," Nadine said, frantically jamming her hand back into her pocket.

"Did you lose it?" His mouth went dry. He'd saved for months to be able to buy that ring.

Nadine's face went pale. "No. I still have the ring, but the diamond is gone!" She continued poking around in her pocket. "It's gone, Joe. The diamond is gone."

"What do you mean it's gone? How could it be gone?"

Nadine withdrew her hand from her pocket and extended it to within inches of Joe's face. "What I mean is that the diamond has fallen out of the setting," she moaned, tears slipping down her face.

There, on Nadine's trembling hand, was a delicate gold band with a gaping hole where the twinkling half-carat diamond was supposed to be.

CHAPTER TWENTY

HOLLY WRAPPED HER scone in a napkin and slid it into the pocket of her coat. "I'll eat this later," she told Marian as they made their way from the café toward Stockton's Jewel Palace.

"Of course," Marian said absently, walking swiftly through the crowd, the bells on her shoes jingling with each step. Holly had to jog to keep up.

Marian finally stopped at an open storefront, cases glittering under the lights. Hundreds of diamonds were just sitting there, begging to be touched. Holly held her breath, but Marian didn't seem to notice.

Good, Holly thought. She doesn't need to know the urge is still there.

"Oh, there's Ralph," Marian chirped. "I'll just go get him." She jingled off in the direction of a chubby man in his mid-fifties.

Holly took another breath. Any one of those pieces would put an end to her money trouble.

I can't do that, she told herself sternly. Marian is trusting me, and so is whoever agrees to hire me.

Moments later, Marian returned, a smiling Ralph Stockton by her side. "Holly, this is Ralph, king of Stockton's Jewel Palace. Ralph, this is Holly Berry. She'll be staying with me for the Christmas season."

"Wonderful!" Ralph exclaimed heartily. "I hope you enjoy our little town. Saddle Hill Christmases are the best."

"That's what I've heard," Holly said, casting a glance at Marian.

"Holly," Marian interrupted. "I was just telling Ralph that you're looking for some seasonal employment. It seems that he's up to his eyeballs right now and could really use an extra set of hands."

"Yes," Ralph said. "Marian has told me some wonderful things about you. If you're available and willing, I'd be delighted if you would come to work with me for the season." Then he added, "I pay well."

"Of course, Mr. Stockton. I would love to work for you," Holly said, wondering what wonderful things Marian could possibly have told Ralph about her. *Come meet my houseguest for the month. I just met her last night and she confessed to having a record for shoplifting. Wouldn't you love to have her work in your store with all this jewelry lying around?*

"You can start right away if you're available," Ralph said, glancing toward the display case holding the star. People were gathering around it again.

"I'd love to." A smile spread across Holly's face. Ralph's positive attitude was infectious.

"Great!" Ralph said.

"Perfect," Marian added. "Now I've really got to get back to the kids. Kris will go berserk if I don't get there soon." She turned to walk away, then added, "He seems even worse than usual this Christmas."

Holly and Ralph watched Marian leave, both smiling at the rhythmic jingling of her feet.

"What would you like me to do, Mr. Stockton?" Holly asked when Marian was out of sight.

"Please, call me Ralph," he offered, then turned toward the ever-growing mass of people around the star. "I'm doing a special Christmas piece this year, and each one is a custom order. The customer will choose their own jewels and metal, then I will make the pieces to meet their specifications. I've had more than a dozen orders so far this morning, with no end in sight. It's a good problem to have, but I need you to help me take the orders so I can start making the pieces."

"When have you told the customers they can pick up their orders?"

"It's supposed to be a three-day turnaround, so the ones that have been ordered today need to be ready on Monday." Ralph suddenly sounded exhausted.

"You're not giving yourself much time," Holly said, her brows furrowed. It was clear that Ralph had gotten in over his head with such a lofty promise. "How long will it take to make each one?"

"Well, the prototype took a very long time. Of course, I designed as I went, so that made it take longer. Also, that one is much larger than the actual pieces are going to be, so of course that added a significant amount of time. I figure I can probably get three done in a day if I really buckle down."

"And you've already gotten a dozen orders. It's only..." Holly glanced at her watch. "One o'clock. Ralph, those numbers don't add up."

Ralph sighed. "I've done the math, too. See why I need help?"

"But, Mr. Stockton—"

"Please, call me Ralph."

"Okay, Ralph. How will my taking more orders for that star help you? I'm not trying to talk myself out of a job, but it seems like more orders will make things harder on you."

"To be perfectly honest, Holly, my store depends on this star. If I don't make enough money this Christmas, I'll have to close the store for good. It has to work, and apparently it's time for me to take on an apprentice. I think you're just what I need."

"But Ralph, I don't know anything about making jewelry. I can help you sell it and take orders for you, but I have no idea how to *make* it," Holly protested.

"You'll be fine," Ralph assured her. "First I'll show you the star, then I'll show you how to take the orders." Ralph led her to the display case. "Excuse me," he said politely, squeezing between the shoppers. He motioned for Holly to join him. "This is our special Christmas star."

Holly's mouth dropped open. It was the most beautiful thing she'd ever seen. She looked at Ralph, whose eyes were glistening, his face lit with pride. She smiled. How wonderful it was going to be to work side by side with someone who was so obviously passionate about bringing beauty into the world.

Holly looked back at the star.

Apprentice. Ralph called her his apprentice. This was her one shot to break the cycle. She couldn't blow it.

She rubbed her fingers together. They were itching again.

CHAPTER TWENTY-ONE

"THIS CAN'T BE happening!" Nadine cried as she crawled around on the kitchen floor of the café.

Within seconds, Joe was also on his hands and knees, scouring the floor for the lost diamond. "It has to be around here somewhere," Joe said, his voice matching Nadine's panicked tone. "Did you hit your hand on anything that could have knocked it loose?"

"No," Nadine said, frantically groping along the floor next to the cabinets and under the refrigerator. "And I didn't even notice it was missing until I showed it to you."

"And you're sure it was there this morning when you got to work?"

"Yes," Nadine said, then rocked back on her heels. "I showed it to Marian after our meeting this morning. After that, I don't think I looked at it again." She brushed her hair off her forehead with the back of her hand. "I've been so busy." A tear squeezed from the corner of her eye.

Joe scooted closer to Nadine and placed a comforting arm around her. "It's okay, Nay. We'll find it. Besides, there's no law that says you have to have a diamond engagement ring to get married."

Nadine sniffed. "No, I suppose there isn't." She managed a weak smile.

"And you have no idea where it could be?"

"I already told you I don't. It literally could be anywhere around here. I've made so many cookies and muffins and scones…"

They looked at each other.

"You don't think…" Joe began.

Nadine shrugged. "It's possible."

They both looked toward the oven, where banana nut muffins were baking to a golden brown.

"What do I do? I can't just go digging through all the muffins. Not to mention the scones. I'm not worried about the cookies—the mixer did most of the work for those. But I did more for the muffins and scones. I suppose the diamond could have fallen into the batter when I was stirring."

"I think we need to talk to Wanda," Joe suggested reluctantly.

Nadine nodded. "I know, but she's going to be so mad at me."

Five minutes later, after Nadine had finally been able to coax Wanda away from the customers, she stood in front of the couple with her hands on her hips. An imposing figure at five feet eleven inches, Wanda Kirk seemed at least a foot taller when she was angry.

"What's the big emergency?" Wanda demanded. "We've got customers out there that aren't going to feed themselves."

"Well, you see…" Joe began.

"We got engaged last night," Nadine interjected.

Wanda glared at them. "You couldn't wait until after the lunch rush to tell me that?" She turned to leave, but Joe caught her arm.

"It's just that, the diamond from Nadine's ring seems to be missing."

"I'm sorry, but what does that have to do with me?" Wanda snapped.

"I had it when I was baking this morning, but now it's gone," Nadine said quietly.

"Well, what happened to it?"

Nadine pointed toward the cases holding the baked goods. "It could be in there."

"In the case?" Wanda seemed to be growing more impatient with each passing moment.

"In the pastries," Nadine squeaked.

Wanda rolled her eyes and threw her hands up in the air. "Oh, for heaven sake! What do we do now? I can't have a customer choking on that blasted diamond."

Nadine and Joe shrugged.

"Look everywhere else first. If you don't find it, then we'll have to dig through the pastries." She thrust a finger in Nadine's face. "The cost of the wasted baked goods will be coming out of *your* paycheck." Wanda turned and stalked back to the line of waiting customers.

"Yes, Wanda," Nadine said, tears streaming down her face.

"We'll find it," Joe assured her.

"How? A search party?" Nadine buried her face in her hands.

"Yes!" Joe smacked his hands together. "We'll form a search party and find that diamond." With that he was off, apparently going to round one up.

As the door exiting the kitchen swung gently on its hinges after Joe's quick departure, the timer dinged. The banana nut muffins were ready.

Nadine groaned and pulled the muffins from the oven, wondering if one of them held a tiny, sparkling surprise.

❧

An hour later, a small group formed in the Rose Petal Café to help look for Nadine's diamonds. Kris and Marian had just gotten off duty from playing Santa and his merry little elf and were ready to help.

The crowd at the café had thinned out, and Wanda stood formidably at the counter taking care of the stragglers, an angry glare in her eyes.

Nadine stood helplessly against the wall.

On Marian's command, the group consisting of herself, Kris, Joe, and a half dozen others dispersed, each one searching inch by inch to find the missing gem.

An hour passed with no luck.

"We're going to have to search the baked goods," Marian said to Wanda, the thrust of her chin communicating that arguing would be pointless. She was determined to find the symbol of Joe and Nadine's love.

With a resigned wave of her hand, Wanda sighed, "Go ahead." She turned away as the group destroyed hundreds of dollars' worth of pastries. "I can't watch," she groaned.

Within thirty minutes the group had searched each and every one of the baked goods.

No diamond.

The bakery case looked as though a madman with a hand

mixer had come in, determined to turn each delicious sweet back to its original form as dough.

"I'm so sorry, Nadine," Marian said, crumbs speckling her hair. "I'm sure it will turn up somewhere. This is Christmas, after all. Miracles happen all the time."

Nadine nodded and covered her trembling lips with a shaking hand. A fat tear slid from her eye and splashed onto the sleeve of her chef's coat.

"Sorry," Kris said, then plucked half a muffin from the mess in the bakery case, nibbling on it as he left the café.

Six more mumbled "I'm sorries" followed as the search party filed out.

Marian, Nadine, Joe, and Wanda stood alone, eyes scanning the pastry massacre.

Giving Nadine a quick hug, Marian again said, "I'm so sorry, dear." She turned and glanced at the sweet young couple whose Christmas season was off to a rocky start.

"I've got to get back to work. Winston is already going to be fuming that I've missed so much time at my post," Joe said, giving Nadine's hand a quick squeeze.

Nadine nodded. "I have a mess to clean up anyway." She waved toward the bits of pastries scattered in the bakery case and on the floor.

Joe winked at her, then as he walked away thought, I'm going to get Ralph Stockton for selling me such a lousy piece of jewelry.

CHAPTER TWENTY-TWO

PROBLEMS, PROBLEMS, PROBLEMS. That's what these people are, Winston thought bitterly as he walked past the Rose Petal Café, where half of his employees were crawling around on the floor. *They're out to ruin me.*

Winston tried to hold his head high, but his shoulders sagged under the weight of his insubordinate troops.

If they only knew how much we need this season to be profitable, maybe they wouldn't act like such dopes, Winston thought. *I come down hard on them because there's more riding on their success this Christmas than they realize.*

Ralph Stockton isn't the only one facing the possibility of going out of business if there aren't enough sales this year, Winston thought. *Carla Whipple's candle shop, Whipple's Wicks, is in even more trouble than Ralph, but she doesn't let on how dire things are. Carla, bless her, puts on a happy face every morning and treats the customers with such kindness. It's no wonder her store is one of the favorites in town, but there are only so many candles a person needs. Unfortunately* for Carla, in a town this size there just aren't enough people to buy the number of candles she needs to sell to pay her rent.

Winston shook his head. People just don't stay in small towns anymore. That's the problem. They flock to the cities for better jobs. No one is content working in a trade, and they dash off to college in other parts of the state as soon as they graduate high school in hopes of "making a better life."

Whatever that means.

He'd just read a news article last week that said half of these people end up working in restaurants or coffee shops and living in their parents' basements, all of which they could have done with no college degree and without going into tens of thousands of dollars in debt. They could have stayed in their hometown and made a difference instead of improving the economy somewhere else. At this rate, Saddle Hill has more than the mall to worry about.

And the Mountain Craft Festival isn't helping matters. Sure, it draws a crowd from all over, and the out-of-towners certainly do spend some money in the local stores, but they aren't the focal point. The number of people that make an actual living selling their hand-crafted goods is slim, and poor Carla might be the next casualty.

What we need is something that will get Saddle Hill Mall on the map. Something that will attract shoppers from other areas, and get them spending their money *here*, in our stores, helping our own people keep their businesses running. We need people to want to spend their money here instead of shopping online.

What I don't need is my security guard leading the charge and having the rest of my half-wit employees crawling around the Rose Petal Café like loons.

Winston hung his head for the first time since he took over as manager of the Saddle Hill Mall. *Why can't they see that I'm trying to help them, that I'd do anything to keep this place going?*

CHAPTER TWENTY-THREE

BRENDA BLEW BUBBLES from her fingertips and sank deeper into the tub. The nerve of Ralph putting that star out for the whole town to see before I even get a glimpse of it! she fumed. After I've devoted the last three years of my life to that man, he can't even wait a few measly hours to start selling the darn thing.

Trying to find a more comfortable position in the cramped tub/shower combo, Brenda cracked her funny bone on the side. "Stupid Ralph!" she cried, tears burning her cheeks as they ran freely from her eyes. "I hate my life! What did I do to deserve this?"

She'd had so much potential in college. Sure, she wasn't the smartest girl in the room, but she didn't need to be. Using the other tools at her disposal, she'd managed. And she'd been a good actress. She still was. How else could she have muddled through the past three years with Ralph without letting him know what a bore he was. Back then, the school paper raved about her performance in *The Sound of Music*. She'd always thought she should have gotten to play Maria but consoled herself with the knowledge that she was about as far from being a nun as a person could possibly get. Besides, the costume was so drab!

A giggle escaped through her tears. *If they could only see my most recent performance, they'd know how good I really am.*

Brenda sighed. She'd needed a good cry. Life was miserable with Ralph and constantly putting on a happy face for him was hard.

"Not that he deserves it," she said through clenched teeth. "He's ruined my life. Here I am, sitting in a tiny bathtub filled with bubbles from a drugstore. And my clothes! These department stores are a joke. Half of what's in them make me look like I'm going to a barn dance. I should be wearing something from Jersey Belle. Maybe if I hadn't hitched my wagon to Ralph's, I would be," Brenda moaned. "Listen to me whining. I even sound like somebody who belongs here. I've got to get out of this place."

Tapping a slender finger on her chin, Brenda thought about how to make her escape. There were no jobs for her in this God-forsaken town, so she had no money of her own. There was just the meager joint bank account she shared with Ralph and the cash he kept in the safe at the store. She could take some of it, of course. He owed her something for the last three years, but there wasn't enough to get her very far.

She'd need a way to get some fast cash.

But *how?*

She shivered as she realized the bathwater had gotten cold. As she took the nearly threadbare towel from the towel bar and wrapped it around herself, she snapped her fingers. The solution to her problem had been staring her in the face all along. She'd just needed that poor, troubled soul at the café to remind her.

CHAPTER TWENTY-FOUR

AFTER A QUICK soak in the jacuzzi, Sylvia Bell was ready to head out and enjoy the festivities. Even though it had been a short flight, especially compared to the ones she frequently took all around the world, it still felt good to have the hot water swirl around her tired muscles. It was a far cry from the tub/shower combo she'd grown up with.

She slipped off her terry cloth robe and donned a pair of slim-cut jeans, a black turtleneck sweater that, with her dark hair and eyes, gave her a mysterious look, and a pair of riding boots. She hadn't brought a single pair of heels on the trip. Sylvia swept her hair into a low bun and checked her makeup. Low-key and casual, but still expertly applied. A done-up New Yorker was probably the last thing this town needed during the holiday season.

Grabbing her red peacoat and oversized shoulder bag, Sylvia headed down the corridor toward the elevator, then opted for the stairs instead. After being on the plane, then driving on winding roads for two hours in an ever-increasing snowfall, she needed to stretch her legs.

As she descended the stairs into the hotel lobby, the smell of freshly baked cookies tickled her nose. As she walked toward the exit, she passed a table stocked with fresh Christmas cookies and eggnog. Saliva filled her mouth. The trip couldn't get more perfect.

After a glass of eggnog and a cookie, Sylvia finally walked out of the hotel and through the parking lot toward her rental car. A snowflake landed on her eyelashes.

What a great little town, she thought with a smile as she inhaled the clean, cold air.

She jerked the car door open, slid onto the seat, and cranked the engine. Thankful she'd opted to rent a luxury car she turned on the seat warmers and relaxed into the plush leather as the warmth radiated down her back.

It was after three o'clock. Most of the shoppers were probably already home from their adventures, hating themselves for getting up too early and spending too much, though she doubted the prices they paid here were anywhere close to the ones she and her neighbors paid on the Upper East Side.

Sylvia steered her car along the narrow streets, many of which were already becoming slick from the snow.

Ten minutes later, she found the perfect parking spot in front of the tiny mall.

Flipping the collar of her coat to block the wind, she dashed from the parking lot into the welcomed warmth of the mall. She'd looked up a map of the mall online and, if she was right, the Mountain Craft Festival booths were set up in the farthest part of the mall from where she was. To get to it, she would have to pass through the center of the mall where it appeared Santa and his helpers were making their lists and checking them twice.

Once inside the main entrance, she passed a small jewelry store crowded with people oohing and ahhing over something that must be the likes of which this town had never seen. She kept walking, making a mental note to stop and see what all the fuss was about on her way out. There were only a couple department stores and a horde of children bombarding a weary-looking Santa standing between her and the main event.

Finally, after weaving around surprisingly large crowds, she stood in front of men and women dressed in their best flannel and bib overalls hawking their handmade goods. A hundred tables were filled with everything from homemade jams and jellies to hand-carved wooden bowls.

You don't get this in New York, she thought happily.

She picked up one of the few shopping baskets available and made her way around the tables.

A cheery-looking woman with a braid wrapped around her head was busily weaving a basket. Sylvia selected a small one and a medium-sized one, paid for them, then wished the woman a Merry Christmas.

At each table she found something unique, and she wanted it all. Everything was made with such care, the quality far better than almost anything she'd be able to find in a department store. For the first time in years, she actually enjoyed herself as she selected Christmas gifts for her friends and family. Seeing the smiling faces of the artisans that created the pieces and knowing exactly where her money was going made her feel even better.

An hour and a half later, she had several large shopping bags stuffed with her purchases. She glanced at her watch. It was nearing five-thirty and, as if on cue, her stomach growled, reminding her that the closest thing she'd had to lunch was a cookie and a glass of eggnog.

There was a food court nearby, but she remembered from the map that there was a little café not too far away. Wanting to fully immerse herself in the quaint town, she chose the café.

Soon, a steaming bowl of tomato soup and a mammoth-sized grilled cheese sandwich was sitting in front of her. Her mouth watered. On a cold, snowy day, nothing could taste better.

As she ate, Sylvia noticed that the young woman stocking the bakery case seemed to be crying. She squinted to read the name badge attached to the white chef's coat. Nadine.

Poor thing, Sylvia thought, dipping the sandwich into her soup. Nobody should be sad on such a glorious day. She placed the sandwich back on the plate and walked to the case holding dozens of delicious-looking scones, muffins, and cookies.

"Excuse me? May I have one of the pumpkin spice scones?" Sylvia asked gently.

Nadine sniffled. "Of course." She picked up the scone with a square of parchment paper and placed it on a small plate. "Anything else?"

"That's all. Thank you." Sylvia hesitated, then asked, "Are you okay?"

Nadine nodded. "I lost something that was very special to me this morning, and I don't know if I'll ever get it back."

Sylvia placed a gentle hand on Nadine's arm. "I'm so sorry."

Nadine nodded as tears filled her eyes. "My boyfriend and I got engaged last night, and sometime this morning while I was baking, the diamond fell out of my ring. I can't find it anywhere."

"That's terrible."

"We looked everywhere. Joe—that's my fiancé—even formed a search party. We combed every square inch of the café, but it was nowhere to be found." Nadine extended the plate holding the scone toward Sylvia. "But Joe bought it at Stockton's Jewel Palace. Ralph's a fair man. I'll know he'll make it right."

"I passed that store on my way in. There was a big crowd. He must do beautiful work," Sylvia observed.

"He really does," Nadine agreed with a sad smile. "Apparently he unveiled some new design today that has the whole town going crazy. He'll be too busy to worry about my ring." Another tear slipped down Nadine's cheek.

A fresh stab of compassion hit Sylvia's heart. "You said he's a fair man. If that's the case, I'm sure he'll stand by his work."

"I hope so. Joe is pretty hot about this. I just hope he doesn't lose his temper and give Ralph a piece of his mind."

"I wish you all the best, and congratulations on your engagement." Sylvia broke off a piece of the scone and popped it into her mouth. "This is absolutely delicious, by the way. Merry Christmas."

Nadine appeared to perk up a tad. "Thank you. And Merry Christmas to you, too."

Sylvia returned to her table and finished her dinner.

Maybe I should go see what all the fuss is about at Stockton's Jewel Palace, she thought as she deposited her dishes on the tray near the café exit.

In January she would begin working on a jewelry line for Jersey Belle. It wouldn't hurt to get a jump on things and take a look at this guy's work. Maybe she'd get some inspiration for her pieces.

She collected her shopping bags and carried the cumbersome load toward the opposite side of the mall.

This is supposed to be a relaxing weekend, Sylvia reminded herself as she struggled under the weight of her purchases. I didn't come here to work. Maybe I shouldn't stop by today. Besides, his new design will still be there tomorrow.

CHAPTER TWENTY-FIVE

MARIAN AND HOLLY dragged themselves from their cars into Marian's house and kicked off their shoes. It had been a long day. Now seven o'clock, Marian had already been awake for sixteen hours. Lucky for her, she didn't need the eight hours of sleep to function that so many people did. Even Holly had been so busy learning how to help Ralph at Stockton's Jewel Palace during the afternoon that she'd hardly gotten the chance to catch her breath. Now the two were glad to be in the comfort of Marian's living room.

"What a day," Marian sighed as she settled into Roger's favorite old chair.

"No kidding. I only worked six hours today and I'm bushed. Learning the jewelry business is more complicated than I thought. I don't know how you do it."

"I get a renewed energy at Christmastime," Marian chirped happily. "But I have to admit it does get a little harder every year. Aging takes its toll on even the cheeriest of souls."

Holly nodded. Anyone could see that Marian still had

enough spunk to go around, but a woman in her seventies was bound to slow down a little.

"Want anything to eat? I'm starving," Holly said, realizing it had been eight hours since she'd had her late breakfast.

"That sounds great," Marian agreed readily. "Handing out candy canes all morning, then crawling around on the floor of the Rose Petal looking for Nadine's missing diamond sure did work up an appetite."

Holly wiggled her toes, then stood and walked toward the kitchen. "Are you in the mood for anything in particular? I'm a fairly decent cook."

"No need for that. Pizza would be delightful. After today, I'm sure neither of us has the energy to cook. The takeout menu is hanging on the wall next to the phone."

Relieved, Holly went into the kitchen and found the menu stuck between the wall and the phone, just as Marian had said. Even though she'd only done a half-day's work, she was exhausted and in no mood to cook.

"What kind do you want?" Holly asked once she'd scanned the menu.

"Whatever you want is fine. I'm not picky," Marian replied.

Holly lifted the phone receiver and dialed the pizza place. Who still has a phone like this? she wondered. But Marian did seem to use words like dear, lovely, and delightful all the time. She was certainly from another generation.

After ordering a deluxe pizza with extra cheese, Holly returned to the living room. Marian had a fire roaring in the fireplace, a cozy scene with the Christmas tree glowing beside it. She sat on the sofa and kicked her aching, sock-clad feet up on the coffee table.

"Is the mall always this busy after Thanksgiving? When I

got here last night, I didn't even know there could be that many people in this town."

Marian nodded. "It is a small town, but the Mountain Craft Festival attracts shoppers from all over. Artisans come from five hundred miles away to sell their work here. Some of it is really first-rate."

Holly stretched her toes. "I didn't even make it down that way. Not that I have any money, anyway."

Marian's gaze never left the flames dancing in the fireplace. "Working with Ralph should help fix that. He's very generous."

"I've noticed," Holly agreed. "I'm worried about him, though. He's promised a three-day turnaround on this star piece, and he's already gotten so many orders. I don't know how he'll be able to have them ready on time."

"That's a good problem to have, I suppose. Ralph really needs the business. Just between you and me, this Christmas is Ralph's last hope of keeping his store open. Profits have been dropping the last few years, and he's barely been able to pay his rent for the storefront. Not to mention hardly having much of a paycheck himself."

"That's awful," Holly said, shaking her head. "He seems like such a nice guy, and from what I saw today, his jewelry is beautiful. I find it hard to believe nobody would buy it."

"They would if they could, but it's a small town. The economy has been bad the last few years with so many people leaving to find work in bigger cities. Besides, there's nowhere around here to wear nice jewelry. Unfortunately for Ralph, that means nobody is buying." Marian paused, then added, "Were you tempted?"

"Tempted?"

"To take something?" Marian prodded.

Holly let her gaze drift to the tinsel sparkling on the Christmas tree. "I was. The temptation is always there. As I told you, though, I've put that behind me."

They sat in uncomfortable silence when the doorbell rang.

"Pizza's here," Marian announced. "You answer the door while I get my wallet," she said, then disappeared into the kitchen.

Holly rose from the sofa and opened the door. Standing on the doorstep was a perturbed-looking young man, snow covering his shoulders. "That'll be fifteen dollars," he muttered.

Gazing past him, Holly noticed that the snow that had been gently falling as they drove home from work had picked up to an almost blizzard-like pace. "Wow, it's really snowing, huh?" Holly commented awkwardly, hoping Marian would get back with the money soon.

"It sure is, and people like you keep insisting I get out in this mess so you don't have to cook. I almost got myself killed on the way here," the delivery boy grumbled.

Holly placed a hand on her chest. "I'm so sorry! Is it really that bad?"

The boy snorted. "Sure is. In a couple hours all this snow is supposed to turn into ice. The roads will be treacherous by morning. I hope the plows and salt trucks start running soon."

"I'm sorry you have to be out in this…"

"Say it with your tip, lady," he grumped.

"Here you are, Malcolm," Marian said as she returned with the money. "There's a nice big tip in there for you. Take care of yourself out there."

"Yes, ma'am. Thank you, Mrs. Bright," Malcolm replied in a tone that couldn't have been friendlier.

Holly took the pizza and closed the door, watching

through the peephole as he walked gingerly down the front steps, clutching the handrail for dear life. "You must order a lot of pizza for that guy to know you by name."

Marian chuckled. "Oh, no. I hardly ever order pizza. Malcolm was one of my students before I retired."

"So you were a teacher? I bet you were excellent."

Laughing softly, Marian said, "I don't know how excellent I was. My students all thought I was too tough on them, but that was only because they had such potential. I retired last year after forty-one years. When my Roger died, I just couldn't bear all the condolences from the people I'd worked with for years. They treated me like I was this fragile thing that might fall apart at any moment. I decided it was time to start over." Marian's eyes seemed to be staring into a far-off time, then returned to the moment as she slid steaming slices of pizza onto their plates.

The two settled at the table and ate in companionable silence, weary from the first of many exhausting days to come.

"Well," Marian said, dabbing the corner of her mouth with a napkin, "I'm going to call it a night. Winston wants us at the mall by seven tomorrow morning."

Holly looked at the clock. That was only ten hours away, and she was certain she could sleep at least that long.

Marian walked toward her bedroom. "Would you mind throwing the pizza box in the big trash can on the back patio?" she called over her shoulder.

"No problem," Holly replied.

When she opened the back door, she saw just what Malcolm was talking about. Snow was piled several inches deep on the lid of the trash can. As she tossed the box into the trash can, she thought longingly of another slice or two. Marian was barely over five feet tall and couldn't weigh more than ninety pounds, yet she'd eaten most of the pizza by herself.

Just then, Holly remembered the scone Marian had bought her that afternoon was still in the pocket of her coat.

She quickly changed into pajamas and retrieved the pastry, then unwrapped it and took a bite. It was a little stale, but still delicious. As she took another bite, her tooth hit something hard.

"Ouch!" She spit the piece into her hand and brushed the soggy crumbs away.

"Oh my goodness!" Holly exclaimed.

There, laying in the palm of her hand, was a diamond.

Holly smiled, thinking her luck had just turned around. Maybe this Christmas would be okay after all.

CHAPTER TWENTY-SIX

EXHAUSTED, RALPH COLLAPSED into his easy chair and exhaled. The day had gone even better than he could have hoped. The orders for the Christmas star came in a steady stream all day. After thirteen hours, he had orders for twenty-five stars. The cramp in his hand and his tense shoulders reminded him of how much time he'd spent hunched over filling out order forms. None of that mattered tonight, though. His store might be saved!

What a way to start the Christmas season! he thought cheerfully. A smile lit up his round face. Nothing could have made this day any better. He'd even had the good fortune of hiring someone to help him. Even though money was tight, he was lucky enough to need help this season.

"God bless Marian Bright," he whispered.

Holly Berry seemed like a perfectly lovely young woman who was eager to help. Still, it unnerved him the way she looked at the jewelry in the cases. Her thoughtful expression reminded him of someone who was casing the joint.

Shaking his head forcefully, he pushed the thought away.

He had no reason to believe Holly was planning some sort of heist and now wasn't the time to be paranoid. He needed her.

Holly had been genuinely concerned about his ability to fill so many orders for the star. If he were honest with himself, he would have to admit he was concerned, too. If he could make three a day, he would have all the orders completed in eight days, almost three times the promised time frame.

He just hadn't expected so many people to order it.

Somehow, he'd have to find a way to make eight in a day for the next three days. With Holly helping at the store, it might be possible. Not likely, but it might be possible. The challenge would be making sure the quality of his work didn't suffer. He'd have to put in eighteen-hour days like he did when he was first starting out, and Holly would have to run the sales floor while he stayed in his workshop. If the quality suffered, though, he'd have to explain to the customers that he'd miscalculated the time needed to create them.

Not that it would surprise some people if the quality was less than stellar, though, Ralph thought ruefully.

This afternoon, Joe Adler had stormed into the store and all but accused him of selling poor-quality jewelry. Fortunately, the crowd was thin at the time, so no one heard Joe's angry declaration that Ralph's jewelry was junk. It stung that somebody would even suggest his work was anything but first-rate. Ralph prided himself on being a dedicated and conscientious jeweler. In his whole career, he'd never had an unsatisfied customer before Joe. It made him sick to think somebody could be so unhappy with his work.

Ralph shook his head. To think, a stone had fallen out of the engagement ring Joe bought for Nadine. That it would even be possible was ludicrous. Ralph triple-checked every one of his pieces for quality before placing them in the display case.

And why did it have to happen to Nadine? There wasn't a sweeter girl in town.

"She must have really banged that ring on something to make the stone fall out," Ralph had said to Joe.

"No," Joe had snapped. "She said she didn't hit it on anything, and we can't find the diamond anywhere." The fury in his face turned to anguish. "You know how long I had to save for that ring, Ralph. I can't afford another one. I can't even afford to get this one fixed, even if we could find the diamond."

"You know I stand by my work," Ralph said, trying to soothe his angry friend. "I'll fix it at no charge as long as you bring the diamond back in with the setting."

The rage returned to Joe's face and he'd pointed a finger in Ralph's face. "You'll fix it at no charge even if we can't find the diamond. You're not going to swindle me! You'll pay for this, Ralph Stockton. Mark my words, you'll pay!"

Swindle!

Ralph pushed the image of Joe storming off from his mind. He couldn't dwell on his disappointment now. Time was a luxury he just didn't have. He had to get to work on the orders he'd gotten today.

He looked at the clock and groaned. It was nine o'clock. He had to be back at the store at seven a.m. If he got one star done in three hours, he wouldn't get to bed until after midnight.

"That's life," he muttered as he hoisted his bulky frame from the chair. If this keeps the store going for another year, I guess it's worth it."

"Ralph!" Brenda bellowed from the kitchen.

Ralph froze, then his shoulders slumped. The last thing he needed today was one of Brenda's moods.

"Can you come here?" She'd been busily making Christmas cookies for the Christmas bake sale at the mall tomorrow. She was a notoriously bad cook, and Ralph pitied the person who bought her cookies.

"Yes, dear?" he asked as he slowly trudged toward the smell of burnt cookies.

"Frost these for me," she commanded, pointing to a plate of sugar cookies on the counter. "At this rate I'll be at it till ten o'clock."

"I'm sorry, Brenda. I can't tonight. I have to get started making these stars. I have to get at least one finished tonight. I'm not looking at being done until at least midnight."

"Fine," Brenda huffed.

Ralph nodded and walked down the basement steps to his workshop. Apparently there was no avoiding her moods. One good thing about being so busy this season, he thought, is that I don't have to spend as much time doting on Ms. Queen. Her tantrums had gotten worse than usual. For the next four weeks, he would immerse himself in work, dedicating his time to creating beautiful things for people who would truly appreciate them.

Unlike Brenda, Ralph thought wearily. She's not happy with anything unless it has an over-inflated price tag.

Maybe this will be the year she gets sick of small-town life and heads back to the city, Ralph thought hopefully. That would make this the best Christmas celebration ever.

Gathering the supplies to make the first star, he hummed a few bars of "We Three Kings," then stopped. His heart wasn't in it tonight. He just hoped his work wouldn't reflect his mood.

The last thing he needed was more people in this town being dissatisfied with his jewelry. It would be just his luck for Joe to get back at him by spreading the rumor that Ralph did shoddy work. He *had* promised to make Ralph pay for selling him a ring the diamond promptly fell out of.

But certainly nobody would believe that, Ralph assured himself. I've been doing this for thirty years without a single complaint.

Even so, he couldn't afford to slack off now. If the star didn't save his business this Christmas, nothing would.

CHAPTER TWENTY-SEVEN

"HELLO, MY BEAUTIFUL Mrs. Claus!" Nicholas Jingle crowed as he waltzed through the door of the modest-sized home he shared with Suzanne, his wife of seven years.

"Hello, yourself," Suzanne called back. "I'm in the kitchen."

Nicholas walked around behind her and planted a kiss on the back of her neck. "How is the loveliest Mrs. Claus the world has ever known?"

Suzanne laughed. "I'm wonderful. How is the handsomest Santa the world has ever known?"

"Spectacular, as usual," he said, then buried his nose in her hair, which always seemed to smell like fresh cookies.

"That's wonderful," she said, turning her attention back to the cupcakes she was icing. "How were the kids today?"

"Sweet as sugar plums, just like always. Each year it does seem like they want more and more," he admitted.

He gazed at his wife. Though she was in her mid-thirties, she still looked like a college student, especially with her hair pulled back in a ponytail like it was now. The only thing that gave away her true age were the tiny lines around her eyes and at the corners of her mouth. He didn't mind them, though. They came from years of merriment that suited a Mrs. Claus perfectly.

"How was Kris," Suzanne asked cautiously. Nicholas's relationship with his brother was always a sensitive thing to bring up.

Nicholas snorted, the feelings of affection toward his wife gone. "How is he ever? Grumpy. The Grinch has nothing on him, I'm afraid."

"Do you think it's possible you're being a little too hard on him? Just because he's different from the rest of the family, that doesn't mean he should be treated like an outcast."

"Oh, please," Nicholas said, waving off Suzanne's defense of his older brother. "You should have seen him with the kids. He practically grimaced every time one of the tots came to sit in his lap. He hates kids. Why he still even puts up the facade of being Santa is beyond me. All I know is it's pretty darn lucky that he never had kids. Although what woman would ever want to make that kind of commitment to a grouch like him?"

Suzanne frosted the last cupcake and slid the bowl containing the leftover icing in front of her husband. "He doesn't hate kids," she countered. "He just doesn't like what society has turned the season into. I agree with him about that, actually."

Nicholas looked at her as though he was seeing her for the first time. "You've got to be kidding. You *agree* with him?"

Suzanne hesitated. "About some things, yes. I agree with him that people have turned Christmas into nothing but a time of greed and self-centeredness. So few people are focused on what really matters these days. They've forgotten that family and friends are what's important, not stuff. But, the consumerism of our culture has heightened the human propensity to want and expect more, without giving a thought to sharing what we already have with others. I would imagine that as a good and decent Santa, you'd agree with those things, too."

Nicholas grunted. "I find that statement ironic coming from you."

Suzanne winced. "What's that supposed to mean?"

"You're in marketing. Your whole job is to sell things to people."

Rubbing her hands on her apron, Suzanne's gaze met Nicholas's. "That's not fair. I use my marketing background to help non-profit organizations raise money, not get them to buy useless garbage." She placed her hands on her hips and narrowed her eyes at him. "Maybe I should stop marketing for you. I've helped you get a lot of Santa gigs over the years. I can make them stop."

Nicholas's eyes widened. "You wouldn't dare! You know my whole life is dedicated to being Santa. I bring joy to children. Would you really take that away?"

Suzanne dropped her hands and they hung limply at her sides. "Of course I wouldn't do that to you, Nicky. I'm just trying to make a point."

He took a step forward and wrapped his arms around his wife. He'd hurt her feelings, and she'd always been so supportive of him and his desire to be Santa for everyone, the young and young at heart. "I'm sorry, Suzie. I didn't mean what I said. Kris just makes me so mad. This time of year is always so hard for me with Kris's hating Christmas and that we still haven't unwrapped our own bundle of joy. We aren't getting any younger, and I thought we'd have already started passing along our Christmas traditions to our own children. Every year I'm reminded that I might be the last of the line."

Suzanne returned his embrace and her voice softened. "I know how much you want children. If it's meant to happen, it will. And as far as Kris goes, he doesn't hate Christmas. He just has a different opinion than you, and that's okay."

Nicholas sighed. "I guess so." He turned toward the freshly decorated cupcakes. "Those look like they turned out really well."

"They did," Suzanne agreed. "I hope they sell well. The volunteer fire department certainly needs the money."

The annual town-wide bake sale to raise money for the volunteer fire department was one of the most beloved of all Christmas traditions in Saddle Hill. Half the town snatched up the goodies to feed the relatives that descended upon them for the holidays. It was an unwritten rule that everything submitted to the bake sale had to freeze well. Family members raved about the homemade baked goods, and no one ever admitted that someone else had baked them. Nearly everyone participated, though no one's offerings shone as brightly as Patricia Jingle's.

"I'm sure there won't be a single one left. You wouldn't happen to have an extra to share with your devoted husband, would you?"

"For two dollars, you most certainly can have one." Suzanne held out an expectant hand.

Nicholas fished two one-dollar bills from the pocket of his Santa suit and placed them in his wife's waiting hand.

"Thank you, and the volunteer fire department thanks you," she said, slipping the money into the pocket of her apron. "Now, go change your clothes. I don't like snuggling with all that fur."

He nodded and obediently walked out of the kitchen,

wondering what had gotten into his wife. Would she really stop trying to find Santa jobs for him? This was also the first time she'd ever sided with Kris instead of him.

Nicholas removed his red, velvety jacket and scratched his chin. Was it possible she didn't love Christmas as much as he thought, or that she was closer to Kris than he thought? She seemed so nonchalant about still not being able to have children. She wanted them, too, right?

For the first time since they met ten years ago, he was beginning to wonder if Suzanne was the woman he thought she was.

Suzanne stared after Nicholas as he walked to their bedroom without the typical spring in his step. She exhaled. Would this never end?

When she'd first met Nicholas, she thought it was cute how much he loved Christmas. Even their Christmas-themed wedding in July was a creative way to combat the summer heat. The guests had raved about what a great idea it was, but the novelty of a year-round Christmas lost its charm quickly. She didn't even spend Thanksgiving with Nicholas and his family anymore. She had a distant relative in a nursing home about an hour away, so she'd made the excuse that Thanksgiving alone would be too sad for someone so far along in years. Spending the day with someone she barely knew was easier than the false cheer of a Thanksgiving that was only getting in the way of more Christmas.

More and more over the years, she'd begun to feel as though she had more in common with Kris than her own husband. Not that she was in love with him or anything, but she felt as though she shared a bond with him that no one else could understand.

As she dropped each cupcake into its own cellophane bag and twisted it shut, she wondered how her life had turned out the way it had. How did she end up with one of the only men in the world who actually thought he was Santa Claus? He was even following his father's path to gaining weight on purpose. He readily gobbled up any leftover icing or cookie dough he could get his hands on, and he expected her to be fine with it. This morning after Nicholas stepped out of the shower, he'd proudly shown her his soft middle. If he thought she could get excited about his expanding waistline, he was badly mistaken. Suzanne always tried to take care of herself. Nothing to the point of obsession, but she certainly paid attention to her figure.

And the way Nicholas constantly compared her to his mother! "Mom makes the best…" he would say, and then fill in the blank with whatever Suzanne made for dinner. Nothing Suzanne cooked was ever good enough. She'd stopped trying to live up to Patricia years ago. Who would want to be Mrs. Claus, anyway?

Suzanne pulled a stool up to the counter and slid onto it. It was late and she was tired, but she wanted Nicholas to be asleep before she went to bed. Having kids was on his mind again, and she couldn't bear to go through the motions of making him believe she wanted them, too. At one time she'd wanted kids as much as he did, but not now. Not with a husband who would force their children to celebrate Christmas every day and deprive them of the magical feelings of a season that only comes once a year.

Infertile. Barren. Fruitless. Sterile.

Those were the words Nicholas had used over the years to describe Suzanne's inability to give him a child. He'd never considered that he might be shooting blanks.

Another thing he hadn't considered was that neither of them were infertile. It was a truth Suzanne knew would crush Nicholas. As long as she had a say in the matter, there would never be a Christmas with a bundle of joy under their Christmas tree.

CHAPTER TWENTY-EIGHT

"HOW COULD HE leave me alone to do all this work?" Brenda fumed as she slid the last of the frosted cookies onto a platter. It was a quarter past ten, and she'd just finished icing the last one. Before her lay an assortment of shapes, from snowflakes and snowmen to holly leaves and Christmas trees.

Each one seemed to mock her.

To think, Ralph had been so selfish that he wouldn't even help her decorate them. Instead, she'd spent three lonely hours in the kitchen baking and decorating cookies to help raise money for a cause she didn't even care about. Of course she was glad there was a volunteer fire department. They'd come in handy when she accidentally set the oven on fire last year baking Ralph's favorite pie for his birthday, but she still wondered if there wasn't a better way to put the fire out than to douse her entire kitchen with that awful white foam. The only thing that redeemed the whole horrible incident was that she'd gotten new appliances out of the ordeal.

Not without a fight, though. Insurance would cover the oven, but that was it. She'd had to fight tooth and nail to get a matching refrigerator and dishwasher. After weeks of her nagging, Ralph finally relented.

It wasn't like I really *needed* them, Brenda admitted to herself, looking at the gleaming stainless steel beauties. But after all I do around here, it was the least Ralph could do.

The least is right, she thought bitterly.

Still sore that half the town had seen his special star design and he hadn't even bothered to show it to her first, she plopped down on the stool by the counter and inspected her engagement and wedding rings. They were modest pieces, but nothing you'd expect from someone who owns a jewelry store. Most women would be satisfied with something like that, but Brenda wasn't most women. She liked to be noticed. Her mother always told her she was meant to stand out in a crowd, but the few meager pieces Ralph had given her certainly wouldn't get her noticed.

Again, she kicked herself for jumping so quickly into marriage with a man she'd known very little about. She knew Ralph was a jeweler and he'd been pleasant enough and had a big heart. Unfortunately his wallet didn't match. His belly, on the other hand, was a different story.

Brenda worked hard on her appearance, making sure she got regular exercise and carefully watching her diet to ensure she kept her trim figure. She always made sure her hair stayed the shiny honey color she paid a fortune to maintain, never letting those pesky gray hairs that insisted on popping up show their natural color. After all that work, all Ralph could do was complain about how much money she spent. It was worth the investment and putting up with his incessant complaining if it meant she might catch the eye of someone more refined with a thicker wallet.

For now, here she was, playing Betty Crocker in a town like this. She'd always been sure she was destined for bigger things. The biggest thing that had happened in this town in the past three years was the renovation of the local movie theater, where patrons had the choice between a whopping four movies to choose from.

How lame!

She needed to get back to the city. She missed the lights, the entertainment twenty-four hours a day, the sophistication. The little bit she'd tried to bring to this backwater town was wasted on the townspeople. They didn't want or appreciate the finer things in life.

Until today.

The star Ralph had designed for Christmas this year was absolutely gorgeous. In fact, it was one of the most beautiful pieces of jewelry she'd ever seen, including the ones at the fancy stores in the city.

I can't believe he didn't give me one on the first day, she mused. Wait a minute. Yes I can. He never gives me anything. All this time I've dedicated to him without so much as a thank you. Maybe I haven't been obvious enough. I'll just have to try harder to get his attention, to remind him what it takes to make me happy, she resolved. Not that I should have to. I'm better looking than most of the other women in this town, and there's no question that I'm of a different class.

But none of this will matter for much longer, she reminded herself.

Like a zip of lightning through her midsection, she had an idea. She hopped off the stool and quickly covered the plate of cookies with plastic wrap. Brenda grabbed her coat and opened the basement door.

"Ralph, I'm going out for a bit. Don't wait up!" she called down the steps.

An uninterested "That's fine dear," was Ralph's only response.

He doesn't even care that I might be risking life and limb on these slippery roads, she fumed, slamming the door and racing to the car, sure to watch for any slick spots on the sidewalk and driveway.

Maybe in my next life I'll have a garage, she thought wryly as she brushed the snow off the top of the driver's side door and slid in. Cranking the heat and the windshield wipers to full blast, she waited impatiently until she could see well enough to drive.

A smile spread across her face, revealing a row of perfectly white, perfectly straight teeth. After tonight, Ralph would notice her and would have to admit that she wasn't just some servant whose sole purpose in life was to cook and clean for him.

She put the car in reverse and eased out of the driveway, then turned onto the side street covered in snow. As she pulled out onto the main road, she pressed the gas pedal harder, causing the back end of her Mercedes to fishtail on the slippery pavement.

Heart thumping in her chest, Brenda whispered, "As long as I don't get myself killed first."

CHAPTER TWENTY-NINE

LOOKING IMPATIENTLY OVER her shoulder, Patricia Jingle pressed the doorbell of Kris's apartment and held it for several seconds. It was after ten o'clock, and she knew he might already be asleep. It would have been a long day at the mall and dealing with all those kids didn't come naturally to him. He'd be exhausted.

Nearly a minute passed before she heard movement inside the apartment. As she waited for him to open the door, it occurred to her that she didn't know quite what to expect. She'd never been to Kris's place because James always insisted the family gather in their home. They were, after all, the heads of the Jingle family. Besides that, their house always looked the most festive and smelled perpetually like freshly baked cookies. Even their daughter-in-law, Suzanne, a lovely girl whose heart never really seemed to be in it, stopped trying to rise to the occasion years ago.

The deadbolt clicked and the doorknob rattled as Kris opened the door. Surprise registered on his face. "Mom? What are you doing here?"

Patricia's surprise mirrored her son's. "Your pajamas are so…normal."

"Yes, Mom, this is how most people sleep. That shouldn't come as a shock."

"I'm just not used to seeing a man in pajamas that didn't have Christmas pictures on them."

Kris looked down at his blue and gray flannel pajama pants and gray thermal shirt. "Yeah, well, I think once you're over ten years old, you should give up the Christmas jammies."

"I'm afraid your father wouldn't agree," Patricia said, glancing around the living room.

"Dad doesn't agree with me about most things," Kris said, a defensive edge to his voice. "Did you just come here to point out more ways I'm a complete disgrace to the Jingle name, or did you actually need something?"

Patricia cast her eyes downward, tears stinging them.

"Sorry, I didn't mean to snap at you. It's Dad and Nicholas I get so mad at, not you. You shouldn't have to take the brunt of it."

Patricia shook her head. "No, I had it coming. I haven't done right by you, Kris," she admitted, then self-consciously tidied her bun.

"This oughta be good," Kris said.

"May I?" she asked, waving toward the faded and sagging sofa.

He shrugged. "Be my guest."

Patricia walked slowly to the other side of the living room, sat down, and deposited her large tote bag on the floor next to her feet. "What is all this?" she asked, indicating the framed portrait of Shakespeare above the fireplace and the many volumes of his work lined up on the mantle.

"Shakespeare," Kris responded. "Now, what do you mean you haven't done right by me?"

"You must really like his work. How many books do you have up there?"

"Thirty-four," Kris said impatiently. "Mom, why are you here?"

Taking a deep breath, Patricia said, "I should have been a better mother to you, Kris. I failed you and I am so, so sorry."

"But—"

"Please don't interrupt. I shouldn't have let Nicholas and your father come down so hard on you over the years about being different. By standing silently by without speaking up for you, I might as well have said those awful things myself. You are different, and that's okay. It's taken me a while to have the courage to say that, but it's true."

A small chuckle escaped Kris's throat. "Only if by different, you mean exactly like the rest of the world."

Patricia nodded. "Yes, but to the rest of the family, you are different." She tugged at a loose thread on her jacket. "But not as different as you might think, or as different as we let on."

Crossing his legs and interlacing his fingers, Kris leaned back in his chair. "I find that hard to believe."

"It's true," his mother countered. "But you're different in one very good way. You're the only one with the guts to stand up to your father and all his idiotic ideas about this holiday."

Kris frowned. "So I have guts now? When did that happen? And since when do you think Dad's ideas about Christmas are idiotic?"

Patricia bent over and retrieved a stack of papers from her bag, then extended them to her son.

"What's this?" he asked, taking them from her and leafing through the pages.

"My memoir."

"*Forever Mrs. Claus?*"

"That's the title. I've spent the majority of my adult life playing the part of Mrs. Claus and will in all likelihood be in that role till my dying day. Your father will probably even have me buried in some red velvet number." She rubbed her face with her hands and sank against the back of the sofa. "Oh, won't that be awful? Maybe I should be cremated instead."

Kris held up the papers. "Does Dad know about this?"

"No. Oh, no. He would be furious. He thinks I love playing year-round Christmas with him."

"But you…don't?"

Patricia shook her head. For the first time, her son saw that she was being held against her will, the prisoner of an eternal Christmas.

"At first it was fun," she offered. "The singing, the baking, the decorations. But after a few years, all the joy of Christmas just seemed to vanish. It wasn't special anymore. The whole thing became a chore instead of something to be celebrated. Even your father isn't so jolly these days."

"No kidding," Kris muttered, then added, "But you love baking Christmas cookies."

Patricia leaned forward and lowered her voice to a whisper. "I haven't baked a Christmas cookie in over ten years."

His eyes shot toward his receding hairline. "You're kidding! Where do you get them?"

"If I tell you, you have to promise never to utter a word to anyone. If you do, I'll deny it and you'll look like you're just trying to ruin the family tradition. Got it?" Patricia's eyes flashed with the warning.

"Got it," Kris said, crossing his heart.

"Nadine Dobbs bakes them for me," she confessed.

"Nadine? From the Rose Petal?"

"Yes. She's a wonderful baker, and she loves doing it. It's just easier to have her make them for me."

"All this time she's been baking your cookies and Dad doesn't know? How does the house always smell like freshly baked cookies?"

"Candles. No, your father has no idea."

Kris's face glowed. "I'm so proud of you, Mom! You've been pulling a fast one on the whole family for over a decade and nobody had a clue!" He slapped his leg and guffawed.

"Stop it," Patricia said, trying to mask her own giggle.

Kris coughed and composed himself. "How do you know she'll keep your secret? Something like that could ruin you."

Patricia's face became serious. "I pay her very well. Hush money, you could call it. All year long, she makes a dozen Christmas cookies for me every week. If there are any left over, I freeze them and put them back out the next week. He doesn't eat as many when it's not the *real* Christmas season. I think deep down he knows it's not the same."

"You know he'd be crushed if he found out about this," Kris said, smiling as he handed the pages of the memoir back to his mother.

Tears sprang to her eyes. "I know. Despite how ridiculous it is, I still really love that crazy old Santa." Blinking the tears away she looked at her son with pleading eyes. "I'm drowning in Christmas, and you should know that I hate the fake snow he has sprayed all over our yard just as much as you do."

"Are you planning to have that published?" he asked, pointing at the manuscript as Patricia slid it back into her tote. "If you do, your feelings won't be a secret anymore. It'll hurt Dad."

Swallowing hard, she nodded. "I am planning to have it published. I already found an agent. I know it'll hurt him, but I have to get out of the Christmas thing. The book is how I plan to tell him." She glanced around Kris's cramped apartment. "You don't happen to have a spare room in case he kicks me out, do you?"

Kris stood and walked to the sofa and sat beside his mother. "Anything for you, Mom," he said and slipped his arm around her shoulder.

"I've been gone long enough," she said, then stood and retrieved her bag from the floor. "And I know who Shakespeare is, son. I have a degree in English Literature. A long time ago, I taught a few college courses." She exhaled heavily. "But that was before Christmas took over and your father forbade anything but *A Christmas Carol* to be read in our house." Patricia winked at her son. "But sometimes I still sneak in some books I checked out at the library."

They walked toward the door, and Patricia embraced her son, kissed his cheek, and rushed out the door. "No one can know what I've told you," she warned, pausing in the hall outside the apartment door.

"Promise," Kris vowed.

As she descended the steps, Patricia thought, all this time I've let him suffer at the hands of James and Nicholas, and he never knew what the year-round Christmas was doing to his own mother.

CHAPTER THIRTY

BRUSHING THE SNOW off his jacket and stomping his feet on the welcome mat, Joe Adler opened the door of Nadine's small house, where he was greeted by the smell of a chocolate cake in the oven, baking to perfection.

"It smells great in here, Nay!" he called as he walked toward the kitchen.

"Thanks, honey. Come to the kitchen. I can't leave the cake just now," she called.

Joe found Nadine bent over, staring through the glass front of the oven. "Watching it bake? I'm sure there are more exciting things you could do with your time."

Nadine straightened and smiled. "No. It's only got another minute to bake, and I have to make sure it doesn't get too done. What would people think if I brought a dry cake to the bake sale tomorrow?" She bent over again and resumed her post in front of the oven door.

"Nobody would believe you're the one who made it. I don't think you've ever baked a bad thing in your life," Joe said, adoring his bride-to-be.

"That's sweet," Nadine said as her timer beeped. "And completely untrue. It's just been a while." She grabbed her potholders and opened the oven, carefully moving the cake pans to a cooling rack nearby. "How did it go today? I heard Winston had you working a double shift."

Joe groaned. "He did. I wish he would stop being so cheap and just hire another security guard. I can't do it all, and I'm exhausted from trying. All day he didn't let me forget that I wasn't there to break up the fight in the women's lingerie section at Dilly's. Even hiring somebody part time just for the holidays would help."

Nadine took off her cocoa powder-covered apron, circled the counter, and slipped her arms around Joe's waist. She rested her head on his chest. "I know, sweetie. But look on the bright side. Today was probably the worst of it. It'll seem like smooth sailing from here."

"I don't like boats," he said flatly, removing himself from Nadine's embrace.

"Are you okay?" she asked him, wrinkling her forehead. "This seems like more than you just being tired from working a double shift."

"Of course it's more," Joe snapped. "I'm so mad at Ralph I could spit. I bought one of the most important things of my life from him, and it turned out to be a piece of junk."

"Don't say that," Nadine pleaded. "It wasn't a piece of junk. It's a lovely ring. If we ever find the diamond, I'm sure it will go back together with no problem."

Joe shrugged. "I just don't like that this happened to us. I'm not superstitious or anything, but it seems like a bad omen."

"That's silly. It just came loose," Nadine countered. "I've spent enough time being upset today. Whether I have a ring or not, we're still getting married. In less than two months we'll be husband and wife. Our happiness doesn't depend on a piece of jewelry."

"Good thing," Joe said sourly.

Again, Nadine wrapped her arms around Joe's waist. This time, looking into his eyes she said, "Just forget about it. When the holidays are over, Ralph will make it right. I know Ralph. Don't let this ruin Christmas for you."

Reluctantly, Joe nodded. "I suppose you're right." He tilted his head toward the counter that held the cooling rack. "When do I get a piece of that cake?"

"For forty bucks you can have the whole thing. It's for the volunteer fire department fundraiser."

I don't have forty bucks, Joe thought bitterly. I spent all my money on that lousy ring. Instead, he said, "Then do you have a cookie laying around here somewhere? I went all day without getting one of your Christmas treats."

"Check the freezer. Don't take the ones on the top shelf, though. Those are for a special order."

"Oh, yeah? I didn't know you took special orders," he said, rummaging through the freezer.

"It's a long-standing order. I've been making them for years. Just don't tell Wanda. She thinks everything I bake should be property of the Rose Petal Café. She even wanted this cake to be a donation from the bakery. Can you believe that?"

"Actually, I can." Joe selected a cookie in the shape of a wreath from a small plastic container in the freezer and popped it in the microwave for a few seconds. Taking a bite, he commented, "Just like it's fresh from the oven."

"I hope not," Nadine countered. "Microwaves are the antithesis of actual cooking…or baking." She shuddered as she placed the ingredients for her famous chocolate buttercream frosting into the bowl of her mixer.

Joe shrugged. Though he'd never admit it to Nadine, most of the time he couldn't tell the difference between home cooking and cooking by Stouffer's. She'd be crushed.

"What time do you have to be at work in the morning?" Joe asked as he polished off the last of the cookie.

"Early again. Six o'clock. But I get off at two, so it'll be worth it," Nadine said, scraping the sides of the bowl with a spatula. "What about you? Will you be free for dinner?"

"Unless Winston wants me to work another double, I'll be done at five. Want me to cook?" Joe offered.

A smile spread across Nadine's pretty face. So far, they both knew Joe had been unsuccessful in his attempts at impressing Nadine with his cooking skills. Probably because his home cooking was, in fact, cooking by Stouffer's.

"If you want to, but will you feel like it after working all day?" Nadine worried.

"Anything for you, my sweet."

"Okay. How about lasagna? With lots of garlic bread?" she requested.

"Consider it done."

"Want me to bring dessert?"

"Tiramisu. It'll be a real Italian feast." Joe's mouth filled with saliva just thinking about it. Soon they'd be eating all their dinners together.

Nadine nodded in agreement, then said, "If you don't mind, it's been a really long and upsetting day. I just want to get this cake frosted and go to bed."

Joe reluctantly agreed, then walked to the chair where he'd draped his coat and slipped it on.

"I hope you're not upset," Nadine said hopefully.

Shaking his head tightly, Joe said, "Not at all. I'm beat, too." He bent down and quickly kissed the top of Nadine's head, then walked out the front door and into the snow.

Despite the crisp white snow blanketing the ground and the glow of the moon reflecting like dawn, Joe stood with his hand on the handle of the car door with the gnawing feeling that Nadine's lost diamond was a sign of things to come.

CHAPTER THIRTY-ONE

FINGERS SHAKING, THE thief lifted the top of the case holding Ralph Stockton's Christmas star. Realizing the case wasn't wired with an alarm, there was a sigh of relief, then a gloved hand plucked the star from the display.

It was two o'clock in the morning. After watching the mall for hours to make sure each employee, especially the ever-present Winston Marshall, had gone home, it had been time to make the move. For hours, the only sound had been a pounding heart and the occasional siren, probably an ambulance thanks to the slick road conditions. Fortunately, the treacherous highways ensured that only a few people ventured out, opting instead for their warm houses and fuzzy slippers.

It was a stroke of luck that the security firm Winston hired to patrol the parking lot hadn't shown up. At least that was one less thing to worry about.

The thief took a moment to admire the piece. Ralph really was a talented guy. The care he put into his work was almost enough to make the shadowy figure reconsider stealing it. Shrugging off the momentary stab of remorse, the intruder determined that it was too bad the best thing that ever happened to Ralph's career was being taken right out from under his nose.

Oh, well, the burglar thought. He has it coming. And he wasn't even smart enough to properly secure the thing.

Being alone with hundreds of thousands of dollars' worth of jewelry was almost tempting enough to stick around and pocket more of Ralph's "labors of love," as he called them at least a dozen times a day to anyone who would listen.

But no, it wasn't worth the risk. Sure, the jewelry could be sold, but that wasn't the reason for breaking in.

The star. That would be enough to devastate Ralph. This was, after all, intended to be his bread and butter this Christmas. Without it, he'd have to close his doors forever.

Glancing around quickly then replacing the top of the display case and bidding adieu to the hundreds of diamonds winking beneath the glass, the town's newest criminal disappeared into the shadows along the long corridor leading to the mall exit. Certain there'd been a noise from the direction of Stockton's Jewel Palace, the robber slipped noiselessly out the door and into the winter air, hands sweating inside the black leather gloves. After following the shadows through the parking lot, the crook slid into the driver's seat and exhaled for the first time in hours.

Though the snow had stopped sometime earlier in the night and the sky had cleared, revealing a million twinkling stars, none could compare to the one that now lay nestled in the thief's coat pocket.

CHAPTER THIRTY-TWO

THE SUN REFLECTED brightly off the Saturday morning snow. Marian Bright hummed softly as she spread butter on a toasted English muffin. It was a glorious day to be alive. It never ceased to amaze her how much cheerier a sunny day could make a person feel. Roger, God rest his soul, sank into a mild depression each October and didn't shake it off until late April. Even though he'd never seen a doctor for his change in mood, Marian always suspected the colder temperatures and gloomy skies during the winter months were to blame.

Spooning a pile of mixed fruit onto her plate, she turned slightly to see Holly shuffling into the kitchen, hair disheveled and eyes only half open.

"Good morning, dear," Marian greeted brightly.

"Morning," Holly muttered, heading straight for the coffee pot.

"Would you like some breakfast? We have to be at the mall in forty-five minutes," Marian gently reminded.

"Just coffee," Holly said, her words still slurred from sleep.

As Marian poured, she narrowed her eyes. "Didn't you sleep well? I was out the second my head hit the pillow."

Holly took a gulp of coffee. "Not really. I was up a lot."

"I had no idea. Roger always said I could sleep through an apocalypse." Marian chuckled quietly, but Holly didn't join her. She tilted her head and watched Holly stare into her coffee. "Are you okay? You don't look well."

Holly nodded. "I've just got a lot on my mind. Besides, I feel bad that I'm probably not going to be much help to Ralph. He needs a lot more than I can give him. He's in over his head and I don't even know the first thing about jewelry."

"Let's not worry ourselves about Ralph again. He's a big boy and can take care of himself. He's been managing for years. You just make yourself available to help however he needs it and everything will be fine," Marian encouraged.

"If you say so," Holly acquiesced, obviously unconvinced. "Are you an elf again today?"

A twinkle in her eye, Marian waved her hand down the length of her torso. "What gave it away?" She was already decked out in full elf attire.

"What about that grumpy-looking Santa?" Holly took another long drink of coffee. "I can't imagine the kids are too eager to climb into his lap."

Marian shook her head. "Not this morning. He talked his brother Nicholas into switching shifts with him. Kris will be there later this afternoon."

"Two Santas in one family? That's some tradition, huh?" Holly asked, her eyes looking brighter as the caffeine began to kick in.

"Honey, you have no idea. That family is obsessed with Christmas. They keep their house decorated all year round and even dress the part. I've never seen James—that's the father—in anything but red and white and black patent leather. Poor Kris. He never stood a chance in that family," Marian said, shaking her head sadly. "Frankly, I think I'd prefer his genuine grouchiness to their fake merriment any day."

Draining the last drops of coffee, Holly rinsed the mug and placed it in the sink. "I guess I need to get ready. Do you mind if I ride with you today?"

"Not at all. Just make sure you're ready to go in the next twenty minutes. Winston will have our hide if we're late. He looked ready to can us all yesterday."

"We can't let that happen," Holly said as she turned and hurried down the hall to her room.

Marian cleaned up the kitchen and put the finishing touches on her costume—a Christmas sweater with a wreath of poinsettias on the front and the words *MERRY MERRY* embroidered inside.

Exactly twenty minutes later, Holly emerged from her bedroom, bundled up and ready to face the cold. "I'm ready," she announced.

"Just in time, too," Marian said, the worry lines on her forehead beginning to soften. "Let's get going. I just heard on the radio that the roads are still slick even though the salt trucks were running most of the night."

She pulled open the front door, a blast of cold air whooshing into the house. Walking carefully down the steps toward the driveway, Marian fumed at Roger for not wanting to build a garage. She would spend the next five minutes scraping the windshield, feet freezing in the snow.

She jerked open the driver's side door and cranked the ignition, turning the defrost on full blast. Holly surprised her by grabbing the ice scraper and going to work on the snow- and ice-covered car.

"Just get in," Holly ordered. "There's no need for you to stand out here freezing to death."

Marian got in and turned the radio to the station playing Christmas music twenty-four hours a day. What a lovely young lady, she thought. I can't believe half the stuff she told me at lunch yesterday. How could such a thoughtful person be guilty of shoplifting?

The passenger door popped open and Holly plopped onto the seat, smacking her snow-covered boots together before swinging her feet inside. "Let's roll," she said as she clipped her seatbelt.

"That was fast," Marian commented as she pulled the car out of the driveway.

"You said we had to hurry." Holly winked at her.

Her spirits certainly seem to have lifted, Marian thought as she backed out of the driveway.

The two rode in companionable silence during the fifteen-minute commute. Mentally blessing the road crews for plowing and salting the roads and parking lot during the night, Marian swung her car into the closest parking spot she could find.

Only two minutes from facing The General's wrath, they dashed toward the door and joined the rest of the mall employees for morning inspection with thirty seconds to spare.

That was close, she thought, then noticed the mood of the group was more subdued than usual.

Winston stood behind his makeshift podium, addressing the employees. "Last night we suffered a first in the history of this mall. It's a complete tragedy, and we must band together during this difficult time to provide support for our brother…"

Marian's chest tightened. Bracing herself for the news that something awful had happened to one of her friends and coworkers, Marian asked, "What happened?"

"I was robbed!" Ralph shrieked, his face pale and drawn.

Marian blinked. Surely she hadn't heard him correctly. "Robbed?" To her knowledge, there had never been a robbery at the Saddle Hill Mall.

"Yes! Someone stole my star!" he sobbed.

Marian walked over to him and placed a comforting hand on his shoulder. "Oh, Ralph. I'm so sorry. Do they know who took it?"

"No." Ralph choked out another sob.

Winston chimed in. "Apparently the case the star was in wasn't wired for an alarm to go off if it was tampered with." He shot Ralph an accusatory look. "Also, whoever did this had the wherewithal to avoid the security cameras. I'm afraid we're looking at an inside job."

"Hi, everybody. Sorry I'm late," a cheerful voice said from behind the crowd of stunned employees.

A dozen heads turned to see Joe Adler approaching the group, happier than anyone had seen him in days.

"Did I miss anything?" Joe asked, the smile never fading.

Grim-faced, Winston replied, "There was a break-in at Stockton's Jewel Palace last night. The star was stolen."

The smile drooped. "Stolen? By who?"

"That's what I want to know!" Ralph wailed.

Winston cleared his throat. "Apparently we have no security footage of the robbery, and Ralph didn't have sensors installed on the display case."

"No sensors? What were you thinking?" Joe chided.

Shooting to his feet and knocking Marian's hand off his

shoulder in the process, Ralph bellowed, "I was thinking this was an honest, decent town. I was thinking that none of my *friends* would do this to me."

Once again, Marian placed a comforting hand on Ralph's back. "Ralph, we don't know who did this," she soothed. "It could have been someone from out of town. Let's not jump to any conclusions until we have all the facts."

Nicholas Jingle tsk-tsked from the front of the group. "People just don't have the true Christmas spirit anymore."

"That's even worse," Ralph said, dropping back into his seat. "If someone from out of town stole my star, who knows where it might be? They could be hundreds of miles away by now." He buried his face in his hands.

Marian glanced at Holly, who was looking down at her hands, picking at a fingernail.

"We'll find it, Ralph," Marian promised. "But right now, we all need to get to work. I'm sure Joe and the sheriff can track down the thief. The best thing for you would be to keep busy."

Ralph grunted. "Yeah, I'm sure Joe will try real hard to find him."

Joe turned his attention away from Ralph and looked toward Winston. "I should have been notified of this when it happened. We've already lost a lot of time. I'll get right on it."

Winston nodded at Joe. "Good. And you would have been notified if your phone had been turned on last night." Turning to face the rest of the employees, Winston clapped and said, "Okay troops, let's get back out there. The shoppers won't stop just because we've been robbed." He descended the stairs leading from the stage, indicating to the employees they were to follow suit and get to their stations.

As the group disbanded Ralph reluctantly stood, and

shoulders slumped, walked back toward the scene of the crime. Marian's eyebrows rose when she saw Carla Whipple intercept him and place a comforting arm around his lower back. That's a familiar touch, she thought.

"I'll light some candles for your star. I'm sure it will find its way back to you," Carla said.

Shrugging off the encounter she'd just witnessed, Marian walked to Holly and settled down beside her. "What's the matter?"

Holly shrugged, her eyes still downcast.

"Something is bothering you," Marian pressed. "You'll feel better if you tell me what it is."

Holly took a deep breath and raised her eyes to meet Marian's. "Why did this have to happen? Now, of all times?"

"What? The robbery?" Marian clarified.

"Yes, of course the robbery," Holly snapped, then turned her attention back to picking her fingernails. "I know you think I did it."

"That's a big assumption," Marian countered. "The fact is, I never even considered that until you mentioned it."

"After what I told you yesterday about my history of shoplifting, and then the star suddenly goes missing. How do you expect me to believe you never considered me? You looked at me when you said the thief could have been somebody from out of town. You think I took it."

"Did you?"

Holly shook her head firmly. "I meant it when I said that was behind me. Now that he doesn't have his star, Ralph won't need my help and I'm out of a job. Just when things seemed to be looking up…"

Marian wrapped her bony hand around Holly's. "Ralph

is going to need you more now than he did before. Each and every one of the pieces Ralph creates is special to him, almost like a child. Now the one he held the most dear is missing. Go to work and do anything you can to help him. Be his friend. That's the best thing you can do right now."

Nodding in agreement, Holly wrapped her arms around Marian's slight frame and squeezed her tightly. "Thanks, Marian. I'll do whatever I have to to help him. And I'll do whatever I can to find that star." She stood and walked briskly toward the jewelry store.

Twenty feet away, Nicholas Jingle was getting the stage ready for the children that would start arriving in ten minutes.

He's not allowing the robbery to dampen *his* Christmas spirit, Marian thought sourly as she listened to him whistle "Deck the Halls."

Slipping off her Christmas sweater, Marian vowed to help find the person who took off with Ralph's Christmas star. The only problem, she thought, is that this Christmas it seems like almost everybody had something to gain from stealing it.

CHAPTER THIRTY-THREE

WINSTON MARSHALL CLOSED his office door, leaned heavily against it, and sighed. How could this day possibly get any worse?

He crossed the room to his desk and opened the top drawer, retrieving a small orange bottle. He unscrewed the childproof cap and tapped a little white pill into the palm of his hand. Quickly popping it into his mouth and downing a gulp of the water he always kept on his desk, he closed his eyes and waited. In fifteen minutes, all would be well.

If only I didn't have this stupid heart murmur, he thought bitterly. I could be commanding real troops instead of being reduced to corralling these yahoos and popping anti-anxiety meds every time they screw up.

He opened his eyes and lowered himself into his ergonomic leather chair, the cushion wheezing as the weight of his soft body squished the air out.

"This has to be the worst start to the Christmas season this mall has ever known," he grumbled to himself. "Why does everything always have to happen to me?"

In the six years he'd been managing the mall, he'd never been strapped with such an inept group of employees. If he didn't know any better, he'd think they were all working in tandem to run him off. He knew they made fun of him behind his back and called him "The General," then snickered together when they thought he couldn't hear. But he did hear, and it turned out his employees were just as bad at being quiet as they were running their stores. He knew they meant the nickname as an insult, but the truth was that Winston thoroughly enjoyed it. Thanks to his heart condition, no one else would ever call him "General."

"I think everybody at this mall has gone crazy except me," he whispered, relishing the relaxing effect of the medication kicking in.

First, there's Joe Adler, Winston mused. I don't know where his head is this year, but he's certainly doing a half-rate job. How could he have missed the fight in the lingerie section yesterday? Half his job is to make sure nothing like that happens. The other half is to make sure nothing is stolen. So far this season he's O for two. All he does is complain that I'm giving him too much work, and that I need to hire another security guard. Rubbish! Joe has been handling it on his own for years.

Then, Kris Jingle has to sit there in his Santa costume and scowl at the kids like he's been sucking on lemons all year. Seriously, who's ever heard of a grumpy Santa? Half the kids in town can say they have, thanks to him. Why can't he be more like his brother? Nicholas has such Christmas spirit. What went wrong with Kris? Winston shook his head. That can of worms was best left unopened.

The biggest surprise was Nadine Dobbs. Sweet, sweet

Nadine, making such a mess out of the Rose Petal Café. Never in six years has anyone complained about her. Then yesterday, Wanda Kirk came stomping into my office, fuming because the café was out hundreds of dollars because of Nadine. From her hysterics, Winston gathered that Nadine had done something to deliberately destroy the pastries. That was hard to believe since Nadine was the most conscientious employee at the mall, but Wanda's reaction didn't lie. Something had gone wrong at the café and Nadine was to blame.

And the robbery! How could something so terrible happen in such a quaint little town? Of all the pieces at Stockton's Jewel Palace, why did the star have to be what the thieves took? Poor Ralph was counting on that star to save his store, and I'm counting on Ralph's rent check every month to help pay the bills. If the customers that already ordered one backed out because they thought Ralph didn't have the proper security to keep their gems safe, there was no way his store would live to ring in the new year.

"Not that I give a hoot about jewelry," Winston admitted to himself, "but Stockton's Jewel Palace does add a touch of class around here. It would be a shame to see it close."

Winston shook his head. From all he knew about Ralph's wife, she'd be unbearable if the store closed. If rumors were to be believed, though, it didn't sound like she was terribly easy to get along with anyway.

The only bright spot of the weekend had been Marian Bright, Winston realized. Despite everything, including losing her husband several months ago, she'd been her typical cheerful self, a smiling ray of hope in the midst of the disintegration of my staff.

Winston clutched the edge of his desk with sweaty hands

and raised himself from his chair. Straightening his back, he did an about-face and walked toward the door. With his hand on the doorknob, he took a deep breath, readying himself for battle. He was in charge, and he'd stay that way. No matter what kind of mutiny the Saddle Hill Mall employees had in mind, neither he nor his mall would go down without a fight. He was the captain of this sinking ship, and if it went down, he was determined to go down, too.

He left his office with a renewed sense of purpose, and a determination to do whatever he had to to keep things from getting any worse.

CHAPTER THIRTY-FOUR

SUDDENLY FULL OF the Christmas spirit, Brenda tossed her cell phone onto the sofa next to her and giggled. It serves Ralph right, she thought. He put that star out for all the world to see, and now it's missing.

She almost felt sorry for him. He'd sounded so pitiful on the phone, and if she wasn't mistaken, he'd been crying. As far as Brenda was concerned, though, he'd brought it on himself. Who leaves something that valuable out in the open without so much as an alarm attached to the display? The big dope who thinks everybody in town is his best friend, apparently. Anybody with half a brain would have wired the case. But then, she'd always suspected Ralph didn't have much going on upstairs.

Now, he was probably going to lose the store and become completely despondent. If I stick around, he'll take me down with him, she assured herself. The only thing worse than Ralph's perpetual cheeriness would be Ralph in the throes of depression, sulking and moaning about how he couldn't live without sharing his beautiful creations with the world.

Brenda shuddered at the thought.

He'll go bankrupt, and I'll get squat when I walk out of this marriage. She chewed on the end of her thumbnail, then jerked her hand away. She'd paid a fortune for that manicure, and Ralph complained about it nonstop. Not that that was anything new.

The thought of getting out of her miserable marriage with nothing to show for it almost made her sick. There probably wasn't even a decent savings account to take half of.

That's why he didn't make me sign a prenup. Heat crept up her neck at the realization. I should have known. Instead, I was stupid enough to think I'd hit the jackpot, and if things didn't work out, half the jackpot would follow me out the door.

Whoever stole Ralph's star, however, had the potential to make a fortune!

She lifted herself off the sagging sofa and paced around the cramped living room, allowing the drabness of the decor to sour her mood even more.

"That money should be mine!" she growled.

More certain than ever that she had been wronged, first by Ralph and now by the thief who took the money she could have gotten from divorcing Ralph, she stormed into the kitchen to binge on the cookies she was supposed to donate to the volunteer fire department bake sale.

Choosing to forget about her carefully planned diet, she took the plastic wrap off the plate of cookies she'd frosted the night before. These are desperate times, she thought as she took a bite of the first cookie. She wrinkled her nose. She poured a cup of coffee to wash down the cookie that was at the same time dry and underbaked. She decided she was doing the community a favor by not taking them to the bake sale.

Everybody laughed at her enough already. They didn't need to know she couldn't even make cookies.

The gleeful feeling she'd had a few short minutes earlier had vanished, replaced by the determination that she wouldn't walk away from her marriage empty-handed.

CHAPTER THIRTY-FIVE

MARIAN SMILED AND bent over to wish the chubby little boy who'd just gotten off Nicholas Jingle's lap a Merry Christmas. Without returning the sentiment, the boy grabbed the candy cane from Marian's hand and marched toward his mother, a woman who appeared to have the same disposition as her son.

Looks like he comes by it honestly, Marian mused, wishing people would use the Christmas season as a way to spread cheer. Instead it just seemed to bring out the worst in some people.

Turning her attention away from the sour mother/son duo to Nicholas, who was already listening attentively to the wishes of the next child in line, Marian realized that the grumpy kid before this angelic little girl had done nothing to dampen his mood.

He really is Saint Nick. On the heels of Marian's thought came the wish that Kris was the Santa on duty this morning. Sure, Nicholas loved Christmas and didn't let it get to him when a kid acted like a brat, but all that cheeriness was getting on even Marian's nerves, which anyone would admit was hard to do.

Naturally jolly, Marian realized in early adulthood that there were times she needed to tone it down for the sake of her fellow man—an awareness Nicholas Jingle didn't seem to possess.

Who would have thought I would miss Kris and his grumpy face? Marian wondered as she plastered on another smile and handed a candy cane to the smiling little girl, spirit buoyed when the little girl didn't snatch it from her and said those elusive words this Christmas: "Thank you."

"I'm going to take a fifteen," Nicholas announced to the children, then turned to Marian. "Can you hold down the workshop for me?"

"Sure," Marian agreed, wondering why Nicholas always felt the need to announce his breaks that way. Take a fifteen? Does he think he's a real actor? Marian sighed. Of course he does.

After Nicholas was out of sight, Marian adjusted the hands on the clock sign and hung it on the rope barricade blocking the steps of Santa's Workshop. If Nicholas thought he was the only one entitled to a break and Marian was just going to stand there anxiously awaiting his return, he had another thing coming.

Darting quickly toward the food court, she nabbed a cup of coffee from a kiosk and downed it as fast as she could, scalding her mouth and throat in the process. With the way this weekend was turning out, Marian found it almost impossible to keep a smile on her face. For the first time in sixteen years, her heart just wasn't in elfing this morning. Not even sideways glances at her *MERRY MERRY* sweater cheered her.

Who would have done such a terrible thing to Ralph? Of all the people this could have happened to, why did it have to be him? He was a good and decent man, always willing to help his friends and colleagues any way he could. Generous to a fault, he needed that star to stay in business. Brenda would be insufferable after this. Marian grunted. Not that Brenda was a peach to begin with. Somebody has to figure out who did this to him.

A quick glance at her watch alerted Marian she only had three minutes to get back to her post. If she didn't beat Nicholas back, he'd scold her for abandoning the workshop.

Sometimes he can be a real pain in the you-know-what, Marian thought, walking as fast as her aging but still spry legs could carry her.

As she walked, she rolled all the facts she had around in her head. Sometime last night or very early this morning, somebody broke into Stockton's Jewel Palace and stole the Christmas star. Ralph hadn't wired the display case, so no alarm went off. Also, the store didn't have its own security camera, so the only one that could have caught the thief was the one out in the main corridor, and far as she knew, there was no security footage of whoever committed the crime. It couldn't have been a spur-of-the-moment decision—it would have taken time to figure out the angles of the security cameras and bypass the mall's alarm system. Whoever did this knew what they were doing.

Or have already had a working knowledge of the security system, Marian realized with a sinking stomach.

She hated to admit it, but she wouldn't be surprised if Joe Adler ended up being the thief. Even though she considered him a friend, there was no denying he'd been furious at Ralph after the diamond fell out of Nadine's ring. He did have the know-how to get around the cameras and the mall's security system. For him, the theft would have been easy.

Still, she just couldn't reconcile the Joe she knew with someone who would be capable of something so heartless. Despite his sometimes-gruff exterior, Joe had a kind heart. It would take a lot to convince her otherwise.

Then there was Holly. How much did Marian really know about her? They'd met in an online chat room, and Marian offered to let Holly come stay with her without knowing anything about her. It had been the truth when Marian told Holly she hadn't suspected Holly was the thief. Until Holly suggested it, that is.

But Holly had confessed to having a history of shoplifting. Marian's stomach twisted with guilt. *What have I done?* Marian wondered as she reclaimed her post on the stage, eyes scanning the crowd of restless youngsters waiting for their chance to give Santa their mile-long Christmas lists.

Nicholas ascended the stage and settled into his chair mere seconds after Marian. He shot her a disapproving look that communicated he knew Marian had abandoned the workshop.

What does it even matter? Marian mused. *I have bigger things to worry about than rubbing Saint Nick's whiskers the wrong way.*

For all she knew, Holly was capable of anything and very well could have broken in late last night to steal the star. After all, she had admitted to being short on cash and was completely exhausted this morning, possibly after a late night of thieving.

But Holly wasn't the only one that needed money, Marian reminded herself. She could think of a half dozen others that were strapped this year, and any one of them could have benefited from stealing that star.

Including Ralph Stockton himself.

CHAPTER THIRTY-SIX

EVEN AT EIGHT a.m., the Rose Petal Café was packed. Shoppers were back for round two of their gift-buying extravaganzas and were using Nadine's pastries as fuel.

As Nadine bent over to restock the bakery case, Joe sneaked up behind her and planted a playful kiss on the back of her neck.

Startled, Nadine straightened, nearly dropping a tray of Danish. Her smile at the sight of her fiancé revealed a row of slightly crooked but perfectly white teeth. "Good morning to you, too," she said, the strain of yesterday nearly erased from her face.

"It looks like you'll be having another busy day," Joe said, his eyes sweeping the occupied tables.

"Looks like it," Nadine agreed. "I just hope most of my work doesn't get tossed in the garbage today." She shuddered. It had been terrible to watch nearly every one of her baked goods torn apart and thrown in the trash.

"I didn't buy anything else from Ralph, so there shouldn't

be a reason to ruin your delicious treats again," he said, a lilt in his voice.

Nadine tilted her head at Joe's comments and furrowed her brow. After putting the last of the Danish into the bakery case, she turned to face Joe and narrowed her eyes. "You're in an awfully good mood today. What's going on?"

"Instant karma," Joe replied, still smiling.

"Karma? What do you mean by that?"

"Let's go back to the kitchen where we can talk," Joe suggested, looking out at the dozens of Rose Petal Café patrons. "There are too many people here for us to speak freely."

Nadine followed Joe through the swinging door into the kitchen, then leaned against the flour-coated counter and crossed her arms. "Tell me what's going on, Joe. There's something different about you this morning. When I saw you last night, you were still so angry at Ralph about the stone falling out of my ring. Now you can't get that ridiculous grin off your face. Something is going on, and I want you to tell me what it is. What's all this about karma?" she demanded.

With a theatrical sigh, Joe said, "Oh, all right. Sometime last night, Ralph Stockton's store was robbed. Isn't that great?"

Nadine placed a hand on her chest. "Robbed?"

"Yes!" Joe enthused. "Winston announced it in our meeting this morning."

"That's terrible," she breathed. "Wanda told me to come straight to the café. She said she'd handle Winston if he was mad that I wasn't there. Apparently I had to make up for ruining everything yesterday." Shaking her head in disbelief, she said, "Ralph was *robbed?*"

"Yes!"

"Joe, that's horrible. How could you possibly be so

calloused to actually seem *glad* that happened to Ralph? He's our friend," Nadine chastised.

"I wouldn't call him a friend, Nadine," he corrected. "He's always been more of an acquaintance than anything else. Besides, he should have known that karma would come back to bite him. It always does." Joe's face was as bright as a child's on Christmas morning.

"Would you hush about karma? Karma didn't do this to Ralph, Joe. A person did. A person that has no regard for all the hard work Ralph has done to create the most beautiful pieces. How could anyone do such a thing, especially at Christmas?" Nadine fumed, disappointed that the man she'd chosen to marry would be so pleased about another's misfortune. "He was hanging all his hopes on sales this Christmas to save his store. He won't be able to stay open without them." Nadine paused and lowered her voice, realizing Wanda might be able to hear her. "What did they take?"

"The star."

"The star!" Nadine shrieked mere moments before Wanda marched into the kitchen.

"What's going on in here?" Wanda demanded, hands on her hips.

"Stockton's was robbed last night," Nadine offered. "The thief took off with the Christmas star."

"I heard. It's awful, but the world didn't stop for that. We still have a business to run, and we're selling pastries as fast as we can put them in the case. Get back to work," Wanda ordered, then pointed at Joe. "And I don't want to see you in my kitchen again." She turned on her heel and stalked out of the kitchen.

Joe took a step toward the kitchen door, but before he

could leave, Nadine placed a hand on his arm to stop him. "Please don't be happy about this, Joe. Ralph is our friend, and he didn't deserve this. You should be helping him instead of celebrating the theft."

He shrugged her hand off his arm and pushed the door open. "It's hard to feel bad for him after I spent most of my savings on a ring that fell apart less than twenty-four hours after I gave it to you."

"Did you do it?" Nadine asked before he disappeared from the kitchen.

Without answering, he walked through the door, leaving it swinging gently on its hinges.

Nadine watched helplessly as her fiancé walked away. She'd known Joe was angry but hated thinking he might have been responsible for stealing from Ralph. Even so, she couldn't just forget his giddiness that Ralph was facing bankruptcy.

The timer buzzed, and Nadine walked to the oven to retrieve a batch of cranberry-pistachio scones. She placed the tray on the counter.

"Ouch!" she shouted as her hand bumped the hot metal baking pan. She immediately turned toward the kitchen sink and turned the cold water on, letting it run over her blistering skin.

"What's going on in here?" Wanda growled, pushing the kitchen door open with such force it smacked into the wall behind it. "I'm tired of having to come in here and check on you."

"I just burned myself, Wanda. That's all," Nadine assured her, though the welt forming on the back of her hand was already the size of a nickel.

Wanda narrowed her eyes and assessed the blister. "That was careless of you, Nadine."

Nadine nodded in agreement. In all the years she'd worked for Wanda, she'd never had a baking-related injury.

"What's going on with you the last couple days? Since you and Joe got engaged, your head has been, well…I don't know where it's been. You're distracted, sloppy, and let's not mention the mess you made out of my bakery yesterday because you lost your ring. If your relationship with Joe is going to distract you from doing your work, we might have to make other arrangements," Wanda warned.

Nadine knew "other arrangements" meant she was skating on thin ice. If things kept going wrong, Wanda would blame her and Nadine would be fired.

"No, Wanda," Nadine assured her. "It's not going to keep me distracted. I'm just so excited about getting married. You know how it is." Nadine immediately wanted to bite her tongue. Wanda did know how it was. Four times. For some reason she just couldn't seem to make a marriage stick.

Shocker, Nadine thought.

Wanda nodded, then said, "Once you get your hand taken care of, clean up this mess. We're busy again this morning and will be until Christmas. Get it together. You're the best pastry chef I've ever had, and I'd hate to see you go because you can't keep your head out of the clouds."

"Yes, ma'am," Nadine whispered as Wanda marched back out to greet the customers.

Tears welled in Nadine's eyes. The past twenty-four hours had been a nightmare. Yes, it was wonderful that Joe proposed, and she really was looking forward to being his wife, but since then everything seemed to be unraveling. Joe had been so angry yesterday, but when he seemed to have cooled off last night, Nadine was encouraged. Now he seemed elated that someone stole the Christmas star from Ralph.

This wasn't like Joe. He was being short-tempered and spiteful. This was not the man she fell in love with. Sure, the double shift Winston always made him work the day after Thanksgiving was rough on him. It was every year, but he'd never allowed it to affect him before. The diamond falling out of her ring pushed him right over the edge. After the way he'd been acting, Nadine began to wonder if she knew him at all.

As she gathered the ingredients for a batch of sugar cookies, Nadine whispered, "Oh, Joe. Did you do this?"

CHAPTER THIRTY-SEVEN

DRESSED IN JEANS, a stylish jacket with a fur collar and cuffs, and her trusty riding boots, Sylvia Bell hopped in her rental car and again drove toward the mall. The Mountain Craft Festival was ending today, and she hoped to be able to pick up some of the wooden bowls she'd seen yesterday. She'd also seen a flyer about a town-wide bake sale benefiting the local volunteer fire department. Her diet was off this weekend, and her mouth watered as she thought about some of the things that might be available at the bake sale. As a child, Christmas cookies, breads, and cakes had always been her favorite. Now, in this quaint little town, Sylvia longed to be transported back to her childhood when everything was so simple.

Sylvia was also anxious to get a look at whatever had been unveiled at Stockton's Jewel Palace yesterday. She needed ideas for her upcoming jewelry line, and this sleepy little hamlet could provide the inspiration she needed.

As she pulled into the parking lot, she noted that, unlike yesterday, several police cars occupied the front-row spots.

For a brief moment, she hesitated going in, then assured

herself that whatever it was couldn't be as bad as some of the things that happen in New York. After all, what could possibly go wrong in an idyllic little town like Saddle Hill? Besides, she reasoned, there are a lot of cars in the parking lot. If whatever happened was so bad, they wouldn't still be letting people shop.

Walking carefully from her car to the entrance, careful not to slip on the patches of ice that still dotted the parking lot, she soon realized that whatever happened had rocked the town. Shoppers close to the mall entrance stood in small groups, whispering to one another. Straining to hear what they said, she was disappointed when their words were too muffled to understand.

I'm most interested in Stockton's Jewel Palace, anyway, so whatever happened probably won't affect my mission, she thought as she neared the jewelry store.

Her heart dropped to her stomach as she realized the jewelry store was the reason the police were there. Slowing her pace, she saw yellow police tape stretched around the perimeter of the store. A man who looked to be in his early to mid-fifties alternated between anger and tears. Sylvia assumed he was the owner. Her natural take-charge attitude and curious streak getting the better of her, she slid quietly toward the entrance, hoping to get some idea about what happened. Keeping her back pressed against the wall, she wouldn't likely be seen but should be able to hear what the people in the store were talking about.

After a few minutes of eavesdropping, Sylvia gathered that the store had been robbed the previous night and there were no suspects.

Back still pressed against the wall, she inched her way toward the open storefront.

"Sheriff, you don't seem to understand," the distraught man said. "My star is my last hope for keeping my store open. Without those sales, I don't stand a chance of being open next Christmas."

Sylvia shook her head. Poor man, she thought. What a terrible position to be in. He must be a talented jeweler. There had been a long line to order that star piece yesterday, whatever it was.

"I do understand, Ralph, but you need to realize that right now we have nothing to go on. There is no surveillance footage of the robbery, and no alarm was triggered when it was stolen. We'll dust for fingerprints, of course, but if the thief had the wherewithal to get in and out of here undetected, he was probably smart enough to wear gloves."

Sylvia frowned. Somebody might get away with this?

"Winston seems to think it's an inside job. Start there," Ralph commanded, his tone nearing hysteria. "Now, if you don't mind, I need to do an inventory of my other pieces to make sure everything else can be accounted for."

Sylvia heard heavy footsteps retreating and inched forward a little more. Finally, she stepped up to the crime-scene tape and cleared her throat. "Excuse me?"

The sheriff who'd been talking to Ralph Stockton turned to face her. He didn't look like he could be more than twenty-five, but his uniform said his name was Sheriff Arnold.

"Yeah?"

Summoning her most charming smile, she said, "I wonder if you might be able to help me. I'm a designer from New York, and I was hoping to speak with Mr. Stockton. I'd originally planned to see him yesterday, but he was so busy taking orders for his star that I decided to wait until today. Obviously this isn't the ideal time to talk to him…"

The sheriff grunted. His baby face did nothing to hide his disposition.

Keep smiling, Sylvia told herself. "Anyway, I was wondering if there was a way I could get a peek at the missing star. Perhaps there's a photograph of it lying around somewhere?"

Sheriff Charming grunted again. "Hold on." He turned and walked toward the jewelry case and picked up a sign with the image of a glittering, jewel-encrusted star front and center.

"May I see it closer, please?" she asked, forcing her voice to remain pleasant in the face of this very *un*pleasant young man.

Sheriff Arnold huffed. This time he took a few steps toward her and extended his arms, holding the sign directly in front of her.

Wow! If the real piece is as good as the sign, this guy has some serious talent, Sylvia thought.

"You done now?" the sheriff asked, plunking the sign back on the jewelry case and turning his attention to the small notebook in his hand.

"Yes, I am. Thank you so much." She stuck her hand in the pocket of her coat and pulled out a business card. "If you wouldn't mind, will you please give this to Mr. Stockton?"

"Do I look like your errand boy, lady?" he growled, but took the card from her. "This ain't in my job description, ya know. I'm in the middle of trying to solve a crime."

"I know, and thank you so much for your help. I have the fullest confidence that you'll crack this case in no time," Sylvia said sweetly, batting her eyelashes.

Might as well go back to the Craft Festival, she decided. This is obviously going nowhere.

She made it no more than a few steps before a high-pitched squeal stopped her in her tracks. She tensed.

This can't be, she told herself. It's not possible.

Then, the sorority-girl voice that had mocked her all through college rang in her ears. "Cow Bell!"

Sylvia turned slowly, praying she was mistaken.

"I can't believe this! You look fantastic!" Brenda screeched.

Sylvia cringed. The last thing she wanted, or needed, on her relaxing weekend getaway was to run into somebody like Brenda Morris. She'd made Sylvia miserable for four years, and even though she was no longer the chubby girl who only had aspirations of going into fashion, the nickname still hurt.

"Brenda," Sylvia said, forcing a smile. If she could handle the sharks in the fashion industry, she could handle Brenda. "What on earth are you doing here?"

Brenda rolled her eyes and laughed. "I ask myself the same thing every morning when I wake up. Unfortunately, I live here."

"You live…here?"

Brenda sighed. "Yes, I do. For the last three years, anyway."

"How did that happen?" Never in a million years would Sylvia have pictured snooty Brenda Morris living in such a small town with virtually no social scene.

"I met a guy a few years back, fell in love, and got married. You know how it is." Brenda glanced at Sylvia's empty ring finger. "Oh, perhaps you don't."

Sylvia fought the urge to grab Brenda by the throat and tell her to stop being such a horrid witch, but restrained herself. "I haven't met Mr. Right yet. I've been so busy focusing on my career, I've hardly had time to think about it."

"So, what are you doing these days? Computer programming, right? You were always so good at that stuff."

Sylvia clenched her teeth and shook her head, again restraining herself from giving Brenda a tongue-lashing. "Fashion. Remember? I studied fashion design."

Brenda tossed her silky blond hair over her shoulder and snapped her fingers. "Oh, that's right. We got such a kick out of you wanting to go into fashion." Brenda paused and inspected her flawless manicure. "I guess you found a job doing that, then?"

An unfriendly smile stretched across Sylvia's face. "You could say that, yes. I'm a designer. I have my own line."

Brenda's eyes popped open so wide Sylvia thought they might fall out. "How did *you* get a clothing line?"

Sylvia winced. She was ten years older and wildly successful, but Brenda's ridicule still stung. "Well, I picked up a pencil and started drawing. Then voilà, I had a clothing line."

"Where do they sell your clothes? Target? Walmart?" Brenda asked sourly.

"Actually, my line is Jersey Belle." Sylvia seldom used her status and success to elevate herself, but there was no other way to make Brenda believe she was actually worth something.

"Jersey Belle is *your* clothing line? That stuff costs a fortune!"

"Yes, it does," Sylvia agreed, then shrugged. "It's always been my experience that you get what you pay for." Then she added. "What are you up to these days? In college you wanted to study acting. Did anything come of that?"

Brenda looked away from Sylvia and sighed theatrically. "You know how it is. I was in a few plays, but then I got married and moved here. I was in a couple plays at the community theater, but there is absolutely no talent around here. The last thing I was in was a stage production of *Little House on the Prairie*. I played Caroline Ingalls. Can you believe they wanted me to perform with no makeup? And the wardrobes! They practically wrapped me in yards of awful blue fabric. Gingham! I looked like I was wearing a sack." Brenda shook her head. "Actually, a sack would have been an improvement."

Stifling a chuckle, Sylvia said, "I can imagine how terrible that must have been for you. You've always taken such good care of yourself, and to be portrayed in the worst possible way must have been a real challenge."

"Oh, it was!" Brenda agreed. "Not that I'm afraid of a challenge, mind you, it was just so unprofessional. The mall janitor played Charles Ingalls in that play. Believe me, he was no Michael Landon. Can you imagine? Me and a janitor? Even I couldn't act well enough to pull that off."

I'll bet, Sylvia thought, remembering the few plays she'd seen Brenda in during college. If memory served her right, they had been dreadful.

"So, no, I haven't been acting as much as I'd like. I could go to one of the bigger cities around here, but that's a haul. I have to drive two hours one way just to have my hair done. I couldn't make that trip every day for rehearsals and whatnot."

"Oh, no. I'm sure not," Sylvia consoled. "But at least you have a husband who I'm sure adores you." Sylvia tried to keep the sarcasm out of her voice. She hated this side of herself.

"Oh, yes. He's absolutely crazy about me. He's been under a lot of stress lately, though. I just can't seem to help him snap out of his bad mood," Brenda complained.

And I'm sure you've done nothing to cause his bad mood, Sylvia thought ruefully.

"Anyway," Brenda continued, "he's been working so hard the past month and he snaps at me about nothing. I don't know what he's so cranky about. He gets to play in diamonds all day. How could anybody that makes jewelry for a living be in such a bad mood? That's just nonsense."

"Your husband is a jeweler?" Sylvia asked, hoping it was a coincidence that the person she wanted to talk to about his new design was also a jeweler. If that man was one in the same, Sylvia suddenly questioned the man's taste.

"Oh, yes. Can you imagine how exciting that is? He gives me stuff all the time, special pieces he's designed just for me. When we met and I found out what he did for a living, I knew I had to nab him before anybody else got the chance."

Hoping against hope that it was just a coincidence, Sylvia said, "He wouldn't be the owner of—"

Before she was able to finish, Brenda blurted out, "He owns Stockton's Jewel Palace, right there." Brenda pointed a slender finger at the store that was still roped off. "I'm the queen," she said, clapping happily.

"You always thought so," Sylvia muttered.

"Well, now it's official. In this town anyway."

Poor man, Sylvia thought. He's been robbed *and* he's married to Brenda Morris. Talk about hard luck.

CHAPTER THIRTY-EIGHT

MY MOTHER DOESN'T like Christmas, Kris Jingle thought cheerfully as he walked through the mall entrance. Correction, she's sick of acting like it's Christmas every single day. Finally, someone else in this family has the sense to realize how ridiculous the charade was.

He hadn't been able to stop smiling since she left his apartment last night. He'd gotten undeniable proof that even though he was the outcast of the family, he was the sane one. Even though she'd sworn him to secrecy, the knowledge that his own mother understood and agreed with his point of view put an extra bounce in his step.

"What is this? Do I see Kris Jingle…smiling?" a voice called from the stage as he approached Santa's Workshop.

Kris shrugged off Nicholas's remark and took a deep breath, determined not to let his brother ruin his newly found good mood. He wasn't the weirdo Nicholas and his father made him out to be. He, Kris Jingle was just a regular guy, and the second-in-command of the Jingle family was on his side.

"Seriously, why are you smiling? You never smile," Nicholas

pressed. "Especially with all the cute little kids you had to talk to yesterday. I heard it was awful."

"Leave it alone, Nicky," Kris warned, using the nickname reserved for the times Nicholas needed a reminder that he was the big brother.

"Nicky? Looks like I'm in trouble about something," Nicholas said with a mocking smile.

Kris merely shook his head and went into the little shack that had "Santa's Workshop" painted across it in red-, green-, and white-striped letters. Inside, he donned his battle dress—a fuzzy red suit and black patent boots. Hooking the fluffy white beard over his ears, he braced himself for the onslaught of endless requests.

Santa, can I have a train set? Santa, I want a new dolly. Santa, Santa, Santa. Hearing that name so much made him dizzy.

He forced a smile and emerged just as Nicholas entered the workshop to change into what he called "civilian clothes."

"You're it," Nicholas said, slapping Kris's shoulder.

Can't wait, Kris thought glumly as he settled into the oversized chair. He glanced at Marian and nodded, signaling that he was ready for the next kid in line.

Hours passed, and he'd learned only one thing: kids were just as selfish today as they were yesterday. It made his stomach churn to know these parents would probably buy the little cherubs everything on their extensive Christmas lists. The only thing that kept him going was his conversation with his mom the night before.

Finally, when he was able to take a break, he stood to stretch and started toward the men's room.

Marian, quick as lightning, caught him before he even got

off the stage. "Did you hear?" she whispered in a conspiratorial tone.

"Hear what?" Kris asked. What good was having a break if people wouldn't leave him alone?

Marian lowered her voice even more. "There was a robbery here last night."

"A robbery? That's ridiculous. We don't have robbers in this town," Kris countered, taking a step in the direction of the restroom.

Marian caught his arm. "Apparently we do now, and the police have no idea who did it."

"What did they take?" Not that Kris was interested. He just wanted Marian to tell him so he could have a few minutes of peace and quiet.

"Ralph Stockton's Christmas star!" she hissed. "Can you believe it? Poor Ralph. He's devastated. That's why I'm still here. I took an extra shift so I could keep my eyes open and try to figure things out."

Kris's eyebrows shot toward the Santa hat. "Somebody robbed Ralph?"

Marian nodded, the corners of her mouth drooping into a frown. Kris thought she looked like a distraught bobblehead.

"It's no secret Ralph needed that star to—"

"I know," Marian interrupted. "What will he do now?" She wrung her hands like a worried grandmother.

"I don't know what *he's* going to do, but I know what *I'm* going to do."

Marian's troubled face brightened. "What?"

"Use the bathroom."

Her face fell. "Oh. Well, you better hurry. You've only got a few minutes left of your break."

"I know," he muttered and walked toward the restroom, struggling under the cumbersome suit and stuffed belly.

Who would steal from Ralph Stockton? Kris wondered once he was inside the stall. He's so nice, even I don't feel grumpy around him.

Kris flushed the toilet, washed his hands, and hightailed it back to the line of waiting kids.

I'd hate to be whoever stole that star, Kris mused as he settled into the chair. Sheriff Arnold has been chomping at the bit to get some action in this town. Whoever took it better brace themselves. They're going to go down hard for this.

CHAPTER THIRTY-NINE

BRENDA STOMPED UP the sidewalk in front of the house she viewed as a shanty, nearly slipping on a patch of ice, cursing under her breath. Slipping her key into the lock, she opened the door so hard that the doorknob banged into the wall behind it and bounced back into its frame. She slammed her keys on the wobbly table just inside the door and dropped her purse on the floor, then walked to the living room and plopped on the sofa.

She buried her face in her hands and moaned. "Why? Of all the people that could have showed up in this awful town, why did it have to be her?" If Brenda didn't know any better, she would have thought Sylvia came there on purpose, just to rub her success in Brenda's face.

Brenda had been merciless in college, teasing Sylvia constantly. With her frizzy hair, plump body, and glasses, she'd been an easy target. Sylvia was never anything but nice, though, and there were times Brenda felt almost guilty for giving her such a hard time. Even though she looked like a mess most of the time, their classmates still preferred being with Sylvia, and it drove Brenda crazy. She'd always hoped pointing out Sylvia's flaws would make her seem more appealing instead, but they flocked to Sylvia even more. Even this morning, Sylvia couldn't have been nicer.

"And now she's gorgeous!" Brenda wailed. "Life isn't fair!"

For hours, despite Wanda Kirk's insistence that she leave, she'd sat at a corner table at the Rose Petal Café, licking her wounds and trying to avoid Nadine's judgmental looks every time she ordered the chocolate truffles infused with peppermint Schnapps. It had been too early to drink, so Brenda drowned her sorrow the only way she could—through dessert filled with booze. No matter how many she ate, though, it hadn't been strong enough to take the sting out of losing to Sylvia.

Tears dampening her hands, she lifted her head and fixed her eyes on the ceramic logs in the gas fireplace. She debated turning it on, but still hot with anger and embarrassment, decided against it.

Sylvia, the one I'd decided would fall flat on her face if she tried to break into the fashion world, is wildly successful with her upscale clothing line, Brenda fumed, gritting her teeth. The worst part is, I can't afford to buy even a blouse from her line! And who's to blame for that?

Ralph!

At the thought of her husband, she picked up the yellow glass daffodil he'd given her for a wedding present off the small table next to the sofa and hurled it across the room. It met the stone surrounding the fireplace and shattered to bits.

"This is all Ralph's fault," she growled. "He was supposed to be a wealthy jeweler living in the lap of luxury, not a half-wit palooka living in a Podunk town." She rolled her eyes. Palooka? Podunk? I'm starting to sound like I belong here.

She'd spent the last three years hoping things would turn around, that her urging might light a fire under Ralph and he would finally be motivated enough to ditch this God-forsaken town and pursue the finer things in life, the things that give life value. Instead, the worst had happened. He'd become even more content in this, this…village. Something about how he had everything he ever wanted now that he'd found her, and that he couldn't imagine uprooting himself when all his dreams were finally coming true.

Ugh. What a sap, Brenda thought angrily.

She'd decided yesterday that it was definitely time to end things with Ralph and was going to wait until after Christmas. Even she didn't feel right about breaking his heart during the holidays. But the truth was, she just couldn't stand being the queen of Stockton's Jewel Palace anymore. She'd already given it three years and sticking it out for another month was too much to ask. It was time to move on.

Resolved, Brenda stood, her gaze falling on the glass shards that littered the hearth. She felt a momentary stab of regret. She really did love that daffodil.

Shrugging, she said, "That's just one less thing to tie me to that man."

Briefly debating whether or not to clean up the broken glass, she decided to let Ralph clean it up himself. The mess was because of him, after all.

Turning on her heel, Brenda glanced briefly over her shoulder at the house she'd shared with Ralph, complete with its threadbare carpet and outdated wallpaper, then turned toward the bedroom. It was time to pack her bags and get the heck outta there.

Carefully packing the nicer things she'd managed to

acquire during her marriage, she wondered what kind of life she'd be stepping into.

Her marriage was a sham. It always had been, and it had held her back long enough. Cow Bell was rich and thin and gorgeous while Brenda had only managed to make it as far as the community theater.

Now it was her turn to shine.

Even though she wasn't sure where she would go from there, she assured herself, "At least things can't get any worse."

CHAPTER FORTY

MARIAN HUSTLED PAST the shops, teeming with shoppers, toward Stockton's Jewel Palace. Claire, a stocky fifty-something woman who insisted she could out-merry Marian, had just relieved her of her elvish duties.

Let her just try to be a merrier elf, Marian thought. Especially working alongside Nicholas Jingle. That guy's cheeriness is worse than the root canal I had last year, and I'm about as happy as they come.

She picked up her pace, weaving around the mall patrons and their overstuffed shopping bags. Roger would have a fit if he saw all these people lugging around bags of things nobody really needs, she thought. Sudden tears stung the backs of her eyes. She'd never get used to how abruptly memories of him would pop into her mind. Shaking off the ache that had become a frequent companion the last several months, she dodged the consumers who plowed through the crowds, not paying any attention to the people around them.

Marian felt horrible about the way she'd left things with Holly after the staff meeting this morning. She'd been visibly hurt at even the idea that Marian would suspect her of the robbery.

Under the confident exterior, Marian could tell that Holly was a fragile and troubled girl. Even if she didn't want to admit it, she couldn't be certain Holly was innocent. There was certainly motive and opportunity. Ralph would have showed her the store, and a smart girl like Holly would have noticed the security system was lacking.

Slowing her pace as she approached the jewelry store, Marian glanced around for her houseguest, but the only person on the sales floor was Ralph.

She must be in the back, Marian reasoned.

"Hey, Ralph. How are things?" she asked gently. Compassion for her friend flooded her. Poor guy still looked nauseous and forlorn.

Deep lines creased Ralph's forehead, his mouth sagged. He waved his hand around the store. "Not so good. Hardly a customer all morning, thanks to the police tape. Thankfully no one has canceled their order for the star yet. I've tried to keep myself busy working on the orders I already have, but I have to man the floor until Holly gets back from her lunch break."

Marian's shoulders dropped. "Holly isn't here? I was hoping to talk to her."

Ralph glanced at his watch. "Actually, she should have been back by now."

"I see…"

"I could really use her help, too. I can't make the stars and be on the sales floor at the same time," Ralph complained. "Not to mention cleaning up the mess the sheriff and his minions made with their fingerprint dust. Things are stressful enough today without her bailing on me. I haven't even had time to take an inventory of my other pieces to see if anything else is missing."

"I'm sure she hasn't bailed on you," Marian said with more conviction than she felt. "Do you know where she was planning to have lunch? If she lost track of time, she might still be there." A knot settled in Marian's stomach. Somehow, she knew Holly hadn't lost track of time.

"I thought she was just going to grab something quickly at the food court, which is why I don't understand why she isn't back yet."

Marian turned and began walking in the direction of the food court, the bells on her shoes jingling with each step. "I'll find her," she called over her shoulder, then said under her breath, "I have to find her."

A sick feeling came over as she scanned the food court, searching for Holly. She was nowhere to be seen.

Maybe I should have expected this. It's possible she hasn't put her shoplifting behind her like she said, and that working in a jewelry store was more temptation than she could handle.

Quickening her steps, she walked across the mall to the Rose Petal Café just in case Holly changed her mind about eating in the food court. Searching the faces of the customers, Marian was disappointed again to realize Holly wasn't one of them.

Marian caught Nadine's attention, who was taking inventory of the bakery case. "How are you this morning, dear?"

"Better than I was, still not as good as I could be," Nadine answered in a gloomy voice.

"I'm so sorry to hear that." On a normal day, Marian would have consoled Nadine and spent as much time as necessary to bring a smile back to her face, but today was anything but a normal day. "You haven't seen Holly in here, have you?"

"Holly? Who's that?"

"Oh, you know. The girl who was in here with me at lunch yesterday. Tall, thin, red hair. She's helping Ralph out for the holidays."

"Oh, her. Yeah, she was in here. She bought a scone. Something about each bite containing a little surprise. It was weird," Nadine said absentmindedly as she counted the muffins.

"I'm sure it was a compliment," Marian said hurriedly. "Do you know where she went?"

Nadine's face scrunched as she thought. "We've had such a busy day, it's hard to remember." She snapped her fingers. "You know, I think she said something about getting Ralph a little gift to cheer him up. I thought that was really nice of her. Ralph certainly needs some cheering up. Try the candle shop. You might find her there."

"Thanks!" Marian called as she raced in the direction of Whipple's Wicks.

Maybe Holly is innocent after all. She'd been so worried about Ralph overextending himself with all those stars, and now she wants to do something nice for him. That doesn't sound like somebody who'd steal his most prized possession right out from under his nose. Right?

When Marian arrived at Whipple's Wicks she was greeted by the competing scents of cinnamon, pine, and…was that burning wood? The sign to her left announced that the scent of the month was "Fireplace."

Who would buy that? Marian thought, looking around for Holly. Her gut told her she needed to find Holly soon.

"What can I do for you, Marian?" Carla Whipple asked as

she stood from her task of restocking the shelf on the opposite wall with candles.

"I was actually looking for somebody. Her name is Holly Berry. She's tall, slender, long red hair. Have you seen her?" Calm down, Marian told herself. You sound panicked. Carla will think something is wrong.

"There was a girl with red hair in here about fifteen minutes ago. I'd never seen her before, and figured she must be a stranger in town," Carla offered.

"Yes, she's staying with me this month and is helping Ralph around his store during the holiday season."

"That explains it, then."

"Explains what?" Marian asked, her heart thumping in her chest. Is this what Roger felt like before he died? she wondered, then immediately dismissed the thought. She had a job to do and that kind of thinking would get her nowhere.

"She said she was looking for something that might cheer Ralph up, that he's having a hard time right now. I said 'No kidding. Poor man got robbed blind last night.' The girl didn't seem to appreciate my comment too much."

I wouldn't either, Marian thought, and Ralph certainly wouldn't. What an insensitive thing to say. "Did she find anything for him?"

Carla shrugged. "She spent a lot of time looking at these candles. These are selling like crazy." She waved a hand toward the ones she was restocking.

Marian walked over to the shelf and picked up a candle called "Christmas Cheer." No wonder Holly was looking at that one. Ralph could sure use some of that. She raised it to her nose and sniffed. It smelled like snickerdoodles.

"How long ago did she check out?" Marian placed the

candle back on the shelf. All the different scents were giving her a headache.

Carla shook her head. "She never did. I was about to ask her if I could help her decide what to get, and she was gone. Just disappeared. I could have used the money, too," she mumbled under her breath.

"Thanks, Carla. I've gotta go."

"Don't you want to buy something?" Carla called after Marian as she made a quick retreat.

Ignoring Carla's plea for business, Marian walked into the bustle of shoppers, not knowing where to go next.

Where could she be?

Nagging at her mind as she tried to figure out what to do, was the thought that if Holly did steal the star, she would have had a very good reason to disappear.

CHAPTER FORTY-ONE

SYLVIA ABSENTLY RAN her fingers around the rim of a smooth wooden bowl at one of the booths set up for the Mountain Craft Festival, oblivious to the intricacy of the work.

"Can I help you with something ma'am?" the man in the bib overalls running the booth asked.

She looked up and smiled faintly. "Yes. I'd like to buy this, please."

"That'll be a hundred and twenty dollars," the man said, a sheepish look on his face. "Each of my pieces is handmade, which accounts for the elevated price tag. You won't see any mass production here."

Sylvia nodded and retrieved her credit card from the handbag. "I understand. You do beautiful work," she commented as the man swiped her card in a portable machine. "Much nicer than what you can typically find in a retail store."

"Thank you," the man replied, a twinkle in his faded blue eyes. "I learned the craft from my daddy, who learned it from his daddy. It's sort of a family business," he said, handing the card back to Sylvia and wrapping the bowl in tissue paper before placing it in a bag.

She took the bag he extended toward her. "Thank you. And Merry Christmas," she said, trying to shake the gloom that had dampened her Christmas spirit.

Of all people in this world, why did she have to run into Brenda Morris? A weekend that was supposed to be relaxing and surrounded by total strangers, and Brenda showed up. Sylvia didn't even take pleasure in watching the envy flit across Brenda's face when she mentioned her clothing line. As successful as she was, Sylvia still felt like the chubby, frizzy-haired girl she was in college. The years had melted away, and she still envied Brenda's confidence and beauty.

That was years ago, Sylvia reminded herself. Just because you ran into somebody that treated you as an insignificant nobody in college doesn't mean you have to let her ruin the rest of your weekend. You're better than that, Sylvia Bell, she admonished herself, and you have never used your status or success to make another person feel inadequate. That was the lesson you learned all those years ago, and Brenda is the one who taught you.

With a renewed sense of confidence, Sylvia straightened her shoulders and perused the other tables overflowing with handcrafted goods. After selecting several other items from hand-dipped candles to a hand-stitched quilt, she braced herself against the weight of her shopping bags and headed toward the entrance. As she approached Stockton's Jewel Palace, she noticed the police tape had been removed. Only a few customers strolled around the floor, pausing occasionally to peer into the display cases. It was a stark contrast to the crowd that had gathered in the jewelry store yesterday. The man she assumed was Ralph Stockton sat in the corner, his shoulders hunched. To Sylvia it looked like he carried the weight of the world on his back.

I can imagine, she thought. He *is* married to Brenda Morris, after all. She shook her head in pity. Poor man.

"Good afternoon," was Ralph's solemn greeting as Sylvia entered the store.

"Hello," Sylvia replied, intentionally making her voice warm and comforting. In her experience, even the smallest amount of kindness from a stranger was enough to turn a bad day around. "May I put my bags somewhere while I look around?"

Ralph waved a hand toward the corner behind his cash register. "Be my guest."

Depositing the bags where he'd indicated, Sylvia noted that he was several years her senior. Brenda must have been digging for gold with this one. Literally.

She walked slowly down the length of each display case, lowering her face to within inches of the glass. Ralph Stockton did amazing work. What he was doing in this sleepy little town was beyond her. He could be quite successful in a larger city.

"Your pieces are beautiful," she said, admiration lacing her words.

Ralph's face brightened. "Thank you. I'm featuring a special piece this Christmas, but unfortunately the model for it was stolen last night."

"I saw the police here this morning, but I did manage to get a peek at the poster. I must say, the picture was beautiful."

He waved off her compliment. "That picture didn't do it justice. It's the work of a lifetime, and somebody just walked out of here with it. They probably ruined me. I won't be able to stay in business without it."

"I'm so sorry," Sylvia said. She meant it. Ralph seemed like a genuinely nice guy—a rarity in her world. What he was thinking when he married someone like Brenda Morris, she didn't know. "If you're still taking orders for it, I'd like to buy one."

A smile illuminated Ralph's face. "Yes, of course." He walked quickly from his post behind one of the display cases to the table in the far back corner. "If you'll just come over here, we can start filling out the necessary paperwork. It's a custom order, so yours will be different than any of the other ones I create. A truly one-of-a-kind piece."

"Great," Sylvia said, then followed his lead and stood on the opposite side of the narrow table.

He already had the pen in his hand, poised above the order form. "Name?"

"Sylvia Bell."

"That's funny," he said, scratching her name onto the form. "My wife went to college with someone named Sylvia Bell."

"That's me," Sylvia offered, cringing at the things Brenda must have told him about her. "I ran into her this morning while the police were here."

"You're that Sylvia Bell?" Ralph eyed her curiously. "From the way Brenda described you, I would have expected someone a little…different."

"I was different back then. But somehow, when I was talking to Brenda this morning, it felt just like old times." That's putting it mildly, Sylvia thought.

Ralph gave her a knowing look. "Brenda can be unkind."

The corner of Sylvia's mouth dipped into a frown. "I guess she told you she wasn't particularly nice to me."

He shook his head. "I've been there."

She felt an instant kinship with this man. Of course he'd been there. He seemed like a kind and caring man, not at all the kind of man Brenda would typically fall for. Unless there were a lot of dollar signs in his bank account, apparently.

Ralph cleared his throat. "What kind of stones and metal would you like?"

"That depends. What are my options?"

"Whatever your heart desires. As I said before, this star will be truly unique to your taste."

"In that case, black and white diamonds set in platinum."

Ralph raised an eyebrow. "That's not very festive."

Sylvia shrugged and smiled. "It will go with anything. Besides, there are a lot of chances to wear black in my line of work."

Ralph went back to filling out the order form. "What do you do?"

"I'm in fashion," Sylvia offered.

Head still bent forward, Ralph chuckled. "That must just kill Brenda."

Remembering the blatant envy on Brenda's face this morning, Sylvia's smile widened, despite her best attempt to stop it. "Yes. It must."

"If you'll just fill out the rest of the form, I'll calculate the total payment based on the stones and metal you've selected." He pushed the order form across the small table.

"Of course." As she filled out her address and credit card information, Ralph's fingers flew across the buttons of the calculator. As she signed her name at the bottom of the form, Ralph turned the calculator around so she could see the grand total.

"Does that seem like a fair price?"

Sylvia raised her eyebrows at the price. Given the attention to detail evident in the other pieces she'd seen, she expected to pay at least twice the amount he'd just shown her. What she'd already suspected was confirmed: Ralph Stockton was a decent, ethical man who wasn't gouging the prices on his jewelry. He probably wouldn't make more than a couple hundred dollars above the cost of materials for these stars. He certainly couldn't be rolling in the dough at these prices.

That must kill Brenda, too, she thought, liking Ralph even more.

CHAPTER FORTY-TWO

WINSTON TAPPED HIS thumbs impatiently on his desk. Joe certainly was taking his time. He'd been summoned nearly an hour ago. That Joe was the only other one that would have had the capability to shut off the mall alarm system and bypass the main security cameras hadn't stopped nagging at him all day. He'd been acting differently today, there was no question about that. Some asking around revealed that he'd been pretty heated about the diamond falling out of Nadine's engagement ring.

Motive.

As far as Winston knew, no one else in town would have a reason to want to hurt Ralph. During Wanda's tirade yesterday about Nadine tearing up the café, he'd managed to decipher Joe's name. Maybe it was all connected.

A brisk knock on the door pulled Winston from his wondering. "Come in," he said brusquely.

"You wanted to see me?" Joe asked, poking his head in the door.

"Yes. Come and sit." Winston pointed to the chair across from him.

"I've only got a minute," Joe said. "We've got tons of shoppers again today, and I wouldn't want to miss another fight."

Winston's mouth twisted into a grimace. The nerve Joe had to mock him to his face. "This will only take a moment. I just need to ask you a few questions about the theft last night."

"Sure." Joe crossed the cramped office and settled into the high-backed chair Winston had indicated. Both the chair and his boss had seen better days. "What's up?"

Winston brought his fingertips together under his chin and leaned back in his chair. "I've been thinking about the theft, Joe, and I've got some concerns."

"I'd say so," Joe replied. "Somebody robbed the place."

Winston shot him a withering look. "I could do without the sarcasm. My concerns are legitimate. There is a thief in this town, and who knows where he'll strike next."

Joe straightened in his chair. "I understand that, Mr. Marshall, but it's been, what, a decade since the last robbery? I'm sure it's an isolated event and won't happen again," Joe encouraged.

"Yes, yes. I'm sure you're right," Winston agreed. "But there's something that's been bothering me, and I can't just ignore it."

"Oh? What's that?"

"You."

Joe's forehead wrinkled. "Me? I'm bothering you? Look, if this is about the fight I missed yesterday—"

"It has nothing to do with the fight. I keep thinking about who would have had motive to steal the star. I mean, a real motive. Of course we've got people here that might have had it in them to do something like this, but for what purpose? Money is always a good motivator, and we've certainly got people here that could use the extra cash, but something about the money angle just doesn't ring true for me. That got me thinking about what a stronger motive could be, and I think I've come up with something pretty solid."

Joe hesitated a moment before asking, "Which is?"

"Revenge."

"Revenge, huh?" Joe thought a moment. "I guess it's possible."

"Yes. It makes perfect sense. But that got me thinking. Who would want to take revenge on someone like Ralph Stockton? He's the nicest man in town." Winston tapped his chin for emphasis.

"I think you've been watching too much TV, Winston."

Winston stood. "I don't think so." Then pacing around his office said, "Think about it. Someone feels wronged by Ralph, and seeing no other way to get justice, hatches a plan to get even."

"Winston, I really don't have time for this," Joe sighed, then stood and hooked his thumb over his shoulder. "I really need to get back out there."

"Wait a minute. This is where it gets interesting."

Joe didn't move.

"From what I gather, there's only one person in town that has a motive for revenge." Winston stopped pacing and turned to face his security guard. "You."

"Me? You've got to be kidding. Why would I need revenge against Ralph?"

Winston took a step toward an exasperated Joe. "Why

don't you tell me?" He crossed his arms over his chest and leaned against his desk.

"I swear, I—"

"Save the defense for court," Winston said flatly. "I know about Nadine's ring, and I have witnesses saying they heard you talk about making Ralph pay."

Joe's mouth formed a hard line. "Wanda."

"I'm not going to name my source, obviously, but I would say the intel is reliable."

"Source? Intel? You're not a real investigator, Winston. I can't believe you're going to take the word of an ill-tempered witch over mine!"

"Settle down, Joe. There's no need for name-calling. I just want you to explain yourself. Other than me, no one else would have had enough knowledge of the security system and how to bypass it. That leaves you." Winston's voice softened. "Try to understand the position I'm in."

Joe reclaimed his seat in the worn chair and leaned forward. He ran his fingers through his tousled hair. "I'll admit I was mad, spitting mad. Embarrassed, too. I did want to get back at Ralph, and I went to Nadine's house last night, still thinking about what I could do to hurt him. I'd thought of spreading the word that his jewelry was trash, that his work was shoddy. But Nadine reminded me of the Ralph we all know. He's always stood by his work, and I realized that if he could, he'd make this right, too. When I got to thinking about it, I knew Nadine was right, so I decided to let it go. I'm about to marry the most amazing woman on the planet. How can I let something as trivial as a broken ring take the joy from that?"

Winston thought a minute. "Hearing about the theft

didn't seem to dampen your spirits this morning. You smiled all the way through the announcement."

Joe rubbed the back of his head and looked at the floor. "I'm not proud of it, but I was a little happy to hear someone had stuck it to Ralph. I know it was petty, but I felt vindicated."

"Okay, then. Get back to work. Don't think you're in the clear yet, though. You're still my number-one suspect," Winston warned.

"I hear ya," Joe said, then stood and turned toward the door. He paused with his hand on the knob and turned back toward his boss. "It might be time for you to consider that there might be a lot more people around here that have much more to gain by stealing from Ralph." At that, Joe opened the door and disappeared into the hall leading toward the mass of shoppers.

Winston stroked his chin. If what Joe said was true, and there were more people out there with something to gain from stealing from Ralph, he was back to square one.

As he tried to focus on the duties of running the mall, the thought irked him that it was very likely the thief was still in their midst.

CHAPTER FORTY-THREE

DODGING JOE SO he didn't run into her, Marian made her way down the back hall of the mall where Winston's office was located. Holly had been missing for hours, and the sinking feeling in Marian's stomach made it impossible for her to focus on anything but getting to the bottom of what was happening at the Saddle Hill Mall.

First, Stockton's Jewel Palace was robbed. Then, Holly disappeared. The logical connection would be that Holly took the star and ran, but Marian couldn't stand the thought of that being true. She brought Holly to Saddle Hill, and felt responsible for the things that were going wrong.

She needed to run her theories by somebody, and Winston was the only person she was fairly certain wasn't responsible for the theft.

Knocking on his office door, she heard a clipped "Who is it?" from the other side.

"Marian. I need to talk to you, Winston."

"Very well. Come in," he said in an annoyed tone.

She opened the door and observed the frazzled man

slouched over his desk, his fingers flexing in his hair. The small office looked as though a windstorm had blown through. Papers were scattered on the desk and spilling over onto the floor. His office didn't match the impression she had of The General.

"What do you need, Marian? I'm very busy." Winston never took his eyes off the paper he was holding.

"I wanted to talk to you about the theft at Stockton's Jewel Palace," she said. "I've got some ideas, and I want to run them past you."

Finally turning his attention to Marian, he looked at her coldly and said, "And what makes you qualified to have an opinion on the matter?"

Marian narrowed her eyes at Winston the way she had when one of her students had gone too far. "I'm fairly certain I'm allowed to have an opinion about anything—or anyone—I want," she shot back, holding Winston's cold glare until he looked away.

"I really don't have time for your theories, Marian. This place doesn't run itself." His eyes went back to the paper in his hand.

She took a step closer to his desk. "Is there some reason you don't want to hear what I have to say? Perhaps you're worried that I think *you* had something to do with the theft?"

"That's ludicrous!" Winston snapped, laying the paper on his desk with a slap. "You have some nerve coming into my office and making accusations like that."

Marian went closer and sat in the chair Joe Adler had vacated only minutes ago. "I'm not accusing you of anything. Just pointing out that you also had motive to steal Ralph's star. I'm also telling you I might be more qualified to give you an opinion that you want to give me credit for." She thrust her jaw forward and waited. It was time for Winston to know she meant business. She wouldn't let this drop until the thief was captured and the star was found.

Winston's mouth formed a hard line. "Okay, then. Humor me. What was my motive?"

"Two come to mind right away." Marian held up her hand and ticked them off on her fingers. "The first is publicity. Our sales have been down the past few years. Ralph facing closure is proof of that. Maybe you thought getting the mall's name in the paper would get people to remember it still existed. Maybe get people to shop locally instead of driving a couple hours to a bigger city. The second motive is money. You saw Ralph's star. Between its size and the intricacy of the work, it would be worth a small fortune. Maybe you wanted to sell it and sink the money into the mall to keep it afloat. Or, better yet, maybe you'd cut your losses and run once you had the money in your pocket." Marian paused. "How's that for motive?"

Winston appeared to be deep in thought. "Not too shabby, I suppose. Except that you're forgetting one very important thing. Ralph's store is more valuable to me open than the money I'd get from selling the star. The star wouldn't pay rent for long. Ralph's store staying open, however, would provide a steady stream of income for this mall. Simple as that. And as for the publicity angle, why would I be stupid enough to risk going to jail just to advertise for the mall? A TV or radio commercial would be less risky."

"Well, I never said my theory was perfect, or that I thought you did it, but I do think you need to hear what I have to say about who *could* have had a reason to steal it."

Winston leaned back in his chair and clasped his hands

together behind his head. "By all means, tell me who might have had a reason to rob Ralph."

Marian chose to ignore Winston's condescending tone and pressed on. "From what I've been able to see, there are three really strong motives for someone to steal from Ralph: Revenge, money, and passion. First, we have to consider Joe Adler. From what I've heard, he's been pretty mad at Ralph because—"

Winston stopped her. "I've already talked to Joe. Who else might have had a motive?"

Marian's mouth drooped. It was no wonder everybody called him "The General." He was about as warm and fuzzy as a cactus. "It's important not to rule anybody out at the moment. We've got Joe, who was really angry at Ralph about the diamond falling out of Nadine's ring. He has a motive for revenge. We've also got to consider that Ralph's wife, Brenda, might feel wronged by him."

"His wife? Why on earth would she want revenge on Ralph? What on earth has he ever done to her?"

"I don't know if you've noticed or not, but she doesn't really fit in with the Saddle Hill culture. She always looks miserable when I see her. If she blames Ralph for getting her stuck in a town she hates, she might want revenge for that. In case you can't tell, she's not the most pleasant woman."

Winston's forehead creased as he considered the possibility.

Pressing on, Marian said, "Then we've got the money aspect. It's no secret that the stores in this mall are struggling. Ralph is on the verge of closing his doors, but so is Carla Whipple. Also, I don't know if you're aware of this, but the Rose Petal Café is holding on by a thread. Why do you think Wanda was so mad yesterday when the pastries had to be destroyed looking for Nadine's diamond? It's because Wanda is counting on every single sale to stay in business. Nadine let that fact slip one time when I mentioned the Rose Petal Café must be such a lovely place to work."

"I wasn't aware of the situation at the Rose Petal. At this rate, I'm not going to have any tenants left," Winston groaned. "This will just be an empty building, and I'll be occupying a permanent spot in the unemployment line."

"Unless you stole the star," Marian ventured. "You're another one that needs the money, whether you want to admit it or not."

"Listen here—"

Marian shook her head. "I already told you I don't necessarily think you had anything to do with the theft," Marian said quickly. "Another person that could be responsible is Holly Berry, the young lady who is staying with me this holiday season and is helping Ralph."

"I've seen her. She looked especially upset this morning when I announced the star had been stolen," Winston remembered.

"She already cares about Ralph a great deal and has worried that Ralph has too much on his plate this Christmas. She has doubts that he'll be able to get the star orders filled on time," Marian offered. She hesitated a minute, then said, "She also has a record."

"A record. One of those big, black, vinyl circles?"

Marian shook her head impatiently. "No, Winston. A *police* record. For shoplifting."

Winston threw his hands up in the air. "Why, in the name of all that is decent, would Ralph hire a shoplifter to work in his store?"

Marian shrugged. "You know Ralph. He always gives

people the benefit of the doubt. Also, he needed the help and she was available. He's drowning right now."

"And he needs the money," Winston said quietly.

Marian nodded in agreement. "Ralph can't be ruled out as a suspect. Making it appear that the star had been stolen, then filing a false claim with his insurance company would give him a financial cushion as he tries to save the store."

"Maybe Ralph and Holly are working together," Winston suggested.

"I don't think so," Marian countered, then hesitated before telling Winston the really damning evidence against Holly. Finally, she said quietly, "Holly appears to be missing."

"Missing? What do you mean she's missing?"

"I mean she was here, and now she's not," Marian explained, as if to a child. "She took her lunch break and hasn't been seen since. The last place I'm certain she was is Whipple's Wicks. She was looking for something to cheer Ralph up."

"That doesn't sound like something someone that robbed him would do," Winston admitted.

"My thoughts exactly," Marian agreed, "which leaves us with the third and final motive I've come up with: Passion."

Winston grunted. "Ralph hardly seems the passionate type."

"I know, but to some degree he must be. He has a wife, after all. A very beautiful wife."

He picked up his pen and tapped it impatiently on his desk. "But a wife that wants revenge, apparently."

"That was just a theory. I didn't say it was a perfect theory," Marian acquiesced, then reminded Winston, "Certainly Ralph must have had relationships before Brenda. He was fifty when they met. That would be a long time to live without ever having a love interest."

"Keep working on it," Winston said, then picked his paper back up and turned his attention to it.

Marian stood and watched her boss for several seconds before leaving his office.

As she walked down the back hall and into the holiday bustle, she was discouraged by the fact that any one of the people she'd mentioned would have a reason to steal from Ralph, including Ralph himself.

The most disheartening thing of all, though, was the knowledge that no matter who was guilty, she'd be helping send one of her friends and colleagues to jail.

CHAPTER FORTY-FOUR

JOE ADLER QUICKENED his step as he approached the Rose Petal Café. If Winston suspected he stole the star, he could only imagine what Nadine thought. She'd been hurt and disappointed when he talked about getting even with Ralph, and this morning when he was so cheerful after the robbery, she looked at him with disgust. He hadn't even considered the possibility that she would think he'd be capable of something so cruel, but when she asked him flat-out if he took it, he was so stunned by her question that he'd just walked away.

Now he could only imagine how that made him look.

Even though it was ridiculous to him, he realized that people thought he had a legitimate reason for wanting to hurt Ralph, and he had to make sure Nadine understood he would never hurt another person that way.

When he walked into the café, Joe noticed the lunch crowd had thinned out considerably. His eyes scanned the restaurant and settled on Nadine, sitting alone at a small corner table. She was slowly swirling her spoon in a bowl of soup, but Joe had yet to see her take a bite.

She looks so sad, and it's because of me, he thought. The last person in the world he would ever want to hurt was miserable because of him.

"Hey, beautiful," he said softly when he reached her table. "Is there room for one more?"

She didn't look up but nodded faintly.

Settling into the chair opposite her, he reached across the table and took her slender hand in his. "I think we should talk," he suggested.

"Yes, I think we should," she agreed as she pulled her hand out of his grasp and leaned back in her chair.

Joe's shoulders tensed. She was distancing herself from him. "I know what you think, Nadine, but it isn't true."

She shrugged a shoulder and flicked her eyes toward the shoppers hurrying from store to store. "It could be true."

Joe leaned forward, closing the distance she'd just created. "Nay, I swear to you, I didn't steal that star from Ralph. You have to believe me."

She raised her doe-brown eyes to meet his. It was the first time she'd looked at him since he sat down.

"Are you sure about that?"

This time it was Joe who created the distance between them. He leaned back in his chair.

"Of course I'm sure. I think I'd notice if I was stealing from people. How could you even think that?" he hissed.

"Oh, I don't know," Nadine snapped. "Maybe because you were so mad at him and were threatening to get even with him. It's quite a coincidence that his most-prized possession goes missing the very next day. Or, maybe it was because you were so happy that he'd been robbed and might have to close his store, talking about all that karma stuff. You've been anything but decent since my ring broke, and I'm starting to wonder if you're the man I thought you were."

The words hit Joe like a punch in the gut. "Nadine, I was angry because the ring that was supposed to be a symbol of my love for you broke. I only want the best for you, and I was mad and embarrassed that it only lasted a few hours. I thought Ralph should be held responsible, yes. I still do. But last night when I left your place, I realized you were right. Marrying you is the most important thing in the world to me. The ring doesn't mean much next to that." He reached for her hand again. "I need you to believe that."

She dodged his attempt and picked up her spoon and resumed swirling it around in her bowl. "I want to, but you were so unkind. It was awful."

Joe spread his hands in front of him. "The only thing I'm guilty of is being human. It was wrong to be happy. Ralph has always been a friend, and I should be helping him instead of celebrating his misfortune, and that's what I intend to do as soon as I convince you that I had nothing to do with the robbery."

Nadine dropped the spoon and grasped Joe's hand. "I do believe you. Now, please help Ralph," she pleaded. "He might lose everything."

"I will," he promised.

She tenderly kissed his fingers, then said, "I've got to get back to work. Wanda will have my hide if I mess anything else up. She's been breathing fire all day, and it's best if she doesn't see you."

She stood and Joe stood with her. "I promise, Nadine. I'll find out who did this. Ralph won't lose his store on my watch."

Nadine squeezed his hand and nodded.

He watched as she walked behind the bakery counter. A promise is a promise, he reminded himself. He'd find the person who was responsible for stealing that star.

Twenty minutes later, Joe sat in the closet-sized room he called an office. Actually, the lingering scent of disinfectant in the air made him pretty sure his office had been the janitor's closet at one time. He stared at the monitors that received the security feed from the cameras in the mall's main areas, and as far as he could tell, the cameras in the hall outside Stockton's Jewel Palace hadn't been turned off. There wasn't even a gap in the time stamp on the bottom corner of the footage. Unfortunately, it seemed to Joe that Ralph had been displaying the star in one of the few areas of the store that a thief could have swiped it and ran without being detected.

Joe shook his head. It didn't make sense. Ralph should have known better. Unless he did it on purpose. Even Ralph couldn't be ruled out as a suspect. He would have benefited greatly from a false insurance claim.

Rewinding the footage to the time the mall closed, Joe scanned the video looking for any movement, some indication of what time the star might have gone missing. After a frustrating hour of watching nothing but a dimly lit store in gray scale, a shadow at the bottom of the screen made Joe sit straight up.

"What was that?"

He rewound it a few seconds and leaned closer to the monitor. There it was again. At eleven o'clock last night, something created a small shadow just out of the camera's view in the vicinity of the star. Of course, there was no proof that the shadow meant anything. Ralph's careless planning made sure of that.

Joe rubbed his tired eyes. "At least I have a time frame to work with," he assured himself.

Confident he had all the information he'd get from the video, he reached to turn it off, but stopped when another movement caught his eye. Someone wearing all black with a hood pulled up over their head walked slowly into Stockton's Jewel Palace. After a few quick glances around, the trespasser moved quickly in the direction of the display cases and took something from the coat pocket.

Joe squinted. "Is that a lock-pick set?"

As he watched, the intruder nimbly jimmied the lock and opened the first display case, taking out one piece of jewelry after another. To his surprise, each piece was placed back in the exact spot from which it was taken. A metal object caught the dim light in the case, revealing a small tool.

"That person is tampering with the jewelry!" Joe shouted to his empty office. "That's what happened to Nadine's ring. It wasn't Ralph's fault. He's not doing shoddy work, somebody is sabotaging him!"

The criminal replaced the last jewel in the case and turned away from the camera.

"I've got to tell Winston," Joe said, hoping his boss would forgive him for not monitoring the mall for the last hour and a half.

Joe walked briskly toward Winston's office, armed with two pieces of information: The star may have been taken around 11:00 last night, and someone who obviously has experience picking locks was trying to destroy Ralph's business.

CHAPTER FORTY-FIVE

AT QUARTER TO four, Marian Bright stood at Santa's Workshop in front of her coworkers. Still clad in her elf costume and *MERRY MERRY* sweater, the ensemble did little to cheer her.

"As you all know, there was a robbery last night at Stockton's Jewel Palace, and Ralph's Christmas star has disappeared," she said to the group she'd called together for an emergency meeting. "I'm sorry to say that so far, we have no leads. Whoever stole it managed to avoid being caught by the security cameras. However, I feel it's my duty to let it be known that the young lady who was supposed to stay with me through the holiday season, Holly Berry, has also gone missing. Whether she is connected to the crime is unknown, but I personally believe she is innocent. Unfortunately, the timing of her disappearance is suspicious and shouldn't be overlooked."

Marian swallowed over the lump in her throat as she looked out at the faces of the people she'd been working alongside for years, faces that were now filled with confusion and uncertainty. Their comfortable and predictable lives in Saddle

Hill had been invaded by a thief. She just prayed it wasn't a thief she was responsible for bringing to town in the first place.

As Marian's fellow employees murmured to one another, Marian announced, "Let's not assume Holly is the thief. She's just a kid looking for a fresh start. But that doesn't change the fact that she is missing, and she must be found. The disappearance of a young woman from our safe little town should concern us all." Just before she stepped off the stage, she added, "Whether she took the star or not, our number-one priority has to be to find Holly."

Descending the few stairs from the stage, she began distributing photocopies of Holly's picture. "Holly is new to town and has only been here a couple of days. Many of you might not have seen her, since she has been working with Ralph and hasn't met many other people. Carla Whipple was the last one we know saw her. Apparently Holly stopped by Whipple's Wicks to buy a gift for Ralph to cheer him up."

Marian cut her eyes toward Ralph, who held the flyer in his hands and was gently shaking his head.

The group disbanded, each person with their eyes focused on the page bearing Holly's picture and whispering among themselves. Only a few mall employees remained. Marian placed the leftover photocopies on a chair and straightened her sweater.

"Do you think Holly stole my star?" Ralph asked, looking as though he'd been betrayed by his dearest friend.

Marian shook her head. "I honestly don't know, Ralph. My gut tells me no, but the fact that she's missing can't be ignored."

"I only met her yesterday, but it didn't look like she was casing my store. She was helpful to me and was very good at the job I gave her to do. She's a natural, actually. I sure could use her."

"I know, Ralph. I can tell you with certainty that she was concerned about you. She worried you might be overextending yourself on the stars and wouldn't be able to fill the orders in the promised time frame. That doesn't strike me as something a person who planned to rob you would feel."

"No, it doesn't," Ralph agreed. "And she was right. I have overextended myself. There were more orders than I expected, and I'm so desperate to keep my store open, I made promises I can't possibly keep. That's why I need Holly. She thinks she doesn't know anything about jewelry, but she's got a terrific eye for detail. She would make an excellent apprentice."

Marian placed a comforting hand on Ralph's arm. "We'll find her and your star, and I'm sure she'll still make an excellent apprentice."

"I hope so," Ralph breathed. "She was trying to find a gift to cheer me up?"

"Yes," Marian said softly. "As I said before, she was worried about you."

As the two stood in thoughtful silence, a flustered Joe Adler raced up to them. "Ralph, I've got to show you something," he said, his breath coming in short bursts.

"Joe, you're hyperventilating. What happened?" Marian worried aloud. "Have you found something?"

Joe inhaled deeply a few times to steady his breathing, then said, "I was just reviewing the security footage from last night. I think I've determined what time the star was stolen. Plus, there's something else you'll find very interesting. Come on." Joe trotted off in the direction of his office.

"I wonder what he found," Marian mumbled as she and Ralph followed Joe's path.

"I don't know, but we're about to find out," Ralph said, moving unexpectedly fast considering his ample girth.

In Joe's office, Marian gulped air to catch her breath. When he's on a mission, he can really hustle, Marian thought.

She and Ralph huddled around the security monitors, watching impatiently as Joe scanned through the security footage from the night before. He pulled up the segment he was looking for and stepped back so they could see.

For the next few minutes, they watched in horror as someone dressed in black carefully withdrew each piece of jewelry, tampered with it, then placed it back where it belonged.

"That person is trying to ruin my business!" Ralph proclaimed.

"Who is it?" Marian asked. "I don't recognize the movements."

"I wish I knew," Joe replied. "After I saw this, I told Winston and got permission to skirt my duties a little longer and quickly scanned the footage from the past several weeks," he tapped his fingers across the keyboard. "When I went back to Halloween, I found this." He pushed play.

As the trio watched the screen, someone in the same black outfit pulled a metal tool out of the pocket, slid it into the lock, and opened the case. Withdrawing the first piece, the burglar held it close, inspecting it carefully, then slipped it into the same pocket that had held the lock-pick set.

"Hey! That person stole from me!" Ralph screamed at the monitor.

Joe raised an eyebrow at the angry jeweler. "Did you not notice anything was missing?"

"I don't exactly check the inventory often. I've always

assumed my pieces would be right where I left them. Apparently that was a lapse in judgment." Ralph sounded indignant.

As the criminal continued to tinker with other jewelry, a silhouette was emphasized by the display lighting.

"A woman?" Marian said in awe as she, Ralph, and Joe watched her remove piece after piece from the display case then replace each one. "I wouldn't have guessed a woman would be involved."

"That's a bit sexist, don't you think, Marian?" Joe scolded, then added, "But yes, I was surprised, too."

Marian shot Joe a look. "It's not sexist since most crimes are committed by men."

Joe ignored her remark. "Any idea who that is?"

Marian and Ralph leaned closer to the monitor. Marian squinted. "She's slender, medium height. Could be anybody."

"That's what I was afraid of," Joe said through a frustrated exhale.

A wave of relief flooded Marian. "I know it wasn't Holly. She wasn't here on Halloween."

"Keep watching," Joe ordered.

A few minutes later, the woman who'd stolen from Ralph tucked a strand of loose hair back under the hood, then turned away, never showing her face.

"Rewind that!" Ralph cried.

As the three of them watched the segment again, Ralph exclaimed, "I know exactly who that is!" He jumped from his chair and rushed from the office.

"Who?" Joe shouted in Ralph's wake.

Marian shrugged. "At least Ralph knows who stole *something* from him. It's just too bad we still don't know who took the star."

CHAPTER FORTY-SIX

BRENDA TOSSED HER food wrappers in the trash can of the tiny fast-food joint she stopped at for dinner, then walked out into the freezing air. The greasy burger would do nothing for her figure, but unfortunately, she'd become used to subpar cuisine while she lived in Saddle Hill.

She'd been on the road five hours with several more to go before she stopped for the night. She'd made it as far as St. Louis before she stopped to eat and hadn't even looked in the mirror as the town she'd called home for the past three years faded into the distance.

There was no use looking back, that part of her life was over. With all the belongings she'd be taking into her new life packed in the trunk of her car, she was both invigorated and nervous about the prospect of starting over. New beginnings had always excited her, and now she would finally have the chance to live the life she'd dreamed of.

Good thing she'd chosen to hyphenate her last name. That would make it easy to drop her connection to Ralph once and for all.

She opened the door of her car and slid into the seat, turned on the seat warmer, and cranked the heat to full blast. As she waited for it to warm, she rested her head against the seat and closed her eyes. There would be no more small-town life, no more marriage to a man who was alarmingly content with mediocrity. The city awaited, and so did a life far beyond what Ralph could even comprehend.

For the first time in years, I can do whatever I want, she thought. I can live absolutely anywhere. There won't be snickers behind my back by Ralph's lousy friends, and I won't have to drive hours just to get a decent haircut and dye job.

She smiled as the heat from the air vents swirled around her. She was headed to southern California where she'd never have to see snow again.

The winters in Saddle Hill were hard. Buckets of snow fell on the picturesque countryside, making the roads almost impassible. Even last night, she'd almost gotten herself killed. Any time the first snowflake fell, everyone would rush to the only measly stocked supermarket in town and pillage all the milk and bread.

"What's the deal with the milk and bread?" she'd asked Ralph more than once. "Do people only eat peanut butter and jelly and cereal around here?"

Yes, she resolved. This time I'm going to settle someplace where the temperature doesn't dip below sixty degrees. She sighed, imagining having perfectly bronzed skin all year round. With my blond hair and dark brown eyes, I'll be gorgeous, she assured herself. Maybe even more gorgeous than Sylvia Bell. She shook the thought away. Sylvia wasn't part of her life anymore. No one was.

She took a moment to indulge in the warmth of the heater,

imagining the sunshine washing over her. Buoyed by the prospect of living in an eternal summer, she vowed to make this the best Christmas she'd ever had.

Flipping on the radio station playing Christmas music twenty-four hours a day, she sang along. She'd long blamed her singing voice for the reason she hadn't made it big in the theater. *Who cares now?* she consoled herself. *There's nobody here but me, and that's just how I want it.*

As she belted out the chorus to "It's the Most Wonderful Time of the Year," an urgent sounding reporter broke into the music to announce that an all-points bulletin had been issued for a Brenda Morris-Stockton of Saddle Hill, Kentucky, on suspicion of grand larceny. The reporter went on to describe the theft at Stockton's Jewel Palace and the developing information that security footage showed a woman breaking into the display cases of the jewelry store, pocketing an unidentified item.

"The bracelet!" Brenda shrieked.

Pulse jumping in her throat, Brenda realized there was no way she could get out of this. Ralph would have given the police the make and model of her car, and it wouldn't be hard for them to find out the license plate number. She wouldn't last a day before being hauled in.

"…she is also a suspect in the theft of a special Christmas piece that was unveiled only yesterday. Ralph Stockton's Christmas star was taken under the cloak of darkness last night. Footage shows this woman in the store around the time of the theft. As of now, police have no other suspects…"

"The star! They're coming after me for the star, too?" Brenda yelled at the radio. "That rat! How could Ralph do this to me?"

Gripping the steering wheel until her knuckles were white,

she took slow, controlled breaths, willing her heart rate to slow down. As she did, the back end of her car slid on the slushy pavement. The sleet that started only a few minutes ago was already making the roads treacherous. It wouldn't be safe to continue driving tonight and getting into an accident would only ensure the police would find her.

Now is not the time to draw attention to myself, she realized. The last thing I need is to stand out or get myself into a position where I actually need the police.

Going against everything she held dear, Brenda got off the interstate at the next exit, resigning herself to having to spend the night in another small town. The local and state police would be out on the roads on a night like this, and one of them was bound to run her plates. Then she'd have no way out.

She guided her Mercedes into the parking lot of a tiny, flea-bag motel with a flashing "vacancy" sign and killed the engine.

"This place looks like it's straight out of a horror movie," Brenda muttered, and with a knot in her stomach added, "And the pretty girl never makes it out alive."

With a bitter taste in her mouth, she knew she had no choice but to spend the night there. Then, in the morning after she'd had time to make a game plan, she'd figure out a way to get to California. All she'd have to do then was blend in with the locals before the police had a chance to drag her in for stealing from that rotten husband of hers.

CHAPTER FORTY-SEVEN

HOLLY BERRY TOOK a steadying breath and stuck her hand in her pocket, feeling around until she found the item that could end her financial problems.

How did I end up like this? Holly thought as she wondered if she'd ever be found. I came here for a fresh start and look at me. I have something that doesn't belong to me and nobody knows where I am. Ralph trusted me and I let him down. He needed me, and I'm not helping him.

The story of my life, Holly thought sadly. A lifetime of making the wrong choice for the wrong reason, and just when I get the chance to do the right thing, I hurt the very people that had enough faith in me to let me try again.

Marian's reputation would be smeared because she's the one who suggested Ralph hire a drifter with a sordid past to work in his jewelry store. Ralph would face financial ruin, and everyone in Saddle Hill will think twice before welcoming a stranger into their midst again.

Tightly closing her eyes, a tear squeezed from the corner of her eye and trickled down her cheek.

She'd failed too many times. Not being there for Ralph when he needed her was just another injustice she'd inflicted upon the decent folks she'd crossed paths with.

No more, she vowed. I have to figure out a way to make this right. With her guilty conscience and nowhere to go, the night ahead promised to be a long one.

CHAPTER FORTY-EIGHT

MARIAN'S ALARM BUZZED in her ear at five-thirty Sunday morning. She slapped the button to turn it off and groaned.

I'm getting too old for this, she thought, but knew her fatigue had nothing to do with her age and everything to do with being worried about Holly.

Hoping against hope, Marian got out of bed, slid her feet into her slippers, donned her red flannel robe, and padded quietly down the hall to the guest room where Holly was supposed to be sleeping. A quick glance in the room confirmed Marian's fears. The bed hadn't been slept in, but Holly's belongings were still scattered around the room like she'd just gone down the hall to the bathroom. It looked like she might return any second, but Marian's intuition told her otherwise.

"Holly?" Marian called, just in case a Christmas miracle had occurred sometime during the night. It is the season of hope, she thought halfheartedly.

Dragging herself to the kitchen for a quick breakfast, Marian decided there would be no Christmas tree-shaped toast or coffee with eggnog creamer this morning. Holly's disappearance and the possibility, no matter how remote, that she had stolen the star had thoroughly dampened Marian's usual joy of the season.

Good thing I'm working with Kris this morning instead of jolly old Saint Nick, Marian reminded herself. She certainly wouldn't be the cheeriest of elves, and Nicholas wouldn't stand for it.

After a quick breakfast of a bran muffin, black coffee, and a banana, Marian hurried through the rest of her morning routine, paying extra attention to applying concealer in an effort to cover the dark circles under her eyes. Finally slipping into her elf costume for the third day in a row, she ruminated on the fact that back in the day, Sunday was considered a day of rest. When she was a child, most stores were closed.

"Now people get up and go shopping and exhaust themselves just to get a good deal," she grumbled to herself as she straightened the bells around the hem of her tunic.

The third Christmas sweater of the season pictured Santa hanging off the side of his sleigh waving and smiling, his cheeks rosy with delight. Below the picture were the words, "…and to all a good night." She slipped it over her ensemble and tried to muster the same amount of joy she usually felt when she wore this sweater. It was no use.

After one last glance in the mirror to make sure she looked the part, Marian grabbed her coat and purse from the hook inside the front door and walked out into the biting cold. Still dark, the sky looked like a well of black ink with not a star in sight.

"Looks like more snow," she said, a white cloud floating in front of her face as she spoke.

She pulled the car door open and slid into the driver's seat, shivering as the cold interior bit through her thin leggings. The engine sputtered in protest as she turned the key. "Sorry, old girl," Marian consoled the car. "Winston wants us there at seven o'clock, sharp. You can do it."

Had it really only been yesterday that Holly so thoughtfully took on the task of scraping the windshield while Marian sat in the car? So much had happened since then. With the robbery at Stockton's Jewel Palace and Holly's disappearance, it seemed like that simple act of kindness was long past.

Marian navigated the roads, still slick in spots, and pulled into the parking lot with ten minutes to spare. Still chilled to the bone, Marian darted from her car to the employee entrance. At Santa's Workshop, Winston was already holding court with the early comers.

"As you all know, we have some new developments in the case of Ralph's missing star," Winston bellowed from his perch. "We now know it was stolen sometime around eleven o'clock Friday night. The footage showed another intruder at that time, who we are assuming was a different person. We believe that intruder was a woman. Unfortunately, other than a shadow in the vicinity of the star, there is no indication she is the one who took the star. I know there is suspicion that Holly Berry, the young woman Marian invited to stay with her during the Christmas season, is the responsible for the theft." He paused and looked at Marian, who dropped her eyes and looked to be carefully examining the pointy toes of her elf shoes. "Let me assure you that we have no evidence to confirm that suspicion. However, in the interest of moving things along, we will be conducting a search of everyone's employee locker just in case one of you is involved."

Protests erupted from the small crowd. "You can't do that…you have no right…"

Winston held up his hand. "I know you don't want us going through your personal belongings, but the lockers are the property of the Saddle Hill Mall, and we reserve the right to conduct a search of said property." He waved to Sheriff Arnold, standing off to the right side of the stage. "The sheriff will be conducting the search with the assistance of our very own Joe Adler."

"Wait a minute," a girl who worked at the cosmetics counter at Dilly's Department Store protested. "Joe works here. Shouldn't his locker be searched, too, by someone other than himself?"

"You're absolutely right," Winston agreed. "I will assist the sheriff in searching Joe's locker. After that, he will take over for me so I can get back to running this place like the well-oiled machine that it is." Winston clapped twice, his signal that the meeting was over. "To your stations, everyone!"

Marian and the rest of the employees watched as Winston, Sheriff Arnold, and Joe Adler retreated in the direction of the employee lounge, which was nothing more than a dimly lit room with old school lockers lining the walls and a cracked vinyl sofa in the middle of the room.

Just before the group dispersed, Carla Whipple placed a comforting hand on Marian's shoulder. "Nobody blames you for bringing a thief to this town. It was just an unhappy coincidence."

Marian's mouth tightened. "There's no proof that Holly is the thief, Carla."

Carla merely shrugged and walked away. Marian watched

as Carla and the rest of the employees went to their appointed "stations," as Winston was fond of calling the stores.

Alone at Santa's Workshop, Marian and Kris Jingle prepared themselves for another onslaught of kids.

"Any word from Holly?" Kris asked, hoisting the sack with his costume over his shoulder and turning toward the shack he used as a dressing room.

"None. I'm worried."

Kris faced Marian and rested a hand on the back of the chair he'd be occupying in less than an hour. "Because she's missing or because you're afraid she took the star?"

Marian sighed. "A little of both, I guess."

"Where do you think she went? People don't just drop off the face of the earth."

Marian fiddled with the sleeve of her sweater. "No they don't. Her car is still parked on the curb in front of my house, so she didn't take it anywhere."

Kris shrugged. "Maybe she took a bus. Legally, she's an adult. She has the right to go anywhere she wants."

"True," Marian agreed, "but the way she left things…it doesn't look like she made plans to go anywhere."

"Maybe leaving everything how it was was part of the plan. It's something that's got to be considered," he suggested.

"I guess so…"

"If she didn't take the star and run, what do you think happened?"

"I wish I knew. The longer she's missing, the more likely something terrible has happened." Tension crept up Marian's neck.

"Well, I guess we'll find out soon enough," Kris quipped,

then went to change into the man who was supposed to be the jolliest in the world.

A welcome distraction, Marian busied herself refilling the candy cane basket and straightening the ropes that were intended to keep the line of children from turning into an uncontrollable mob.

Thirty minutes later, Kris was seated in his chair, and Marian was armed with the best smile she could muster and a basket of candy canes.

Just before the first child took a seat in Santa's lap, Winston approached the stage and cleared his throat. He tipped his head in the direction of Sheriff Arnold.

Dangling a pair of handcuffs and walking toward the stage, Sheriff Arnold said, "Kris Jingle, you'll need to come with me."

Kris's face turned a shade of red that rivaled his velvet costume. "What for? I'm in the middle of something."

"I'm afraid I have to place you under arrest for the theft of Ralph Stockton's Christmas star," the sheriff said coldly.

"That's absurd!" Kris shouted as he was yanked from his chair and the eager sheriff snapped on the shackles. "I've never stolen anything!"

"The evidence doesn't lie, Kris," Winston interjected. "We found the star in your locker."

"No way," Kris protested. "I didn't do it!" he cried over his shoulder as Sheriff Arnold tugged him along.

Marian's mouth hung agape as she looked out at the crowd of children, their little eyes watching in horror as their beloved Santa Claus was led away from his workshop in handcuffs.

CHAPTER FORTY-NINE

JAMES JINGLE LISTENED in disgust as the morning news reported the arrest of his own son.

"How could he do such a thing?" James wailed. "It's not enough that he doesn't want anything to do with our Christmas traditions, but now he's trying to ruin it for everybody else, too!"

At the sound of his distress, Patricia raced down the stairs to the living room only to find her husband with his face buried in his hands, weeping.

"Our son," he said, words muffled by his hands. "He's a disgrace."

Kneeling in front of him, Patricia tugged his hands away from his face. "You've got to pull yourself together and tell me what's going on."

James raised his face to meet his wife's. Tears dripped into his snow-white beard. "It's Kris. He's ruined the Jingle name."

Patricia rocked back on her heels and stood up. "James, will you please leave Kris alone? Just because he doesn't ooze

Christmas spirit every single day of the year doesn't mean he's ruined the Jingle name," she scolded.

"He's been arrested for stealing the Christmas star from Stockton's Jewel Palace, Patty. In front of the children while he was dressed as Santa. The kids saw Santa being arrested! What will that do to their dreams on Christmas Eve? Who wants to think of a convict slipping down their chimney in the middle of the night and lurking around their home? They'll never believe in Santa again!" James choked out another sob.

Patricia slapped her thigh. "Who cares if those bratty little kids never believe in Santa again? It's creepy to think of anyone lurking around your house at night. Even Santa. It's disgusting and a disgrace that you're more concerned about a child you don't know being able to continue to live in a fairy tale than your son who has been arrested. If you ask me, you're the one who's ruining the Jingle name. Not Kris."

Wide-eyed, James stared at his wife of forty years as though she was a stranger. "Patricia! Bite your tongue."

"I will not," she fumed. "I've been biting my tongue far too long. It's time you get over yourself, James Jingle, and realize that the whole world doesn't revolve around you and your neurotic need to celebrate Christmas every blasted day of the year. If you ask me, you're the one that's responsible for the division in this family. You've favored Nicholas over Kris their whole lives, and it shows."

"I'm just trying to uphold the Jingle name."

Patricia held up her hand. "I don't want to hear it. It's up to you to make things right. Whatever might have gone wrong with Kris, you might need to consider the possibility that you're at least partly responsible. If you hadn't spent his entire life bashing him over the head with how different he is, the tension in this family never would have happened." She thrust her jaw forward, then turned on her heel to walk toward the kitchen.

"This isn't appropriate behavior for a Mrs. Claus, Patricia," James admonished.

Patricia whirled around to face her husband. "Maybe I'm more than a Mrs. Claus, James. Have you ever considered that?" She crossed her arms over her chest and kept her icy gaze fixed on her husband.

James furrowed his thick white brows. "What has gotten into you all of a sudden, Patricia?"

Her anger began to melt away and the exhaustion of the last forty years set in. She walked toward her husband and sat in the chair across from him. Grasping his thick hand in hers, she said, "It's not so sudden, James. I'm tired. I'm tired of all this." She waved her hand around the cozy living room at the Christmas decorations. "I love Christmas. I do. Just not all year long."

James pulled his hands from his wife's grip and leaned back in his chair, dropping his eyes to his lap. "How long have you felt this way?"

"A long time, I'm afraid. I just didn't know how to tell you. I knew it would break your heart," Patricia confessed, tears filling her eyes. "It's too much pressure. I can't do it anymore."

"Oh, Patty. I wish you'd said something. I had no idea how you felt," he said, an unexpected tenderness lacing his words. "Have I really treated Kris that bad?"

She nodded. "You have, and Nicholas has been following your example his whole life. Poor Kris didn't have anybody in his corner, so I told him the truth."

"The truth about what?"

"About me. He needed to know he has somebody on his side, to know that I understand where he's coming from." Patricia leaned back in the chair and fussed with the ruffles on her apron. "He needed to know he's not alone."

James turned his attention to the twinkling lights dancing on the Christmas tree. "I never meant to be a bad father," he confessed. "No Santa would. I guess I just started down a path and didn't realize how far I'd gone in alienating him. How did everything get so out of control? How do I make it right?"

The sound of the crackling fire filled the silence before Patricia spoke. "Just let him know you care about him, even if he doesn't love Christmas the same way you do. Let him know that you accept him as your son no matter what. That's all he's ever wanted. Start there."

"I'll try, but Patty, he robbed Stockton's Jewel Palace."

"That's ridiculous. How could they possibly believe he took that star?"

"They searched all the employees' lockers this morning, and Sheriff Arnold and Joe Adler found the star in his." The shame was still etched on his face.

Patricia waved her hand, dismissing the idea. "Impossible. Kris would never steal that star. He doesn't have a reason to."

James shrugged. Maybe if he wanted to take some of the joy out of the Christmas season..."

Shooting her husband a withering look, she warned, "Stop it right there, James."

"Sorry, dear. Habit."

"A habit you need to break right now. I suggest you change your clothes and head down to the jail to see Kris. Now, more than ever, he needs to know you care about him."

A look of surprise crossed James's face. "Change? What

will I wear if I don't wear this?" he asked, waving his hand the length of his of his red overalls. He hadn't worn anything but Santa-approved apparel in forty years.

"Clothes. Normal clothes. You still have some tucked away in the back of your closet."

James hoisted himself out of his chair and stood, admiring his wife. Though her hair was now gray and her skin wrinkled, she was just as beautiful as she was the day he married her. He walked slowly toward the stairs leading to their bedroom, then turned to face her. "I remember why I fell in love with you, Patty."

She cocked an eyebrow. "Oh yeah? And why is that?"

"Because you're spunky. I'm afraid that got lost in all our merriment." James smiled a small, sad smile and walked slowly up the stairs, wondering what he'd say to Kris when he got to the jail. He had a long way to go to make things right with his son.

Had Kris been trying to get my attention when he stole the star? James wondered, then remembered Patricia's insistence that Kris would never take it.

If that was true, who would hate him enough to put it in his locker and let him take the blame?

CHAPTER FIFTY

SYLVIA CLICKED OFF the radio and shook her head. Kris Jingle, the grumpy-looking mall Santa she'd seen yesterday, had been arrested for stealing the star from Ralph Stockton. On top of that, the news reported that there was a warrant for Brenda's arrest due to suspicion that she also stole from Stockton's Jewel Palace. Brenda, who always seemed to have it all, was going to be arrested for stealing from her own husband.

"I guess you can never tell about some people," she muttered to herself. "Apparently even Saddle Hill isn't immune to crime."

She pulled the collar of her plush robe closer to her neck and relished the feeling of total relaxation. It would be her last day in Saddle Hill before flying back to New York tonight. The long weekend had been exactly what she needed to replenish the energy she'd used creating her new line. Fresh country air and the small-town pace had done wonders to renew her excitement about getting started on the jewelry line in January.

I'd really love to have a few more days here, Sylvia thought. I forgot how much I love small-town life. She immediately dismissed the idea. Her employees would be at the office bright and early tomorrow, and so would she. They were even more excited about getting an early start designing the jewelry than she was. She smiled at the thought of the new adventure she'd be undertaking in less than twenty-four hours.

The really thrilling part of the actual design work wouldn't begin until after the new year, but for the next week she'd be narrowing down the list of jewelers she was interested in collaborating with. The only problem was, during the past few days she realized there was another name she wanted to add to the list.

Ralph Stockton's work was stunning. It rivaled any other jeweler who'd sent a sample for her to consider, actually surpassing all but one or two. But the thought of actually working with the others made her feel sick. Even though Sylvia admired their work, dealing with them on a day-to-day basis wasn't something she could get excited about. They were elitist jerks who only cared about the status their creations would bring.

Ralph was a different story. He'd been nothing but kind and respectful when she stopped into his store to order the star. He had no idea she was considering a possible partnership, so there was none of the phony sucking up and sickening sweetness she'd already dealt with from the others. He was kind because that's who he is. It showed in his prices and the way he treated his customers. Talent and compassion were a hard combination to come by in her world, and the thought of it being an actual possibility was beyond appealing.

That settles it, she thought, unfolding herself from the overstuffed chair in her hotel room. I'm going back to Stockton's Jewel Palace today before I have to leave for the airport. I've got to gauge Ralph's interest in taking his business to the next level. The money he'd make from helping me develop my line of jewelry would be more than enough to save his store. He'd be able to stay in the town he loves and work with me remotely. Now that Brenda is probably out of the picture, he'd be able to devote more time to his designs instead of walking on eggshells around her.

Sylvia's mouth curved into a mischievous smile knowing that if Ralph agreed to work with her, he'd become a wealthy man and Brenda would never see a dime of it.

Shame on me, Sylvia thought as she crossed to the small closet where she'd hung her clothes for the weekend. Brenda had been obviously unhappy when they spoke yesterday. Perhaps she was just trying to find a way out of the life she hated. An unexpected stab of compassion for Brenda hit her. Flashing back to her college days, Sylvia definitely knew what it was like to want desperately to get away from something—or someone—that caused misery.

Selecting an ivory poncho and slim-cut jeans, she slipped off her robe and dressed for the last day of her mini-vacation. She'd have one more lunch at the Rose Petal Café, do a bit more shopping at the Craft Festival, and present Ralph with the offer of a lifetime. After that, she'd pack up and be on her way home.

"Too bad," she muttered as she took one last appraising glance in the mirror before heading out the door. "I'd love to stick around and see Brenda try to charm her way out of this one."

Feeling a tad guilty about her pleasure at Brenda's trouble, Sylvia reminded herself that her bad feelings toward Brenda would only hurt herself. Brenda didn't know and probably didn't care that Sylvia was still nursing the pain from all those years ago. Brenda never cared about anything that wasn't about her.

The best way to get even with her for all the ways she hurt me, Sylvia decided, is to not let all those cheap shots keep eating away at me. That, and to make her soon-to-be-ex-husband a very wealthy man when Brenda won't be able to touch a bit of it.

CHAPTER FIFTY-ONE

MARIAN RUBBED HER thumb in circles on the side of her coffee mug and stared at the wisp of steam circling into the air.

Kris Jingle had been arrested!

She shook her head as she replayed the scene in her mind. The children had been devastated, their parents horrified when Kris was led away by Sheriff Arnold. Marian herself had been flabbergasted. Sure, Kris could be a bit irritable, even downright grouchy at times, but to think he was responsible for the theft was preposterous. There were at least a half dozen other people who worked at the mall that would be better suspects. Now that Santa's workshop had been shut down until Nicholas's shift began, Marian had extra time to figure out who, besides Kris, could have stolen the star. As she sat in the Rose Petal Café sipping her coffee, she considered who else might have had something to gain from stealing from Ralph.

First, there was Winston. The mall was his baby and he'd do anything to get publicity. For him, it was all about the number of shoppers, and very little to do with the people themselves. A sleepy little town like Saddle Hill didn't typically draw tourists, but if something happened to put it on the map, it might increase the volume of people walking through the front doors. If that happened, nothing else would matter. Also, he had a master key to all the lockers and could have easily slipped the star into Kris's when no one was around.

Marian quickly dismissed the notion. Winston and Ralph were friends, at least as far as someone like Winston Marshall was capable of having friends. It wasn't likely that Winston would do anything to hurt Ralph. Also, the only kind of attention the mall would get from this would be negative because no alarm had been triggered. If she knew Winston, he was probably working like a madman to do damage control about the whole ordeal.

And speaking of security systems, Marian thought, Joe would be the one person who knew exactly how to bypass it. Only he and Winston have the codes to activate and disengage the alarms. Joe could have easily slipped in during the night, turned off the alarms, stolen the star, and slipped back out again without anyone being the wiser. He was awfully mad about the diamond falling out of Nadine's ring. There were rumblings around the mall that Joe had even threatened that Ralph "would pay" for what happened. Unlike Winston, Joe wasn't motivated by an unnatural affection for the mall and wouldn't care one way or another if the whole thing was closed.

Marian raised the mug to her lips and took a slow sip of the coffee. *I suppose It's possible, she thought.* She gazed over the rim of her mug and watched as Nadine restocked the bakery case. That was a girl a man would do anything for. Even steal. The only thing that kept Marian from telling Winston that Joe would be a much better suspect than Kris was that

Nadine would never consider marrying a man who would steal from a friend.

She lowered the mug and rapped her fingers on the table. *Then there's Holly. So far, she seemed the most likely suspect, or had been until the star was found and Holly was still missing. Never mind that Holly was a stranger in town with itchy fingers, she went missing when the star was stolen, but only after talking to Marian about it. Did she get scared and take off, leaving the star in the first open locker she found in an effort to distance herself from the crime? Or was she so afraid it would get pinned on her that she panicked and ran?* Marian's gut told her that was the most plausible scenario.

"What were they thinking, arresting Kris?" Marian asked herself in a sharp voice. An elderly lady at the next table glanced in her direction, a questioning look on her face. Marian ignored the woman and got back to thinking.

No, Holly wasn't involved. Her disappearance had to be purely coincidental. A sense of urgency gnawed at Marian. *Holly had been missing for twenty-four hours, and no one reported seeing her after she stopped by Whipple's Wicks to find a gift for Ralph. But where did she go from there?*

Chewing on her bottom lip, Marian moved down the line of potential suspects. *We know Brenda stole at least one thing from Ralph, and that she tampered with his jewelry on at least two occasions. But the video footage from that night showed Brenda entering the store from a different direction. She came through the entrance at the top of the screen, and the shadow at the bottom of the screen disappeared the same way it appeared. It wouldn't have made any sense for her to sneak in without being caught on camera, then go around the perimeter undetected, just to walk back in from an angle* she would have known would be in view of the camera. Even Brenda wasn't that bold. Or stupid.

Marian sighed. Of course she couldn't dismiss the possibility that Kris *had* been responsible. But what about motive? As far as Marian knew, he didn't need the money he'd get from selling the star. He had no vendetta against Ralph. He hated being Santa, but as far as Marian knew, that was his only pitfall. She didn't care what Winston, Joe, and Sheriff Arnold said. Nobody could make her believe he'd stoop so low as to go out of his way to make someone else miserable just because he didn't like stuffing his fuzzy red and white suit with a pillow and hooking an itchy white beard over his ears. Beneath his surly exterior, Kris was a kind-hearted man who just wanted the freedom to do his own thing without having the judgment of his entire family thrust upon his shoulders.

Poor man, Marian thought, draining the last bit of coffee. She scowled at the bottom of her mug. It had gone cold.

From somewhere in the back Wanda Kirk barked orders at Nadine.

Now, there's one I could see doing something horrible just to make herself feel better, Marian thought wryly. Misery seemed to be the fuel that got her through her days, and the more of it there was, the happier she seemed to be.

Assuming Wanda's best feelings could even be described as happy.

All day long she squawked at Nadine for one thing or another, often reducing the poor girl to tears. It's no wonder she can't make a marriage last, Marian mused. Anybody that stuck around would probably die of unhappiness. She smiled sadly as she remembered Roger's words about Wanda: "If you're going to be miserable, at least have the courtesy not to drag everybody else down with you." He had her pegged. Roger had everybody pegged. Ralph had certainly dodged a bullet when he broke off his engagement to that one!

Ralph had dodged a few bullets, if Marian remembered correctly. She couldn't be sure who it was, but Marian thought she remembered that Ralph had been involved with someone else not long before he met Brenda. Unfortunately for Ralph, he'd broken it off when Brenda showed so much interest in him.

Marian unconsciously tapped her chin with an index finger, a sure sign that she was racking her brain. Who was it that Ralph had dumped in order to marry Brenda? No matter how hard she tried, a name wouldn't come to her. Had Ralph and Wanda gotten back together?

Oh, what she would give to be able to pick Roger's brain about what was going on!

As she stood, she pushed her shoulders back and deposited her empty mug on the table with the rest of the dirty dishes for one of the café staff members to collect. As she walked out of the Rose Petal, she was more certain than ever that Kris had been framed.

The problem was, Marian found it impossible to narrow down the list of suspects. It seemed to her that this Christmas, almost everybody had something to gain from stealing from Ralph.

CHAPTER FIFTY-TWO

JAMES JINGLE ADJUSTED his flannel button-down shirt and tugged at the waist of his jeans. It had been years since he'd worn civilian clothes and felt as uncomfortable in them as he'd feared. That could be in part because his waistline had expanded over the years, but mostly because he felt so unlike his true self.

Patricia had insisted he not dress the part of the merry Santa when he went to the jail to visit their son, and immediately squashed his argument that people in jail, more than anybody, could certainly use a little merriment. Her response that he was going to support Kris and not play the part of jolly old Saint Nick at some company Christmas party ended the conversation. That and the icy glare he'd forgotten she was capable of. Patricia was full of surprises today.

Pulling the door open to the sheriff's station, James was greeted by the aroma of stale coffee and gun oil. He took another breath, certain he smelled body odor and vomit wafting from the jail cells in the back of the station. He cringed at the thought of his eldest son being held in a place like this. It smelled nothing like the holiday scents of pine tree and warm cinnamon he'd become accustomed to.

As a way to cut costs and ensure the inmates were securely locked away, the town had voted years ago to attach the new, ten-cell jail to the back of the sheriff's office. In a town like Saddle Hill, even ten jail cells had been unnecessary. A few drunken disorderlies here and there, maybe a domestic argument that got a little too loud, but never any real crime. Until now, that is. To think a *Jingle* had the distinction of committing a crime that would get actual jail time.

"Can I help you?" a young deputy asked without looking up from the service weapon he was polishing.

"Yes. I'd like to speak with my son, please." James's voice cracked as he said the words. Never in a million years would he have guessed he was asking to see his son in jail, although most parents probably don't see incarceration in their children's future.

"And who might that be?" the deputy asked, never raising his eyes from his pistol.

"Kris Jingle."

Patricia's words echoed in his mind: *...you might need to consider the possibility that you're at least partly responsible for this...*

Could that be true? Had the years of blatantly favoring Nicholas really led to Kris getting in trouble now? James felt terrible that it could even be a possibility. Santa would never treat a child that way. Maybe he wasn't as good a Santa as he thought.

Finally, the deputy looked at him and narrowed his eyes. "*You're* James Jingle. You look...different."

James shifted from one foot to the other, growing

increasingly uncomfortable in his "normal" clothes. To him, they felt anything but normal. "Well, yes," he stammered. "I'm trying something new."

The deputy, whose uniform had a patch that said "Nolan" on the front, stood and plucked a key ring off the wall behind him. "It's about time, if you ask me. Your family has the reputation of being a little crazy," he offered, motioning for James to follow him toward the back.

The eldest Jingle winced. Crazy? Try jolly and cheerful. But what does that little whippersnapper know, anyway? James thought defensively. Between the deputy's comment and Patricia's sudden confession, James began to see his charade through the eyes of others for the first time in forty years. He enjoyed it, and Nicholas enjoyed it, but apparently everybody else thought it was obnoxious. His shoulders slumped. Perhaps Kris had been right all along.

James and Deputy Nolan walked through a solid steel door, down a narrow hall, and through another steel door. On each side of him was a row of five cells. Only two were occupied. A dirty, smelly old man who looked like he'd been spending too much time on the business end of a whiskey bottle was in one. His son, looking forlorn and vulnerable, was in the other.

"Kris," James said awkwardly. "How are you?"

Kris sat on a cot bolted to the wall. His head snapped up at the sound of his father's voice. "Never better," he grumbled. "What are you doing here?"

James took a step closer to the cell. "I came to talk to you."

Kris crossed his arms over his chest. "About what? How I'm such a disappointment and no self-respecting Santa would ever end up in jail?"

"No, I just—"

"Then what?" Kris growled. "How I've shamed you and the family name, and am no longer welcome in your home?"

"No, son. I came to apologize. Apparently you've been right all along, and I've been a huge Christmas jerk." He looked down at the toes of the hiking boots he didn't remember buying.

Kris looked bewildered. "You're apologizing to me?"

"Yes, your mother gave me a good talking-to this morning, and basically told me to stop acting like an old jackass. She pointed out that I might even be part of the reason you're sitting in jail in the first place. It seems I've been too tough on you for not wanting to celebrate Christmas all year. From the looks of things, I'm the odd man out. Not you."

A smirk covered Kris's face. "Mom told you she's tired of it, huh? I've gotta say, it does make me feel better that she came clean to you. At least you know I'm not the only weirdo in the family." Kris scratched his face, still red from the irritation of the fluffy white beard. "But how are you the reason I'm in jail? Did you steal the star?"

"Don't be ridiculous," James snorted, indignant at the suggestion. "I've never stolen anything in my life. No, your mother seems to think that if you are guilty, it's because I pushed you into it by coming down so hard on you all the time. Although, she doesn't believe you'd ever commit such a crime," he added.

"Well, she's right. I didn't take it."

"But the radio said the star was found in your employee locker."

"So? That only means somebody planted it there. Besides, who would be dumb enough to steal something then hide it in their own locker? Certainly not me. The lockers are property of the mall. Winston can have them checked any time he wants without our permission. He definitely would if something as valuable as the star went missing. What kind of idiot would put it there knowing it would be found?" Kris narrowed his eyes. "Unless they *wanted* it to be found…"

"Are you suggesting you think somebody put it there on purpose, knowing it would be found and that you'd take the fall for it?"

Kris shrugged. "It's possible. Either somebody wanted me to get in trouble for it, or they panicked and stuck it in the first locker they could get into just in case they were searched."

"But who would do that to you? Who would hate you enough to want to see you get in trouble for a crime you didn't commit?" James's voice rose at the injustice.

Kris crossed his leg over his knee and looked straight in his dad's eyes. "I'm not the most well-loved person in this town, but I don't know of anybody that would want to see me arrested. Do me a favor, though, and keep that possibility to yourself. It's much more likely that somebody put the star in my locker because it was the easiest place to stash it. I never keep it locked."

"But why can't I say anything? If you didn't do it, who-ever is guilty needs to be punished," the plainclothes Santa protested.

"They will. Winston and Joe will find them. Sheriff Arnold is like a bloodhound. He's very excited about solving the case, even though he's wrong. Don't worry, Dad, between the three of them, they'll find the real thief."

"Not if they stop looking," James pushed.

"Dad. Trust them. Trust me," Kris pushed back.

"Okay. Whatever you say."

"Thank you, and please tell Mom she's right. Mr. and Mrs. Claus didn't raise a thief." Kris looked tenderly at his father. What a weird way for them to rebuild their relationship.

Thoughtful silence floated between father and son.

"Visiting time is up!" the deputy called from the direction of the steel door.

James turned his attention back to his son. "I've got to go. Keep your chin up." He stuck his hand through the cell bars and gave his son's shoulder a quick squeeze.

"Thanks, Dad. Remember, don't worry. I'll be out of here to celebrate the real Christmas with you."

James nodded, turned, and walked away, certain his son was innocent.

Now he just had to pray that Winston, Joe, and Sheriff Arnold would keep looking for another suspect.

CHAPTER FIFTY-THREE

RALPH WALKED INTO the sheriff's office, almost giddy about the news that his star had been recovered. Joe Adler had called him an hour ago, saying Ralph needed to get to the station as soon as possible, but hadn't given him any indication about who was responsible for the theft. Now, only minutes away from learning who the culprit was, Ralph wasn't sure he wanted to know. Whoever it was, Ralph probably considered him or her a friend.

Greeted by Deputy Nolan, a kid of about eighteen who no doubt just graduated high school, Ralph's apprehension grew.

"Have a seat in there," the deputy instructed, waving to a room outfitted with a table and a few straight-backed chairs to the right of the main area.

Ralph nodded and went inside. The room was empty, indicating that Joe and Sheriff Arnold hadn't made it there yet. They'd be there in a few minutes, though, and he'd learn the identity of the person that could have put the final nail in the coffin of Stockton's Jewel Palace.

Hushed voices preceded their entry by mere seconds.

Clasping his hands together in front of himself, Ralph began to sweat. His excitement about having the star returned had given way to a bout of nerves as he considered who in this town hated him enough to steal from him.

"Hey, Ralph. Thanks for getting here so fast," Joe said. "I'm sure it was hard to get away from the store."

Ralph nodded and frowned. "Even more difficult now that Holly seems to have bailed on me."

"I heard. Doesn't seem like you can get a break this weekend, huh?" Joe sympathized.

"Nope. Apparently several people I've considered friends are determined to ruin me." Ralph gave Joe a look that communicated he was included in that group.

Joe cleared his throat. "Yes, but I think we can all agree you don't deserve that."

The two made eye contact for several seconds, silently conveying that there were no hard feelings.

Ralph broke the silence. "So, you said you have the person responsible for stealing the star in custody."

"We do," Sheriff Arnold confirmed. "We did a search of the employee lockers this morning, and as Winston suspected, we found it in one of them."

"And?" an impatient Ralph prodded.

"I'm sorry to say we found the star in Kris Jingle's locker," Joe said quietly.

The room closed in on Ralph. "Kris was the one who took my star? But *why?*"

Joe shrugged. "We don't know. He swears he didn't do it."

Ralph unlaced his fingers and ran them through his thinning hair. He exhaled, feeling as though the wind had been knocked out of him. "How could he?"

Joe and the sheriff let Ralph process the information before breaking in. "For now, the evidence points only to him. As of now he's being held without bail, and I promise he'll be punished for stealing from you," the sheriff promised.

He considered the words for a moment, then asked, "Can I have the star back?"

Sheriff Arnold pulled a small evidence bag from his pocket and placed it on the table in front of Ralph. "I'm afraid we have to hang on to it for a little while longer. It being evidence and all. We'll return it to you as soon as we can."

"May I?" Ralph asked, reaching for the bag.

"Be my guest."

Ralph held the bag close to his face, examining the product of his hard work. "It is beautiful, isn't it?"

"Sure is," Joe agreed. "You do great work."

Ralph smiled faintly and put the star down, sliding it across the table to the sheriff. "So, where's the other one?"

Joe and Sheriff Arnold looked puzzled. "What other one?"

Ralph blinked. "The other star. There were two.

CHAPTER FIFTY-FOUR

FRANTICALLY RACING AROUND the motel room, Brenda threw her belongings into her suitcase. She'd planned to be out of this crummy lodge before sunrise, hoping to escape under the cover of darkness. Just like every other plan she'd ever made for her life, this one didn't work out either. The power had gone out some time during the night and the junky alarm clock bolted to the nightstand hadn't gone off. Now it was nearing ten o'clock and the sun had been up for hours. Plenty of time for someone to spot her car in the parking lot and report it to the local police.

Darting to the window, she pulled the corner of the curtain aside and peered into the parking lot. Everything seemed quiet. There were no flashing lights or sirens nearby. There weren't any cars belonging to other travelers in sight.

Maybe I'm still in the clear, she thought. She wanted to be relieved, but the bead of sweat trickling down her spine betrayed her fear.

Get a hold of yourself, she told herself angrily. Once you're out of here, you'll ditch the car and rent one somewhere. You took enough cash from Ralph's safe to make it to paradise, she assured herself.

Throwing her toiletries into her bag, she zipped it and cast one last frenzied glance around the room, making sure she'd left nothing behind that could be traced to her. Assured she had everything, she left the room key on the dresser and yanked the door open. Letting the door slam behind her, she walked quickly through the parking lot and around the side of the building where her car was out of sight to passersby. As she rounded the corner of the building, she glanced up and looked right into the eyes of a uniformed police officer leaning against the driver's-side door of her car.

"Imagine my delight," he began, "when I was responding to a noise disturbance at the motel and happened to spot a car matching the description of someone suspected of committing grand larceny. Lo and behold, I ran the plates and voilà, I find out it belongs to one Brenda Morris-Stockton, a fugitive from Saddle Hill, Kentucky."

Fugitive?

Brenda's eyes darted around the parking lot, searching for a way out. Could she outrun him? Not a chance. She hadn't run in years. It was time to use the only tools she had at her disposal: her looks and charm.

"Officer, it's not what you think. I've left my husband, and I don't want him to come after me. I can only imagine what he'd do if he found out where I was." She batted her eyelashes at him and pooched her bottom lip out slightly, managing to squeeze a single, fat teardrop from her eye.

"I bet," he said unsympathetically. "Most husbands don't like it when their wives steal from them, especially when what they steal is jewelry worth several thousand dollars." The police officer pushed himself off the side of the car with his boot.

"Oh, that," Brenda said, forcing herself to laugh and flicking a strand of her hair over her shoulder. "That was a misunderstanding."

"Did he misunderstand seeing you on security footage breaking into his jewelry cases, tampering with the items, and slipping a diamond tennis bracelet worth ten thousand dollars into your pocket?" the officer challenged.

Brenda licked her lips nervously. "Security footage? At the store? I didn't think those cameras even worked."

The officer smirked. "Obviously. Yes, ma'am, they work, and they caught you red-handed trying to sabotage your husband's business. For your trouble, you get to ride in the back of my freshly cleaned squad car. I've even scrubbed the vomit out of the upholstery."

"But—" Brenda began to protest, then went silent. She'd seen this on TV thousands of times. Anything she said could be used against her. If she ever went to trial, that is. Ralph, the sap he was, probably wouldn't press charges against her, anyway.

The officer approached her and slapped the handcuffs on her wrists. He cocked an eyebrow as he appraised the diamond bracelet she was wearing. "This looks just like the one your husband reported missing. But I'm sure it's just a misunderstanding." The corner of his mouth twitched in amusement.

Clamping her lips shut, she ducked her head as he placed her in the back of the cruiser, then watched as he loaded her suitcases into his trunk. She guessed he'd be accompanying her the five hours back to Saddle Hill. Soon she would be the resident of the jail she'd so often mocked as a Mayberry-esque lockup where the local Barney Fife kept a watchful eye on the town drunk.

How humiliating.

Well, this seals it, she thought ruefully. My marriage to Ralph is obviously over. Even big-hearted Ralph won't let this slide.

Leaning back against the seat, Brenda closed her eyes and envisioned the life she'd dreamed of disappearing. There would be no year-round summer, no eligible men fawning over her, no adventures in her newfound singlehood. Just cinder block walls, steel bars, and an orange jumpsuit. She groaned. This would be even worse than being married to Ralph.

He's so kind and forgiving, Brenda thought desperately. Maybe I can get him to drop the charges and give me another chance. A smile tugged at her lips. He's always found me irresistible. Her smile faded. The hope was hollow, and she knew it. She'd pushed Ralph far enough. Though he'd never said an unkind word to her or discussed the topic of divorce, his late hours at the store and in his home workshop communicated that he was just as sick of her as she was of him.

Now the gorgeous Sylvia Bell is in my town turning heads like I used to. The thought slammed into her mind before she could stop it. She tried to shake off the dread, but it squeezed her chest until she could hardly breathe. Sylvia, the chubby girl Brenda had tormented in college, had everything Brenda had ever wanted: freedom, a successful career, not to mention the stunning good looks she'd managed to acquire over the past decade.

"It's just not fair," Brenda whined from the backseat of the squad car.

The police officer had the courtesy not to reply. A soft chuckle from behind the steering wheel was his only response.

Instead of the annual Christmas parade, Brenda envisioned the entire town of Saddle Hill lining up along Main Street to watch her riding in the back of the police car all the way to the sheriff's office. She imagined reporters from the local paper shouting questions at her while she ducked her head against the cameras flashing in her face.

My fifteen minutes of fame, she thought bitterly. I'll finally have my picture in the paper, and it will be for stealing from my own husband. It doesn't get much lamer than that. No one will want to hire me to act in their plays now.

I'm finished, Brenda resigned. I'm finished before I ever got started.

CHAPTER FIFTY-FIVE

HIS EYES STRAINED from watching a black and white screen for the past hour, Joe rubbed his temples and leaned closer to the monitor. He'd gone over the footage from the night the star was stolen from Stockton's Jewel Palace a dozen times, but so far had been unsuccessful at coming up with an alternate explanation of what happened.

The fact that Kris Jingle had been arrested for stealing the star didn't sit right with Joe. Anybody that knew Kris could tell you he didn't care enough about anything to risk getting in trouble for it. If Kris had a drug habit or something, Joe could understand it. But no, Kris was squeaky clean and not much of a risk-taker. Unless you counted making his family mad. Other than that, he was a goody two-shoes if there ever was one.

A knock at the door of his office broke Joe's concentration. Welcoming the break, he stood and opened the door. In front of him stood a worried-looking Marian Bright.

"Can I talk to you?" Marian asked, twisting the bottom of her sweater in her hands.

"Of course. Want some coffee?" Joe offered.

Marian declined.

Joe arched his back to loosen his spine, then turned and walked toward the small table in the corner of his office that held a coffee maker and a stained mug. He poured a fresh cup for himself and returned to his seat.

"What are you doing?" Marian inquired, motioning toward the monitor on his desk.

Joe took a long drink of his coffee, then said. "I've been looking over the security footage from the night of the robbery to see if I can find anything."

"Shouldn't Sheriff Arnold be doing this?"

Joe snorted. "He's feeling awfully proud of himself for making this bust, and I don't think he's in any kind of hurry to look for a different suspect than Kris."

Marian released the bottom of her sweater and circled behind Joe. She bent toward the monitor. "Do you think Kris is innocent, too?"

He raised a shoulder then let it drop. "Kris has nothing to gain from stealing that star. Winston and Sheriff Arnold can say what they want, but he had no reason to take it. Besides, Kris is smart. When we looked in his locker, the star was laying on top of everything else where it could be easily seen." He looked at Marian. "If you stole something, would you be so careless?"

Marian shook her head emphatically. "Definitely not."

"Me either." Joe rewound the video to the time he saw the shadow at the bottom of the screen. "Look at this."

Marian leaned closer. "What am I supposed to be seeing?"

Joe pressed a few buttons to zoom in, then put a finger on the bottom of the screen. "Here. This is where I saw the shadow that helped me pinpoint the exact time the robbery occurred. If I can see more than just a shadow, I might be able to help Kris."

Marian leaned closer, forcing Joe to move. "Can you play it slower?"

As the video clicked by at half speed, Joe and Marian stared at the screen, unblinking.

"Stop!" Marian shrieked.

Joe paused the video.

"Rewind it just a few seconds," Marian commanded.

Joe did as she requested and played it again in slow motion.

"Stop it," Marian said, then pointed frantically at the screen. "Look!"

"Well, I'll be…" Joe muttered, stunned and annoyed that he hadn't noticed it earlier.

At the bottom of the screen, the damning evidence against Kris Jingle stared back at them. A white fur cuff attached to a red velvet sleeve sat at the bottom inch of the monitor.

It was a Santa suit.

"I guess it was Kris, after all," Joe mumbled. "I really thought I'd be able to find something to clear his name."

Feeling deflated, the duo continued to stare at the screen.

Then Marian patted Joe's back. "Don't give up yet, dear. I think I have a plan."

CHAPTER FIFTY-SIX

IMPATIENTLY DRUMMING HIS fingers on the table at the sheriff station, Ralph looked around the waiting room that also served as an interrogation room, a conference room, and whatever else the community needed it to be. If he remembered correctly, it had also been the site of several town potlucks that Brenda never wanted to attend.

This was a place Ralph wasn't too familiar with before, and now he'd been here twice in one day. He'd only been back at the store a few minutes when Sheriff Arnold called to tell him that Brenda had been located several hours from Saddle Hill and was being transported back.

Already overwhelmed by the betrayal of someone he considered a friend, that his wife had stolen something so valuable from him left him reeling.

When he'd gone home yesterday to confront her about the video footage that showed her breaking into his jewelry cases, he'd been heartbroken to find the glass daffodil he designed for her smashed against the stone fireplace. To him, it had at one time been a symbol of their awakening love, and it crushed him that she wasn't even sentimental enough to hold on to something she once said she treasured.

True, he hadn't really felt anything akin to love for her for a long time, but he was able to hold the good times in fond memory.

Within the first year of marriage, he'd been able to see Brenda for who she really was, and that was when he realized he didn't care for her the way he thought he had. She was selfish and self-centered, and she didn't care that he was already stretched to his financial limits. She always wanted just a little bit more. When her car sputtered and died in front of the grocery store, she demanded a Mercedes. Not just any Mercedes, though. It had to be the best one the dealership had. Whether it was or wasn't, Ralph didn't know. Truthfully, he didn't care. All he knew was the price tag nearly sent him into bankruptcy. Everything Brenda did was expensive. Even the haircuts she drove two hours to get were a hundred bucks a pop every six weeks. That didn't even include the dye jobs and her manicures. He didn't know how he'd been able to afford being married to her for as long as he had.

Ralph straightened in his chair at the sound of the door opening. A muffled voice said, "I've got Brenda Morris-Stockton in the back of my cruiser. Whaddya want me to do with her?"

Sheriff Arnold mumbled a response Ralph couldn't make out, and within a few minutes the door to the interrogation room opened.

He turned his head toward the sound of the gasp behind him.

Brenda stood in the doorway looking disheveled for what he assumed was the first time in her life. Shock, then fear registered on her face. "Ralph, darling. This isn't what you think."

He turned his back to her and realized he was digging the tips of his fingers into the palms of his hands.

She circled around to the other side of the table and took the seat in front of him, wrists shackled together. "Ralph, what they're saying I did, I swear to you I didn't do it." She tried to smooth her hair with her hands, an awkward move with the handcuffs.

Ralph looked at her blankly. "I saw the video, Brenda. I saw you breaking into my jewelry cases and tampering with my pieces. I also saw you slip the diamond tennis bracelet you'd been wanting into your pocket. Remember that?"

"Honestly, Ralph—"

"You don't know the first thing about being honest, Brenda," Ralph lectured. "How many other things have you taken from me during our marriage? Things you thought I wouldn't miss? Was that all I ever was to you? A way to get pretty things?" Hurt and disappointment oozed from his words.

"This has all been a mistake, Ralph. Can't we just start again?" Brenda pleaded, tears pooling in her eyes.

Ralph leaned back in his chair, putting as much distance as he could between himself and his bride. "I don't think so. You stole from me. You shattered something that was supposed to be a symbol of our love. Not to mention you've been going through money like water since we got married, yet you can't seem to trouble yourself to find a job. I can't afford to stay married to you."

"I'll do better, I promise. I've never stolen anything from you. That wasn't me you saw on the security camera. It was probably that girl you had come work for you. The one people are saying might have stolen the star."

Ralph shook his head and looked away. She could do just

about anything to manipulate a person but acting sincere was the one thing she couldn't pull off. Unable to look at her any longer, he started to leave, but paused when the door opened behind him. "Mr. Stockton, I've got something you're going to want to see," Sheriff Arnold said from the doorway.

Ralph turned to face him, then watched as he placed a small velvet bag on the table in front of Brenda, then turned it upside down to empty the contents.

"Do these belong to you?"

Ralph's eyes widened as he looked at the small pile of jewelry, all pieces Brenda had asked for but Ralph wouldn't let her have. A detailed inventory this afternoon had revealed that these pieces had also gone missing from his jewelry case. He hunched forward and began picking through the pile. "Yes, those are mine. All of them." He looked pointedly at Brenda. "She has no right to any of those pieces." He continued separating the glittering treasures until they laid neatly side by side on the table. "The other star isn't there," he said flatly.

"How could I have your star?" Brenda protested. "I heard on the radio that Kris Jingle was arrested for taking the star."

Ralph settled back into his chair and looked at Brenda, his anger giving way to pity. This was the most unhappy woman he'd ever met. She wasn't unhappy because she didn't have everything she wanted, but because she never really wanted the things she already had. For the first time in their marriage, he realized he wasn't the reason for her misery. She would be miserable no matter who she married.

"I made two copies of the star," he explained. "I had the larger of the two on display in the store, and the smaller one was in my safe as a backup."

"You had two and didn't show me either?" Brenda fumed. "That's so selfish!"

Ralph tilted his head at her. "I'm surprised you didn't see it. It was in my safe with my cash, which apparently you have no problem wiping me out of."

"You also broke into his safe and stole his cash? Have you no shame?" the sheriff demanded.

"Of course I didn't break in," Brenda huffed. "The old softy used our wedding date as the combination, as if that was some special day in history."

Ralph's voice softened. "Why did you take the jewelry? And my money? I've done so much for you."

Brenda settled against the back of the chair and placed her manacled hands on the table in front of her. "Because when I left you, I knew I'd get diddly squat. There was nothing to get. This jewelry is my alimony."

Ralph began to chuckle, warranting a puzzled look from his soon-to-be-ex-wife.

"What's so funny?" Brenda demanded. "Don't you understand I've been robbing you blind, you big dope?"

"You thought you were going to make money off that?" he guffawed, slapping his leg, his reaction raising Brenda's ire even more.

"I don't know what you think is so funny, Ralph," Brenda growled. "I gave you some of the best years of my life, and this was my payback."

"Yes, I guess it was," he said, wiping a tear from the corner of his eye. He hadn't laughed that hard since before he and Brenda were married. Then, composing himself, he looked at her and pointed to the jewelry on the table. "Those aren't real diamonds."

"What?" she exclaimed. "They're fake?"

"Afraid so. It seems you robbed my very lovely cubic zirconia section of the store."

"What were you doing with fakes? Do you cheat your customers?" Brenda said indignantly.

"Look who's pointing fingers about cheating people," Ralph snapped back, his jolly mood suddenly gone. "Of course I don't cheat them. The case is clearly labeled. They're all CZ. Except the tennis bracelet. That one is genuine."

"Will you be pressing charges for those pieces, too?" the sheriff asked.

Ralph looked at Brenda. Naked hope crossed her face.

"Oh, yes," he said. "I'm pressing charges for grand larceny and breaking and entering. I want every one of those pieces to be in the charges against her." He stood and reached for the doorknob. "She won't be getting another thing from me."

Just as he turned the knob, the door swung open.

"I want to press charges against that woman for holding me hostage!"

CHAPTER FIFTY-SEVEN

A RUMPLED HOLLY Berry pointed an accusatory finger at Brenda.

"Holding you hostage? You're crazy." There was venom in Brenda's words.

"Brenda, is this true?" Ralph asked.

"I don't know what she's talking about," Brenda muttered and looked away from the others in the room.

"Liar!" Holly shouted.

"Quiet, both of you," Sheriff Arnold ordered and turned toward Holly. "Have a seat and tell us what happened."

Holly lowered herself into the chair next to the one Ralph reclaimed and began. "I knew how upset Ralph was about the star being stolen, and how much he was counting on it keeping him in business. I wanted to do something nice for him, just to let him know someone cares. I don't have much money, so I went to Whipple's Wicks to pick something out. I figured I could afford something there, and Carla really does have some lovely things. When I was smelling some of the candles, she started talking to me." Holly paused and motioned toward

Brenda. "She looked sad, and I asked her if there was anything I could do. She shook her head and said she was having marital problems and that she feared it wouldn't last much longer. I tried to comfort her and said I wished there was something I could do. I gave her a tissue, and she dabbed her eyes, saying I'd already done more for her than I realized. She asked if she could just get some things off her chest in private, and she led me to a small hallway in the back of the store. Before I knew it, I'd been shoved into a supply closet that must have originally been built as a bomb shelter, because no matter how much I yelled, nobody came."

"Don't be ridiculous," Brenda huffed. "What would I possibly have to gain by locking you in a closet? I don't even know you."

"Maybe not, but I had a lot of time to think while I was stuck in there. I remembered there was someone nearby when I was telling Marian about my unfortunate past, and a face came to memory. It was you. You'd been eavesdropping on my conversation with Marian and knew I had a history of shoplifting. It occurred to me that you probably wanted the suspicion thrown on me." She turned to Ralph. "The whole time I was in that closet, I was so afraid you'd think I was the one who stole your star."

Ralph stood and placed a comforting hand on Holly's shoulder. "I could never for a minute convince myself that you stole it, Holly. To me, you're nothing more than a very competent and enthusiastic apprentice who is quickly becoming a friend."

Relief brightened Holly's face. "Thank you, Mr. Stockton."

He smiled. "I told you to call me Ralph." To the entire

group he said, "Now, if you'll excuse me, I need to get back to the store. I have a business to run."

Ralph walked out the front door with a spring in his step that had been absent for a long time.

The sheriff jerked his head toward Brenda. "So what you're saying is this woman locked you in a supply closet at Whipple's Wicks?" he confirmed.

"Yes. I've been stuck in there since yesterday afternoon, which explains why I look like this." Holly waved a hand the length of her torso.

Brenda snickered.

Holly glared at her. "At least I'm not in handcuffs."

"This time, sticky fingers," Brenda quipped.

"Ms. Berry, you can file your complaint with Deputy Nolan out front," Sheriff Arnold said dismissively, then as Holly left the room nodded toward the pile of jewelry still sitting in the middle of the table. "It looks like your foray into shoplifting is going to get you some time behind bars, Mrs. Stockton."

"That's Ms. Morris. I have a hunch I won't be hanging on to the Stockton name for much longer."

"Fair enough," the sheriff said.

Brenda tried to cross her arms over her chest, then let them drop. "I'm not saying another word until I have a lawyer."

"That is, of course, your right." Sheriff Arnold stood and jerked Brenda up with him. He escorted her from the room, down the back hall, and placed her in the cell.

As it clanked shut behind her, she cursed the day she hitched her wagon to Ralph Stockton.

CHAPTER FIFTY-EIGHT

AFTER SIGNING HER statement for Deputy Nolan, Holly said, "I need to get cleaned up and get to the store to help Ralph with the stars. Those suckers are selling like hotcakes, and he's already behind as it is."

As Sheriff Arnold came over to the deputy's desk, Holly said, "Have you found out who took the star?"

The sheriff nodded. "We found it in Kris Jingle's employee locker at the mall."

Holly furrowed her brow. "Isn't Kris Jingle the grumpy-looking Santa who doesn't like kids?"

"Yep."

A thoughtful moment passed. Holly shook her head. "I don't think he did it."

The sheriff snorted. "How would you know? You don't even know the guy."

"I have my own past," she confessed. "I can spot people like me pretty quickly. Kris Jingle seems to be a what-you-see-is-what-you-get kind of person. He'd have to be to show his dislike of kids so openly. From what I do know of him, he isn't sneaky enough and doesn't have a reason to take the star," Holly reasoned. "You might want to look for another suspect."

With that, Holly turned and walked out of the station into the cold, crisp air, thinking how nice it would be to get back to the work she was doing for Ralph. For the first time in her life, Holly looked forward to doing something, and as long as Ralph was willing to teach her, she'd do her best to learn.

The frigid air burned her lungs and she walked quickly toward the mall. It was at that moment she realized just how close she'd been to having her past catch up with her. She needed, and wanted, a new start, and Saddle Hill was just the place to get it.

But first, there was something very important she had to do.

CHAPTER FIFTY-NINE

"SO KRIS REALLY did it?" Nadine asked Joe as they sipped hot chocolate at one of the café's corner tables during her break.

Joe nodded solemnly. "It looks like it. If I hadn't seen it on the security footage with my own eyes, I wouldn't believe it, either." He took a long drink of his hot chocolate, careful to avoid choking on a marshmallow. He'd never had the heart to tell Nadine that he hated marshmallows in his hot chocolate. Setting the steaming mug back on the table, he said, "Marian thinks she might have a plan to prove Kris's innocence, but I don't see how that's possible. The sheriff is pretty confident they've got the thief in custody, and he's feeling pretty proud that he's solved such a big crime."

"Poor Ralph. I'm sure it hurts to know someone he considered a friend was the one who robbed him," Nadine offered as she watched her own marshmallows melt into foamy white mounds.

"Ralph considers everyone a friend, but yes, I'm sure it does. Something about this just doesn't add up, though," Joe said, thinking out loud.

"You saw him, Joe. He's on video stealing the star. What doesn't add up?" Nadine's worry was evident in her voice.

"I didn't actually see *him*. Just the sleeve of a Santa suit. It just feels wrong, somehow."

Nadine's face brightened. "If you just saw the sleeve, it could have been anyone. You can rent those at any costume shop. Maybe somebody wanted to frame Kris, or maybe they just hid it in the first place they could. The locks on those lockers are about as cheap as they come. A toddler could pick them," she volunteered.

Joe pursed his lips. "That's true. Unfortunately, Sheriff Arnold is pretty much finished looking for another suspect. Marian and I are on our own to make sure the right person is behind bars. But how?" Joe slapped the table in frustration.

Nadine jumped. "Don't do that," she warned as Wanda glared at them from behind the counter.

"Sorry," Joe muttered. His gaze settled on the young woman approaching them.

"Is that who I think it is?" Nadine whispered.

Joe nodded.

"Nadine Dobbs, right?" asked the young woman when she reached the table.

"Yes," Nadine replied cautiously.

"I'm Holly Berry. I'm staying with Marian Bright during the holiday season."

"We know who you are," Joe said sharply, "and I have to say you've caused quite enough trouble around here already with your little disappearing act."

Holly visibly winced. "I heard that you lost the diamond from your engagement ring. I was in here on Friday and got one of your delicious scones, and when I ate it later that night,

I found this…" She held out her hand, and laying there in her palm was a twinkling diamond.

"My diamond!" Nadine jumped up and threw her arms around Holly's neck. "Thank you so much!"

Holly closed her hand around the diamond so she didn't drop it in the force of Nadine's hug.

Joe stood. "We're glad to have that back. Thank you for returning it." His voice had softened and he smiled at Holly.

"I understand some details about my past have gotten around, but it's all behind me, and I want everyone to know I wouldn't steal something like this," she said, then opened her hand and carefully dropped it into Nadine's. "Or Ralph's star," she added.

"We know you didn't take the star. They already have the thief in custody," Joe assured her.

"I heard. Anyway, I need to get back to the store to help Ralph. Drop by and I'm sure he'll have that diamond back in the setting in no time," Holly said, then hurried out of the café in the direction of Stockton's Jewel Palace.

"What do you know about that?" Nadine beamed, her hand closed around the diamond. "A Christmas miracle."

Joe wrapped his arms around his bride-to-be. "Indeed it is."

Nadine deflated slightly in his embrace. "If only Kris Jingle could get a Christmas miracle."

"I know," Joe agreed. He was quiet a moment, then released Nadine. "If anybody can make that happen, Marian can," he said, looking hopefully off in the distance.

"What can she do?"

"If she has a plan, and we can figure out how Kris was framed and who did it, maybe we can get that person to confess. She can be a persuasive old bird, and I'm going to help her." A smile tugged at Joe's mouth. He released Nadine and stepped back. "I've got to go."

"Good luck," Nadine encouraged, "and wish me luck in not making Wanda madder at me than she already is," Nadine said, casting a cautious sideways glance toward her boss, who was still scowling.

"Just be your sweet self and she won't be able to not love you." Joe gave Nadine an encouraging wink, then blew her a kiss.

Nadine smiled and returned to the kitchen, bouncing slightly as she walked. Joe smiled at the idea that he had a part in returning some joy to his usually bubbly fiancée.

As he watched Nadine, he pulled his cell phone from his back pocket and muttered. "If we're going to get Kris out of this mess, I've got to talk to Marian."

CHAPTER SIXTY

NICHOLAS JINGLE SCOOTED the last kid in line off his lap and stood, trying in vain to stretch the spasm out of his lower back. After Kris was arrested early this morning, Winston said he didn't plan to open Santa's Workshop again until tomorrow morning. He'd said the kids were traumatized and nobody would be interested in returning to the scene where Santa had been led away in cuffs.

Ever concerned for the joy of the season, Nicholas persuaded Winston to open Santa's Workshop and offered to work the extra hours. Marian stood nearby with a basket of candy canes for all the children who returned. The corners of Nicholas's mouth dipped as he studied her. For the cheeriest person in town—aside from the Jingles, of course—she certainly wasn't playing the part of the cheery elf this afternoon. She was distracted and grim-looking. The worst indignity she'd inflicted upon Santa's Workshop this afternoon was that she'd had the audacity to answer her cell phone while there were children present. What nerve! That was definitely not appropriate elf behavior.

What's the matter with people this year? Nicolas wondered. If Marian is unhappy and slacking in her role as an elf, Christmas in this town is definitely falling apart. She's the only other person in Saddle Hill who could rival the cheer of the Jingle family. Kris excluded, of course.

His lips twisted into an unconscious grimace. Of all the things Kris could have done to rebel against the family, being arrested for stealing Ralph's Christmas star was just about the worst. He hadn't spoken to his dad yet, but Nicholas was sure he was ready to die from embarrassment. It wouldn't even come as a surprise if Kris was officially disowned from the family for this one.

"Oh, well," Nicholas muttered. "We make our choices. Kris has certainly made his over the years."

He twisted at the waist one last time in an effort to relieve the muscle tension and nodded at Marian, releasing her from her duties. If he didn't know any better, he'd think she just frowned at him.

Shrugging off her reaction, he retreated into Santa's Workshop and shucked off the red velvet suit. Sweat stains drenched the armpits of his undershirt. He needed water. Nobody realized how physically demanding it was to be Santa. If one didn't properly hydrate, they could get dizzy and let a kid fall off their lap. That was a tragedy no child should ever have to endure.

That and watching their beloved Santa Claus handcuffed and arrested.

Nicholas dabbed his face and neck with the small towel he kept in the workshop for that purpose, then dressed in his most festive civilian clothes. He smiled. It always drove Kris crazy when he and their father referred to normal clothes as "civilian." Kris always said they didn't need to act like they were going into battle. Nicholas and James assured him he couldn't be more wrong. They were soldiers for Christmas cheer going into battle against the Gloomy Gusses of the world. Then they'd look at each other and laugh while Kris continued to scowl. Sometimes they'd even call Kris "Gus" behind his back.

Ready to get home to one of Suzanne's delicious dinners, Nicholas exited the workshop with his duffel bag thrown over his shoulder as if he were carrying a sack full of presents. He took one last cursory glance around the stage to ensure everything would be ready to go tomorrow morning, noting that Marian had already taken off and was nowhere to be seen.

That was quick, he mused.

With Kris in jail, the burden this Christmas fell solely on Nicholas and James Jingle. Not that it's a burden at all, Nicholas reminded himself.

As he descended the steps, a breathless Joe Adler jogged toward him.

Joe gasped for air. "Nicholas, thank goodness I caught you. We've got a problem. You've got to come to the sheriff's station."

Nicholas dropped the duffel bag at his side. "What's wrong?"

Joe solemnly shook his head.

Nicholas's eyebrows bunched together. He took a step forward. "What is it? Is Kris okay?"

"It would be best if you came with me to see him. I'm afraid we might not have much time." Joe said, then turned and started jogging to the front doors.

Nicholas fell into step beside him. "Joe, tell me what's going on. Is something wrong with Kris?"

"Just come with me," Joe urged.

The two jogged briskly to Joe's car. Joe cranked the engine and drove in the direction of the station.

A few minutes later, after riding in total silence, they pulled into a parking spot. Joe and Nicholas jumped out of the car and dashed inside.

"Let's go in here," Joe suggested, motioning to the interrogation/conference room.

Nicholas followed him.

Marian sat somberly at the table, her eyes fixed on the men as they entered.

"What are you doing here?" Nicholas demanded, then glanced between Marian and Joe. "Tell me what's going on. I'm starting to get freaked out."

"We've had a new development in the case. We have conclusive proof that Santa Claus robbed Stockton's Jewel Palace," Joe offered.

Nicholas placed a hand on his chest. "So Kris really did it. I was hoping that by some miracle, he didn't actually stoop that low to ruin Christmas. As you can imagine, we're all horrified that he would bring this kind of shame on the Jingle name. Absolutely horrified." He shook his head for emphasis.

"I can imagine," Joe said in the tone of a confidant. He leaned forward and lowered his voice. "I have video footage of Santa taking the star."

Nicholas licked his lips. He really needed water. "Don't let that get around. I'm afraid Santa is already getting a bad name in this town. You know, with Kris getting himself arrested in front of all those children this morning."

"Oh, yes. The children. They did look frightened," Joe agreed.

Nicholas dropped his eyes to the floor and shook his head,

as though mourning the innocence lost by dozens of children at Santa's Workshop. "Poor kids. They should never have had to witness that. Sheriff Arnold should have waited until Kris was finished with his shift to arrest him. How will they ever believe Santa will come to their homes to bring presents on Christmas Eve night when they know he's locked in the slammer?" Nicholas's voice was sorrowful. "And who wouldn't be scared thinking a criminal is coming down their chimney in the middle of the night and lurking around the living room?"

"Sorry 'bout that. Justice doesn't wait, I'm afraid."

"What do you think the kids will say when there's no Santa in that chair tomorrow?" Marian asked quietly.

Nicholas narrowed his eyes at her. "What's that supposed to mean? Of course there will be a Santa in that chair. It'll be a stretch, but I can cover Kris's shifts. We might have to cut our hours short, but I can assure you that each child in this town will have the chance to sit on Santa's lap."

"You own a Santa suit," Marian said, raising sad eyes at Nicholas.

"Yes, I do. So does Kris. So does Dad. So do a lot of people. What's your point?"

"It could have been you on the security footage Joe saw," Marian said matter-of-factly.

Nicholas snorted. "Don't be absurd. You're a mall elf, and you're a mall security guard. Neither of you have any authority to make me stay here," he said, turning his attention to Joe. "Now, if you'll excuse me, my wife has dinner waiting for me." He pushed himself back from the table and stood.

"You're right," Joe conceded. "I don't have any authority to make you stay here. He does, though." Joe motioned in the direction of Sheriff Arnold, who was now standing in the doorway with his arms crossed over his broad chest.

"I'm going to have to ask you to stay. I've got some questions about what you were doing when the star was stolen Friday night."

Nicholas looked frantically at Marian, who he'd considered a friend until this moment. His shoulders slumped at the realization that she wasn't going to come to his defense. He returned to his chair and sat down heavily.

Kris had managed to dampen his Christmas spirit after all.

CHAPTER SIXTY-ONE

"TELL US WHAT happened Friday night at Stockton's," Marian said gently as Sheriff Arnold settled into the chair directly across from Nicholas.

"What are you hoping I tell you?" Nicholas's voice was disdainful.

"The truth, for starters," Joe snapped. "Your brother is sitting in a jail cell and you have a chance to help him. Now's your chance."

Sheriff Arnold already thought this was a waste of time but had agreed to let Marian and Joe give their plan a shot. If something didn't happen soon, he'd wash his hands of the whole scheme and Kris would stay in jail.

Nicholas had always been Marian's least favorite of the Jingles, and at the moment she'd love nothing more than to reach across the table and shake some sense into him. If her hunch was right, and Nicholas had stolen the star and planted it in Kris's locker to just to humiliate him and get him in trouble, Nicholas would be facing years of jail time. Instead, he was willing to let his brother take the fall.

What a guy, she thought. I'm sure glad he's not my brother.

"We know Kris didn't take that star. We also know we're looking for somebody with a Santa costume that would have a reason to want to get Kris in trouble," Marian said sternly.

Nicholas straightened. "First of all, it's not a costume. It is a uniform that deserves respect. Second, why would somebody steal the star just to get Kris in trouble?"

Marian rolled her eyes. As much she loved Christmas, she, like the rest of the world, thought it was a costume. Obviously Nicholas disagreed.

"Marian seems to think you stole the star and pinned it on Kris because you're trying to get back at him for something," Joe piped in. "Maybe for not taking Christmas as seriously as you think he should. Something along the lines of making him pay for ruining the family."

Nicholas turned his head away and stared at the wall.

Desperate times, Marian thought. She had one other card up her sleeve, and it was now or never. "You know, I'm worried about how all this might affect Kris's health." She forced tears into her eyes and chewed her bottom lip.

"What's wrong with Kris's health?" Nicholas asked, looking for the first time like he cared about the plight of his brother.

"Well, a doctor came to check on him because he complained of chest pain after he was arrested. It would seem Kris has a heart condition he's been keeping to himself. If he gets too upset, it could be the end of Kris Jingle." A tear slipped from Marian's eye and she sniffed. "That would really ruin Christmas, don't you think?"

Nicholas's eyes darted around the room. "Kris has a heart condition? I didn't know."

"He didn't want anyone in the family to find out. He said

everybody already thinks he's weak. He said he'd rather die with no one knowing something was wrong with him than face the family with a major health condition." Another tear slipped down her cheek. "I'm afraid he might get his wish."

"I don't want Kris to die!" Nicholas wailed. "Will he be able to get the treatment he needs?"

Marian raised a thin shoulder and let it drop, her chin quivering. "I'm not a doctor. All I know is what I was told. Treatment may or may not be an option. Only time will tell, I suppose. Who knows if he'd even accept treatment. He might rather just fade away than continue to be the pariah of the family."

"Yeah. After all, he's still pretty young and has never even been married. Poor Kris hasn't known much happiness in his life," Joe added, shaking his head sadly.

Sweat trickled down the side of Nicholas's face. "Aren't you going to say anything?" he asked Sheriff Arnold.

A simple shrug was the sheriff's only response.

Nicholas's breath came in short bursts, his heart raced. "I did it! I took the star from Ralph's store. I wanted to stick it to Kris for being such a downer all the time. I swear, I had no idea he was sick. Please, let me see him," he begged.

Sighing, Sheriff Arnold stood and left the room, the keys to the cells jingling on his hip. He returned a few minutes later with Kris at his side.

Nicholas sprang to his feet and threw his arms around his older brother. "Kris, I'm so sorry! I wanted to get back at you for ruining Christmas every year, but I had no idea you were dying. I don't want my big brother to die! Please, please forgive me for pinning this on you," Nicholas begged, sobbing into his brother's neck.

Kris rolled his eyes toward the ceiling and pushed Nicholas away from him. "Dying? I'm not dying. Where'd you get that idea?"

Tears still streaming down his face, Nicholas pointed an accusatory finger at Marian, whose eyes were now dry. Joe smirked beside her. "Marian told me you had a secret heart condition and the stress of being in jail could kill you. She said you were having chest pains."

Marian winked at Kris.

Chuckling, Kris said, "Is that so? Actually, I was having chest pains. The last kid that sat on my lap was a tad on the hefty side. I think I pulled a muscle helping him get down."

"You lied?" Nicholas wailed at Marian. "How could you?"

Marian shrugged. "You lied. What's the difference? Except that your lie would have put your own brother in jail for years. Either way, we got the information we needed." Marian turned toward Sheriff Arnold. "Well?"

"Under the circumstances, it would seem that you're free to go, Kris." The sheriff then turned toward Marian and Joe. "Good work, you two. I might have to deputize you."

Kris turned to his brother. "I'll tell Mom and Dad what happened. I'm sure they'll blame me for getting you into this. Thanks for confessing, though. I knew you had it in you to do the right thing, even if they had to drag it out of you."

He thanked Marian, Joe, and Sheriff Arnold, then left the station a free man, thanks to his friends.

"I've got a freshly vacated cell for you, and if we hurry, the bed might still be warm," the sheriff said, then grabbed Nicholas's elbow and guided him through the door, where they disappeared down the corridor.

Joe placed his hand over Marian's. "Nice hunch, partner.

But I think Christmas just got a little less jolly for the Jingle family this year."

Marian nodded. "The right person is in jail, though. The question now is, who stole the other star?"

277

CHAPTER SIXTY-TWO

THE NEWS OF Holly's return had rippled through the employee grapevine, and Marian walked as quickly as she could to get to Stockton's Jewel Palace. Still invigorated by her role in getting Nicholas Jingle to confess to stealing Ralph's Christmas star, she needed to see Holly to make sure she was okay.

I never should have doubted her, Marian berated herself as she noticed the crowd of shoppers had thinned substantially since Friday morning. The Mountain Craft Festival was wrapping up and all the shoppers were home, probably eating dinner and arguing about how much they spent over the weekend. Then they'd go back to work tomorrow so they could earn money to pay for the things they'd already bought.

Roger would be appalled.

On the bright side, the kids would be back in school so the lines to see Santa would be much shorter. During the day, only the kids who were too young to be at school would come to see Santa.

Not that there was much of a Santa to see. With Nicholas

in jail for stealing the star, James Jingle might just have to start working twelve-hour shifts again.

Marian stepped into Stockton's Jewel Palace and paused. Holly, still looking a bit disheveled from her ordeal, was standing behind the counter with Ralph talking in hushed tones. Placing a hand on her chest and shaking her head, Marian took a step forward and tenderly said, "I'm so glad you're okay, Holly. I was so worried."

Holly raised her head and studied Marian.

Marian's heart sank. Had she heard that I told everyone about her past?

After several seconds, Holly smiled faintly. "It's good to see you, Marian."

Relief flooded her. "I was so afraid you'd be upset with me."

A knowing look flitted across Holly's face. "You were afraid I took the star and passed that concern along to everyone else." She dropped her eyes. "I told you that part of my life was behind me."

Even though she hadn't believed Holly was responsible for the theft, she'd planted the seed of doubt in the minds of her coworkers. Nobody would have been looking at Holly like she was a criminal if Marian hadn't opened her mouth. She felt about an inch tall. "I'm so sorry," she whispered, tears stinging the backs of her eyes.

Holly reached forward and squeezed Marian's hands. "I understand why you might have thought I was involved. I might have wondered the same thing if I was in your position. I want you to know I'm finished with that. I have a new life now, and work to do. We've got to catch up with the star orders so Ralph can get them filled on time. Obviously I was of no help to him while I was locked in that closet."

Marian looked at Ralph and smiled. Ralph stood by Holly's innocence and had taken her under his wing, offering to teach her the ins and outs of creating the beautiful pieces he so proudly displayed. That's just like Ralph, Marian realized. No matter what happened next, Holly's life would be better because she'd met him.

Everyone's was.

Just as Marian turned to go, she said to Ralph, "I heard Brenda was arrested this morning. I'm so sorry."

Ralph's mouth formed a grim line. "Unfortunately, she stole more from me than I realized. Luckily for me, though, she was arrested in a small town outside St. Louis. She was actually wearing the bracelet she stole from my store and had several other pieces in her luggage. I honestly thought she might have taken the other star, but the sheriff searched her bags and didn't find it. She denies having any involvement and is appalled that anyone would think she would do something so horrible." Ralph snorted. "Can you believe that?"

"I'm so sorry, Ralph," Marian said again. "You should know that Nicholas Jingle confessed to stealing it and framing his brother. He was mad at Kris for always being such a downer at Christmas and wanted to get even. He didn't do it to hurt you. He did it to hurt Kris," she offered, hoping it would help Ralph feel better.

"Now if I could just find the other one," Ralph mumbled. "If somebody is looking for money by selling it, they're going to be really disappointed when they find out the gems aren't real."

"They're fake?" Marian asked in surprise.

Ralph rolled his eyes. "Why can nobody believe that? Brenda was spending money so fast I could barely pay my bills. There's no way I could afford to use real stones in the models. Of course the ones I'm making for the customers are genuine, though," he assured them.

"Wow," Holly admired. "If you can make something look that good with glass, I can't wait to see what the real ones look like."

Ralph beamed in response. "Yes, well, if anybody is ever going to see the real thing, I've got to get started filling more of the orders. I'm hopelessly behind. If you'll excuse me…"

The phone on his small desk rang. He crossed the room to answer it. After a few minutes, Ralph replaced the receiver and turned toward Marian and Holly, who were watching him with interest.

"You've got to love a small town. Since Nicholas confessed, there won't be a trial. I don't think I'll get so lucky with Brenda, though. She still swears she's innocent of any wrongdoing, even though they found the pieces in her possession. Apparently I need Joe to help me update my security. It looks like I can't trust people to do the right thing anymore, and I certainly don't need this happening again." Ralph bent forward and flipped through a stack of order forms on his desk. "It's time to get back to work, Holly."

"You've got it, Ralph," Holly responded with a smile. "Marian, I'll be home late tonight. I've got to help Ralph get back on top of things. Don't plan on me for dinner."

Marian bobbed her head in agreement and turned to walk out of the store.

"And Marian?" Holly called after her.

Marian stopped and faced her young houseguest.

"No hard feelings."

She nodded, then ducked her head to keep her emotions at bay and walked out of the store.

Such a forgiving girl, she thought. I hope her reputation can recover from my running my big mouth.

The day that had started so rough was turning out okay, after all. Nicholas was behind bars, right where he belonged. Brenda, too, and Kris was getting back to life as usual.

But what about that other star? Marian wondered. If those closest to Ralph didn't know the stones weren't genuine, it was likely the thief wouldn't, either.

Money, passion, revenge. One of them had to be the motive. It always was.

Nicholas had been getting revenge on Kris for supposedly ruining the Jingle family Christmases by stealing the star and framing him.

Brenda was just plain greedy and wanted the jewelry she thought Ralph owed her.

That leaves passion. But who would be passionate enough about Ralph to want to see him hurt?

A memory from several years ago slammed into her mind. She snapped her fingers. "I think I know who took the other star."

Feeling lightened by her revelation, Marian smiled to herself as the bells on her elf shoes jingled a merry cadence with every step she took.

An attractive woman Marian only vaguely remembered seeing the past couple days flashed a megawatt smile at her and strode toward Stockton's Jewel Palace.

Whatever is going on in that pretty head of hers sure has put a bounce in her step, Marian observed as she walked outside toward her car.

And what I might have figured out has put a bounce in mine.

CHAPTER SIXTY-THREE

SYLVIA MARCHED INTO Stockton's Jewel Palace, unable to get the smile she'd had since hearing the news of Brenda's arrest off her face. It was shameful, she knew, but Brenda had it coming. Brenda had made her miserable for four years, then expected everyone to forgive her if she batted her eyelashes and pouted.

That wouldn't get her out of this.

"Mr. Stockton, I heard the good news!" Sylvia exclaimed as she walked into the jewelry store. "I'm so glad they recovered your star."

Ralph smiled up at her from his desk. "Yes. It's wonderful. Now if I could only get the other one back."

Sylvia gave him a puzzled look but forged on. "Well, I hope I'm about to make your day even better." She glanced at Ralph's hand, noting he wasn't wearing his wedding ring anymore. That was fast, she thought, but didn't blame him in the least. His wife *had* stolen from him, after all.

"How so? Are you planning to order more stars? Maybe with actual color this time. Black and white is so dull. You seem like a vibrant woman who would prefer something with a little zest." Ralph winked at her.

Sylvia chuckled. "I'm afraid I won't be ordering any more stars. As I told you before, I'm a fashion designer in New York. My clothing line is Jersey Belle, which I don't expect you to have heard of."

"Oh, I've heard of it," he assured her. "Brenda wouldn't stop bugging me to let her buy your clothes. No offense, but it's way too expensive for me."

"None taken," Sylvia said, smiling. She liked Ralph more every time he opened his mouth. He was honest to his core, and that was refreshing in a world where personas were created just to impress. "I wanted to talk to you about a jewelry line I'm going to start working on in January. I've been trying to decide what jeweler I'd like to hire to create the pieces, but I hadn't been able to settle on anyone. Now I know why. When I came in and saw your star and the rest of your work, I knew you were the jeweler I wanted to work with."

Ralph's mouth hung open. "You want me to design jewelry for Jersey Belle?"

"Yes. I assure you our partnership will be extremely lucrative for you. You'd make more than enough money to keep your store open. Of course you'd work remotely so you wouldn't have to leave Saddle Hill, although a few trips a year to New York might be required. Does that sound like something you'd be willing to consider?"

Ralph didn't say anything.

Sylvia held her breath as she waited for his response.

"You say I could stay here?" Ralph finally asked.

"Yes."

"And I'd make enough money to keep my store?"

"And then some," Sylvia assured him. "You could probably open a dozen more stores, if you wanted."

Ralph smiled. "I'd be designing jewelry for Jersey Belle, and you'd be my boss?"

"In a matter of speaking, yes, but I'm not a jeweler. We'd collaborate and I'd give the designs my official stamp of approval, but you'd be the one really in charge of designing the pieces. It would actually be more of a partnership than an employer-employee situation."

Ralph's mouth twisted into a mischievous smile. "This would kill Brenda."

Sylvia had to force herself not to smile with Ralph. It really would.

"I'll do it," Ralph agreed, his round cheeks flushed with excitement.

"Excellent!" Sylvia enthused, clapping her hands. "When I get back to New York tonight, I'll call my attorney and have him start drawing up the agreement." She glanced at her watch. "I need to get going so I don't miss my flight." She extended her hand toward Ralph. He grabbed it and pumped her arm up and down. "It's been a pleasure. You'll hear from me soon."

She pried her hand from Ralph's grip and walked quickly out of the store toward the parking lot. Her suitcase was already in the trunk of the rental car. She'd be cutting it close, but as long as the weather cooperated, she should make her flight.

As she slid into the driver's seat and backed the car out of the parking spot, she thought of the irony of how her relaxing weekend had turned out. She'd set out to leave work behind for a few days, but now was on the verge of having a signed contract with a talented jeweler. It was probably the most productive vacation she'd ever had.

To top it off, her nemesis from college days was sitting behind bars for grand larceny.

"I couldn't have planned this weekend any better if I tried," she said through a smile then hummed the first few notes of "We Three Kings."

I wonder where that came from, Sylvia thought as she eased the car into the recently plowed roads. It's appropriate for this weekend.

A star had led her to something special this Christmas, too.

CHAPTER SIXTY-FOUR

MARIAN TOOK A sip of her chamomile tea and tapped her fingers on the kitchen table. This weekend had been the most unusual kickoff to the Christmas season she could ever remember. In the forty years she'd been a resident of Saddle Hill, the town had never been turned on its head quite like this.

Two Santas had been arrested, Holly had been locked in a storage closet overnight by Ralph's vindictive wife who'd also robbed him, and one of the stars was still missing. If Marian was right about who took the second one, it wouldn't be missing much longer.

But how do I prove it? Marian wondered as she relished in the warmth of the herbal tea.

Still clad in her elf costume, the hem of the tunic jingled as she bounced her leg up and down. It had been a long time since she felt this restless. A problem solver by nature, figuring out how to pin the theft of Ralph's other star on thief number two was driving her crazy.

But she had an idea. If she was going to get a confession,

she'd need to play the sympathy card. It had already worked once today, maybe it would work again.

She walked over to the phone hanging on the wall and dialed Joe Adler's cell phone.

"Are you still at the mall?" she asked as soon as he answered.

"Aren't I always?" he replied glumly.

Marian noticed that the noise of the shoppers in the background was mild compared to the last couple days. She glanced at the clock. It was Sunday, so the mall had shorter hours.

"I think I've come up with a way to get a confession from the person who stole the other star."

"You know who took it?"

"I think so. I can be at the mall in twenty minutes. Don't leave until I get there," Marian ordered.

"Who?"

"I'll tell you when I get there," she promised.

Joe agreed to meet her by the main entrance in exactly twenty minutes.

Marian hung up the phone and jingled over to the coat closet to retrieve her jacket. With the car still warm from her trip home, she was quickly back on the road, determined to prove that somebody in town did have a reason to want to hurt Ralph.

Exactly twenty minutes later, as promised, Marian dashed into the mall, noting that the stores would be closing soon. They'd have to hurry.

She nodded at Joe as she approached him and without slowing her pace, brushed past him. "Come on."

Joe jogged to catch up with her. "It's time for you to tell me what's going on."

"First, call Sheriff Arnold. He needs to be here."

The two continued their brisk pace as Joe made the call, struggling to keep up as he spoke.

"He'll be here right away," he said when he disconnected the call. "Apparently we have some credibility with the law enforcement in this town after getting a confession out of Nicholas."

Marian smiled, pleased with herself that she'd been able to help find the truth about the robbery. Now, if everything went according to plan, she'd be able to solve the other one, too.

"Who did it, Marian? You promised to tell me."

"I will. What are the main reasons people commit a crime?"

Joe rolled his eyes. "Winston warned me you might do this."

"What are they, Joe?" Marian repeated impatiently.

He shrugged. "I don't know. Money?"

"That's always a good one. That's why Brenda stole from Ralph. Of course, the jewelry she stole were mostly fakes. Serves her right," Marian added under her breath.

"She was also trying to get revenge on him for not giving her the lifestyle she thought she deserved."

"That's true, which brings us to the second reason to commit a crime. Revenge. That's what we saw with Nicholas. He stole the star and then framed Kris to get back at him for ruining Christmas." Marian continued to hustle down the corridor. "What's another reason?"

"Will you please just tell me who you think did it?" Joe was finally losing his patience.

"Passion."

"Who would be passionate about Ralph?" he huffed.

Marian winked, then said, "You know, Joe, you really should work on your stamina. You're letting an old lady outrun you."

"Noted," Joe said sourly. "Who would be passionate

enough about Ralph to rob him?" He stopped and snapped his fingers. "Wanda! They were almost married a few years ago, if I remember right."

Marian shook her head and waved at Joe to catch up. When he did, she said, "Ralph was in a relationship when he met Brenda, but he broke it off just before he asked Brenda to marry him."

Joe's forehead wrinkled. "Really? I didn't know he'd dated anyone since Wanda."

"Most people didn't. They kept it pretty quiet since she'd been recently divorced. It didn't last long, I'm afraid, but she's been carrying a torch for him ever since."

"Who?" Joe demanded.

Marian stopped in front of Whipple's Wicks and pointed inside.

"Carla Whipple?" he asked incredulously.

Marian raised her eyebrows and smiled. "I'd forgotten about it, too, but after Ralph's star was stolen she tried to comfort him. The way she touched him reminded me of how someone in love would have done it. Then I remembered how crazy Carla had been about him and began to suspect she wasn't over him."

"But why steal from him? Especially if she still loves him?" Joe's gaze was fixed on the short, middle-aged woman with a dark blond bob straightening the candles on the shelves inside the store.

"Let's ask her." Marian led the way into the store that was filled with all the scents of Christmas. Though the smell was overwhelming, Marian felt sad that such a cheery place was going to be the scene of a person's arrest.

As Marian and Joe approached Carla, she greeted them

with a smile. "Hey there, you two. I'm afraid I've already closed the register, so I can't ring up any more purchases."

"We're not here to buy anything, Carla," Joe said gently.

Carla's smile dropped. She looked from Joe's serious face to Marian's and wiped her hands on her apron. "Okay, then. What can I do for you?"

Marian took a few steps forward and took Carla's hand in her own. "What can you tell me about Ralph's star?"

Carla licked her lips. "I heard Nicholas Jingle stole it and tried to pin it on his brother. Not that anyone should be surprised if Kris really had stolen it. He's a grump."

"Not that star. The other one. The one he kept in his safe. What happened to that one?" Marian asked, making herself sound as sympathetic as she could.

"How should I know?" Carla's face hardened as she jerked her hand away from Marian's grasp. "I didn't know there was another star."

"Carla, I know how much it hurt you when Ralph broke off your relationship to marry Brenda. I also know you still care about him. Ralph's hurting right now, and you know why. If you could take some of that hurt away from him, I know you'd want to."

Her face fell. "Ralph deserves to hurt for a while."

Marian glanced at Joe. "Finish locking up for her. We're going to Winston's office."

Joe nodded and began the task of closing up Whipple's Wicks for the last time.

CHAPTER SIXTY-FIVE

SEATED IN WINSTON Marshall's office, Marian held Carla's shaking hand as she encouraged Carla to tell her story.

"We're your friends, Carla. Please believe that we want to help you," Marian said, never taking her eyes off the woman who was so obviously heartbroken.

Carla dropped her eyes to her lap. Her chin quivered as she spoke. "Ralph and I were good together. We had a lot of fun, yes, but it was more than that. Then, out of the blue, he tells me he met someone else and that he's planning to propose. Then he had the nerve to bring that…that witch to this town! It was humiliating. When I met her and saw the kind of person she is, I couldn't believe he preferred her over me. She thought she was too good for this town, and any idiot could see she thought she was too good for Ralph, too. Everyone except Ralph. He's such a good guy. Nobody is too good for Ralph." A tear formed in Carla's eye and rolled down her cheek.

"Why don't you tell us what happened," Winston said in a voice more compassionate than Marian thought possible.

Carla sniffed and nodded her head. "I didn't plan to steal

from Ralph. I really didn't. Sometimes I go to his store after hours to look at the pieces he's been working on. When we were together, he'd take me there late at night sometimes so I could be the first one to see his work. When he broke things off, I didn't get to do that anymore. His jewelry is so beautiful, I still wanted to be the first one to see the new pieces." She paused to shrug. "He'd somehow managed to get the password for the mall's alarm system so he could come in and work late, and I found it in his office one day. After we split up, sometimes I'd sneak in to take a peek. I knew the combination of his safe back then, and I wanted to see if he'd changed it." She raised her watery eyes to Marian's. "The combination used to be the anniversary of our first date. When I tried that combination, it didn't work. Then I put in his wedding anniversary to that awful woman, and it popped right open."

Marian gave Carla's hand a squeeze. She was so sorry for this woman. "When did you decide to steal the star?"

Carla blew her nose on the tissue she had balled up in her free hand. "Not until I saw it. It was breathtaking, his finest work for sure. I could tell he put his whole heart and soul into creating that star. I missed him and wanted a piece of him. The star represented the best of him, and I wanted to keep that with me. It was everything I love about him."

Marian turned to look at Joe and Sheriff Arnold who were standing side by side in the back corner of Winston's office. "Get Ralph," she mouthed to them.

Joe disappeared quietly through the door.

Marian turned her attention back to Carla. "So you opened the safe and saw the star. Overwhelmed by loneliness for him, you took it as a way to remember the good in him. Is that right?"

Carla bit her lip and bobbed her head up and down. "I just wanted a piece of him to hold on to. I know it's been three years, but I still love him."

Marian squeezed Carla's hand tighter. Carla wasn't a criminal, stealing from Ralph to gain something. She was a heartsick woman who'd lost someone she loved dearly and was desperately trying to remember what they'd had.

Sheriff Arnold poured a cup of coffee and offered it to Carla.

"Thank you," she said, dropping the tissue and taking the mug.

As she drank, Winston's door opened. Joe entered, Ralph close behind.

Ralph stopped in the doorway, and with all the compassion Marian had ever seen, he looked at Carla. "I'm not pressing charges."

Tears spilled down Carla's cheeks and landed with a splash in her coffee. "Ralph, I—"

"I was wrong," Ralph admitted. "You were nothing but caring, and I gave you up. I never deserved you..."

"Ralph," Winston interjected. "She stole from you. As much as we all like Carla, she has to be held responsible for taking that star from you."

"Consider it a gift. You can't arrest her for accepting a gift." Ralph's eyes shone with fresh affection.

The room was stunned into silence.

Finally, Sheriff Arnold said, "I guess I'm not needed here. Have a good evening." He brushed past Ralph with a nod and a smile.

"In that case, I really must get back to work. This mall won't save itself," Winston said with his typical formality.

Marian and Joe filed out of Winston's office, Carla and Ralph far behind.

A grin spread across Marian's face as she looked over her shoulder, studying her two friends who seemed to be on the verge of a reconciliation.

"It looks like this Christmas is already full of miracles," Joe observed.

"Yes, I believe it is," Marian agreed. It did her heart good to see two people who had so much in common finding their way back together.

Despite the frenzy of the season, some people were realizing what is truly important.

She smiled again. Roger would have been so pleased.

EPILOGUE

Christmas Day

"TO THE SADDLE Hill Mall employees, who really did save Christmas and could teach the rest of the world a thing or two about what really matters!" Winston exclaimed as he raised a glass of eggnog in a toast to his troops.

"Hear, hear," echoed around the room as everyone raised a glass to join Winston's toast.

This year, Christmas wasn't just about opening presents and having dinner with family, it was about celebrating friends and coworkers who had become a different kind of family.

All because of The General, Marian thought wistfully. It had been at Winston's suggestion that each one of the mall employees, along with their families, don their finest Christmas attire and celebrate together in the sole ballroom at the Saddle Hill Inn. The past month had been difficult for each of them, but on Christmas Day, they'd all come together in a celebration of hardships conquered.

With warmth spreading through her chest, Marian glanced at each person who'd become so dear to her, helping her not only get through the loneliness of her first Christmas without Roger, but who had also helped her see the best in humanity.

Joe and Nadine were cuddled together, the returned diamond winking brightly on her left hand. Marian knew tonight was a different kind of celebration for them. They hadn't been able to wait until January to be married, and confided in Marian and swore her to secrecy that they'd eloped last night, on Christmas Eve, to ensure they wouldn't have to miss another Christmas Day as husband and wife. They would announce their marriage soon, but for now it was their own little secret that Marian felt privileged to be included in.

Next to the new Mr. And Mrs. Adler, Kris Jingle sat between his parents, the joy of the season written on his face for the first time in years. James Jingle wore a regular suit with not a stitch of red. Patricia wore a sleek navy blue gown she'd bought just for the occasion. Marian knew Patricia had her own reason to celebrate. Her memoir, *Forever Mrs. Claus*, had been picked up by a publisher and her story of living as Santa's wife for the past forty years would be in the hands of readers by next Christmas.

Marian smirked as James shifted uncomfortably in his seat and tugged at the front of his suit jacket. It would take him a while to get used to civilian clothes, but he looked happy. From what Marian could gather, he'd finally gotten over his shame that Kris was ordinary, and he was making his own effort to live a normal life.

Poor Nicholas had been allowed to come home for Christmas and was on house arrest. James had gotten special permission for him to attend the celebration, but out of embarrassment, Nicholas refused to attend tonight's gathering. It didn't help matters that his wife, Suzanne, had filed for divorce and moved back to Alabama to live with her parents.

The picture of hope and generosity, Ralph Stockton beamed between Sylvia Bell and Carla Whipple. Ralph had let it slip that Sylvia was there with a contract for him to sign, making him the official designer for the new Jersey Belle line of jewelry. From the looks on their faces, Marian was certain the emerging partnership was the best Christmas gift either of them could have hoped for. An unexpected surprise for Marian was that she had gotten the chance to meet another member of the Christmas name support group. Sylvia was a lovely woman who was bringing such joy to the community through her partnership with Ralph. Now that their paths had crossed, Marian looked forward to getting to know Sylvia better.

A tear stung Marian's eye at the sight of Carla Whipple, leaning close to Ralph as he draped his arm affectionately across the back of her chair. It hadn't taken long for the two of them to reconcile, and Marian suspected wedding bells would chime in the near future. She wished them a long life of happiness together.

Marian also knew Ralph hadn't accepted any of Brenda's phone calls from jail, which she guessed were Brenda's feeble attempts to ask Ralph to drop the charges and give her another chance. Instead, Ralph had successfully had his marriage to Brenda annulled, claiming she misrepresented herself when they were married. The judge happily obliged.

Holly Berry sat next to Marian, content that she'd found the new start she so desperately wanted. With Ralph's new business venture, Marian knew he was giving more of the day-to-day responsibilities of Stockton's Jewel Palace to Holly. She'd even admitted to Marian that she really did have a knack for jewelry. Ralph, elated with the turn his life had taken and overcome with gratefulness for Holly's help during the Christmas season, had even made a copy of the star for her as a special Christmas gift. A lump formed in Marian's throat. After a lifetime of letdowns and disappointments, Holly had finally found her home.

Marian wiped a tear from her eye as she glanced around at the smiles on each of her friends.

If only Roger was still with me, she thought wistfully. He would have loved to see how the town came together this Christmas.

Holly gently patted Marian's hand, a gentle reminder that she wasn't alone. Even though Roger was gone, Marian still had a family.

A season that had begun with so many difficulties and had the potential for so much heartbreak, was ending with a spirit of joy and goodwill.

Filled with gratitude for life, Marian could hardly wait to see what next Christmas would bring.

Acknowledgements

MANY THANKS ARE in order for the creation of this book.

To my editor, Dierdre Stoelzle, who provided a keen eye for detail and encouraging comments while suggesting ways to make the story better.

Chrissy, at Damonza, for creating a beautiful book, inside and out.

Becky Willard for helping me overcome my awkwardness to get a good photo for the back of the book.

Thank you to my mom, Cindy, for reading through it and offering (always constructive) criticism, and for constantly correcting my grammar as a child; and to my dad, Larry, for passing on to me the love of writing and creativity.

Thank you to Joanna Penn for being such an incredible resource for authors and providing instruction and advice for all things writing.

To my husband, Billy, and daughters, Zoe and Nora, as well as many friends and family who have encouraged me through this process.

Finally, to you, the reader. Thank you for taking a chance on an unknown author and picking up this book. I hope you have enjoyed reading this story as much as I enjoyed writing it.

See you next time!
Erin